PRAISE FOR *ONE*

'Lean, crisp writing and a tightly paced plot set in an all-too imaginable future make for a page-turning, thought-provoking read' Jo Callaghan

'With a terrifying vision of a global climate emergency, a jaw-dropping government conspiracy and some truly devastating twists, Eve Smith has conjured one hell of a speculative thriller' Tom Hindle

'All-too convincing, and scientifically plausible. As much a warning as an entertainment. It scared the hell out of me' Paul E. Hardisty

'Amazing, beautiful writing, jam-packed with clever ideas on every page ... A brilliant read' Helen Fitzgerald

'Wow! Set in the heat of climate-crisis Britain, *One* is a novel simmering with great intelligence and insight that never fails to be terrifyingly and thrillingly plausible' James Goodhand

'The reader is hooked and dragged at breakneck speed through a climate-ravaged and resource-starved Britain. Sharp perception and intense images shine out of every page. Eve Smith is a master storyteller for our troubled times' Simon Conway

'A chillingly plausible tale of societal corruption and control, written with a brilliantly realised world, great pacing and a storyline that is both thrilling and deeply moving. Thought-provoking, moving and gripping, *One* proves Smith a top author in the speculative-thriller genre' Philippa East

'This brilliant book immerses us in a dystopian future where a green-tech paradise conceals a family-planning hell. As an illegal excess child who survived China's One Child Policy, this gripping and unsettling tale brought back all my worst memories from that time and reminded me of how easily the abhorrent practice of forced birth control could come back in a not-too-distant future' Shen Yang

'A terrifyingly plausible vision of the future. This is a page-turning thriller that raises troubling issues about the balance between saving the planet and our individual human rights. A brilliant piece of speculative fiction!' Guy Morpuss

'A powerful warning and a gripping thriller' Greg Mosse

'A gripping and pacy thriller set in an all-too plausible and terrifying future' David Beckler

'A chilling, poignant novel that holds a mirror up to our world, *One* is a story about personal responsibility, bodily autonomy and sisterhood, just when we need it most, Sensational' Vikki Patis

'Another taut and terrifying thriller from Eve Smith' Louise Swanson

'What. A. Book! A terrifying, yet plausible read. Too scary to imagine in reality, and yet...' Heather Fitt

'Horrifying and gripping in equal measure, *One* is a jaw-dropping glimpse of the catastrophe around the corner ... Astonishing' Lucy Martin

'Pulses with great ideas, and more deliciously terrifying ones. Compulsive and addictive' Adam Simcox

'Eve Smith is the queen of the near-future thriller! Pulse-pounding and heart-rending in equal measure, this book is a tour-de-force which, though set in a dystopian society, allows us to view our own in a whole new way' Louise Mumford

'Another belter from the breathtaking imagination of Eve Smith. Meticulously crafted, no detail is overlooked, producing a thriller so authentic it doesn't feel speculative at all. Just terrifyingly real and viscerally affecting. Bravo' Sarah Sultoon

'An absolute rollercoaster ride of a novel. Emotive, propulsive and compelling ... Eve Smith is a visionary storyteller' Awais Khan

'Gripping, pacy, frightening and deep – I love a story that leaves me having big thoughtful discussions with others afterwards, and this definitely did. A very brilliant, masterful book'
Sarah K. Jackson

'A tense thriller … Very cleverly weaves in current issues to keep it grounded in the "would they? could they?" scenarios'
Fiona Sharp, Waterstones

'Her best yet. Not just original, thought-provoking and scarily relevant, it is, first and foremost, a fantastic read I devoured in one sitting' Simon Bewick

'Another prescient tale that will keep you up reading long after the rest of the world has fallen silent' Suzy Aspley

'A wonderful writer who weaves scarily possible versions of society into the real world … doubly moving for me due to two of my adopted children, victims of the one-child policy themselves'
Claire Sheehy

'A masterpiece set in a dystopian Britain … a breathtaking page-turner much in the vein of *Black Mirror*, with vibes of *Logan's Run* and *Soylent Green*' Patty Dohle, Waterstones

'There are not enough superlatives for Eve Smith's new thriller … A must read' Dr Gerry Lee

'Gripping, thought-provoking and so authentic! Five huge stars'
Suzey Breckon

'As speculative/climate fiction goes, *One* is a frightening glimpse into a "what-if" future, with its roots firmly placed in the now. If you only read one cli-fi book this year, then make it this one'
The First Eleven Minutes

'Quite frankly, a nightmarish vision of the future of Britain based on the foundation of environmental collapse and societal control'
Emerald Book Reviews

'Hits you all at once, a stunning blow that leaves you gasping for more ... will keep you mesmerised and captivated'
Surjit's Book Blog

'A marvellously entertaining read, super-addictive and thrilling from start to finish' From Belgium with Booklove

'Definitely one of the best speculative fiction novels I've EVER had the pleasure of reading. It's so exquisitely written ... An emotive, breathtaking read' The Book Review Café

'Eve has yet again written a story that forces you to sit up and pay attention ... A thought-provoking, emotional and compelling read that makes us wonder why, in 2023, women's reproductive rights are still being controlled' Secret World of a Book

'A thrilling, tension-packed conspiracy story that grabbed my attention and held it right to the very last page'
Jen Med's Book Reviews

'I could not read it fast enough but had to put it down once or twice as the subject is not unbelievable ... Eve Smith is a consummate writer who leaves nothing to the imagination'
Sally Boocock

'Eve Smith is a master at pulling threads from current headlines and weaving them into a compelling work of fiction ... the queen of speculative thrillers' Canada Hardcover

'Eve Smith once again shows why she is the best author of speculative fiction ... a story that provokes thought, anger and a fear of what could be our own future world' My Bookish Blogspot

'A phenomenal author and one of the best of our time. Each book just gets better and better' Little Miss Books

ABOUT THE AUTHOR

Eve Smith writes speculative thrillers, mainly about the things that scare her. She attributes her love of all things dark and dystopian to a childhood watching *Tales of the Unexpected* and Edgar Allen Poe double bills.

Longlisted for the Not the Booker Prize and described by Waterstones as 'an exciting new voice in crime fiction', Eve's debut novel, *The Waiting Rooms*, set in the aftermath of an antibiotic resistance crisis, was shortlisted for the Bridport Prize First Novel Award and was selected as a Book of the Month by Eric Brown in the *Guardian*, who compared her writing to Michael Crichton's. It was followed by *Off-Target*, about a world where genetic engineering of children is routine.

Eve's previous job at an environmental charity took her to research projects across Asia, Africa and the Americas, and she has an ongoing passion for wild creatures, wild science and far-flung places.

Follow Eve on Twitter: @evecsmith; Instagram, Facebook, TikTok: evesmithauthor; or contact her via her website: www.evesmithauthor.com.

Also by Eve Smith and available from Orenda Books:
The Waiting Rooms
Off-Target

ONE

EVE SMITH

ORENDA
BOOKS

Orenda Books
16 Carson Road
West Dulwich
London SE21 8HU
www.orendabooks.co.uk

First published in the United Kingdom by Orenda Books, 2023
Copyright © Eve Smith, 2023

ONE Party logo illustration ©Aaron Smith

Quotation on page vi from *More Than One Child: Memoirs of an Illegal Daughter* by Shen Yang, © Shen Yang 2021, English translation © Nicky Harman 2021.

Eve Smith has asserted her moral right to be identified as the author of this work in accordance with the Copyright, Designs and Patents Act, 1988.

All Rights Reserved. No part of this publication may be reproduced in any form or by any means without the written permission of the publishers.

This is a work of fiction. Names, characters, places and incidents are either products of the author's imagination or are used fictitiously. Any resemblance to actual events, locales or persons, living or dead, is entirely coincidental.

A catalogue record for this book is available from the British Library.

ISBN 978-1-914585-74-6
eISBN 978-1-914585-75-3

Typeset in Garamond and Century Gothic by www.typesetter.org.uk

Printed and bound by CPI Group (UK) Ltd, Croydon CR0 4YY

For sales and distribution, please contact info@orendabooks.co.uk

For Dave

'In the process of growing up, all excess-birth children have faced unendurable disappointments. These have torn us apart and inflicted wounds that will never heal, and which still cause us pain...

Sunshine Lü, Wei Wanjun and me, as well as millions of others who were born as excess-birth children and lived their lives hidden away, we were all sungrass blooming brilliantly in the darkness...

We have walked out of the shadows, toward the light.'

—Shen Yang, *More Than One Child,*
Memoirs of an Illegal Daughter

'But always – do not forget this, Winston – always there will be the intoxication of power, constantly increasing and constantly growing subtler.

Always, at every moment, there will be the thrill of victory, the sensation of trampling on an enemy who is helpless.

If you want a picture of the future, imagine a boot stamping on a human face – for ever.'

—George Orwell, *1984*

ONE

**Generations failed us.
But we kept our promises
and stemmed the Crisis with actions,
not empty words.**

Our **N**atural **E**arth

The **ONE** Party
For your child, and theirs.

CHAPTER 1

A hazed pink stripes the sky, mirrored in the regiments of roof panels, imbuing the street with a crimson glow. I love this hour, when tentative hues give rise to shape and form. The birds agree; their chorus swells with seesaw chirps and trills. Robins, blackbirds, goldcrests.

Possibly a finch.

Kane steps forward and scans the road. I check the time and count to four.

Today is a four day.

'Clear,' says Kane.

We tread softly past houses huddled in semi-circles, all facing the sun: last-generation builds, patchworks of recycled brick and stone. The Hydrail hisses in the distance. Our appointment is at number twenty-four. Which is good, because that's six fours.

Kane unclicks the gate.

Red and green eyes wink at us from the walls: bricked in bottles. Some people consider these designs too gaudy, but I like them. They remind me of those glass pebbles Mum and I found one summer on a beach in Wales, by the village that fell into the sea.

Someone's up: a light is on. No one leaves lights on overnight: a needless waste of your resource quota. I approach the door and wait for the house to announce me. A blind flicks, and the light snaps off. I sigh. Here we go.

I address the camera: 'My name is Ministry Representative Houghton. I work for the Ministry of Population and Family Planning.' I pause while their system authenticates me. 'I am here to investigate an offence under section twenty-five of the Population Planning Act. You are legally obliged to grant me access.'

Silence.

I imagine the hushed discussion, refining alibis, perhaps some wild escape plan. Kane's already interrogated the layout. He's got all exits covered.

I count to four and rap on the door.

'This is your first warning.'

The light switches back on. And another.

Kane moves into position, in front.

In mythology, Kane is the god of procreation. Kane also means 'little warrior'; I picked it specially. I never say it out loud, though. We're not supposed to give them names, in case we become attached, fret about their demise. It's one of the reasons the Ministry doesn't programme them with personalities.

A man with a long, oval face opens the door. He attempts a smile, which wilts as he clocks Kane. A woman with pale skin and curly black hair is clamped to his side. Her gaze moves over my face and lingers, predictably, on my eyes.

I finger my Ministry badge while Kane completes his checks.

'Are you Samuel and Linda Charring?'

My feed has already confirmed their identities, but it's a procedural relic we're obliged to follow.

The man nods. More of a twitch. He's clutching his wife so tightly the skin around his cuticles has bleached.

I clear my throat. 'Linda Charring, your medi-profile indicates that your hCG hormone levels are elevated and you have not menstruated for fifty-nine days. In the last month, you ordered folic acid and vitamin supplements.'

Her breath flutters.

'This data indicates that you are knowingly pregnant. Yet you have failed to report to a family planning centre.'

Neither of them responds.

'You have one son registered, living at this address. Is that correct?'

Her eyes flit to the stairs.

'Each couple is permitted one child in their lifetime. Giving birth to a second child is prohibited by law and constitutes a birth crime.'

The husband steps forward. 'Look,' he begins, 'we didn't mean to ... It's not like this was planned. It just...' his arm flaps like a limp tentacle '...happened.'

My jaw stiffens. The same old excuses ... As if conception were some unfortunate mishap, beyond their control. The Ministry provides free contraceptive implants that never run out. How difficult can it be?

'Mr Charring, your wife deactivated her Destine implant.' I pause. 'You are both adults. You are aware of the consequences.'

The wife pushes in front of her husband, shielding her belly with her arm. 'I won't. You can't.' Tears bloom. 'It's my baby!'

It was much harder, when I started. Witnessing the anguish of mothers.

Our training reels helped me with that.

Emaciated migrants fleeing camp after camp. The bloody wars over food and water. Acres of crops decimated by pests or sun.

The Charrings' child won't starve, or drown in floods that consume whole cities. He won't die a slow, painful death from disease or burn in a wildfire that incinerates his home.

'Please ... can't you make an exception? Just once?'

She gazes at me as if I am some benevolent deity, empowered to forgive her sin.

I didn't slog my way up to executive grade three, with my condition, by turning a blind eye.

'We'll absorb the child's resources into our quota,' she continues. 'There'll be no excess, I swear.'

I take a breath. 'We tried that before. It doesn't work.'

This is how we got into this mess. Bending the rules, trusting people to make the right choices. While the climate spiralled out of control.

The husband slumps. He knows it's pointless. But not her.

'I won't do it,' she says, in a raw whisper. 'Go ahead: arrest me.'

Kane makes a slight whirring noise. I cross my fingers under my sleeve four times.

We're both alert to this stage: when defence ramps up to defiance. This is what we've trained for: PMC. Probable moment of confrontation.

'It's my right. My human right.' Her lip quivers. 'We never used to have these laws. They're … barbaric!'

I don't explain that our own profligate consumption compelled them, and the failure to protect our borders. That ONE's policies saved us from lawlessness and famine.

I have learned the hard way that such logic does not help. It's more liable to provoke an attack.

'UK citizens have the right to live in a healthy, prospering environment. This is enshrined in our constitution. Stability and security come at a price. Your family quota has been exceeded. This pregnancy must be terminated. If you refuse to attend your clinic, then the procedure will be enforced.'

She pulls away from her husband. There's a faint pinging: probably a medi-alert for her escalating heart rate.

'You and your damned rules,' she growls.

I brace myself and think of Niko, curled in his basket.

'No compassion. No mercy.' Her eyes glitter. 'About as human as that silicon shit-heap beside you.'

Before I have time to react, Kane raises his arm:

'ABUSE WILL NOT BE TOLERATED!'

Both of them flinch.

'Linda, sweetheart.' The husband glances up the stairs. 'Think of our son.'

She cradles her stomach: 'What about *this* son? Or daughter?' She glares at me. 'Maybe one day you'll be on the other side of this door. Then you'll feel something.' She turns and sobs into her husband's chest. 'I can't do it, Sam ... I just can't...'

I apply the distraction technique and count the spindles on their staircase: four, and four more. They taper towards the bottom, like miniature oars.

'Please ensure your wife attends her appointment. Failure to comply is a birth crime and will incur a significant resource penalty and house arrest.'

The husband's gaze lifts to mine. 'People will look back at this, and they will judge you for what you do.'

He ushers his wife down the hallway just as a small face peeps over the banister, striped pyjama legs slotted between the spindles. The boy stares at Kane and then me, his mouth a perfect pink zero.

I arrange my lips into what I hope is a smile.

The boy's eyes do not budge.

I consider lifting my hand in a wave. Anything to break that unblinking stare. But such a gesture might appear trivial.

And I wouldn't want to be inappropriate.

CHAPTER 2

It looks like a pile of rags, dumped by a dusty track.

A constant flow of people trudges past, clutching baskets and babies and bags. They stumble across deep cracks in the earth that look like a maze game I once played. The presenter is reeling off numbers – huge numbers, bigger than we've ever counted to in school. But then the camera moves closer. And, poking out of the rags, I see a leg.

A girl's leg.

...Every five seconds, a child dies from hunger...

It doesn't look like a girl's. More like a machine's, before they coat them with silicone. Just skin hanging off bone.

They zoom in on her face.

It is my face.

But the cheeks are hollows. Black pits where my eyes should be.

Something flickers. Not one thing, many. A swarm. Crawling, wings glistening, burrowing into my—

I wake with a cry. My fingers claw at my face, even as I register it's just the nightmare. The same nightmare that's haunted me ever since they showed us that reel at school.

I sit up. The sheet is slicked to my skin. Niko stirs in his charge-basket and opens one eye. He clambers onto the bed and spoons into my belly. Dawn births familiar shadows: my floating desk, the robotic tree, its CO_2 filters glinting darkly. I cross and uncross my fingers three times. Because three feels right for today. Everything in threes.

A high-pitched beep tears into the room. Niko bolts upright as my screen lights up like a solar flare.

I haul the blanket around my shoulders and scurry to my desk, Niko clacking along the tiles behind. A thick red bar flashes on our family dashboard. It's only Wednesday and my grandparents have already overshot their week's resource quota. Typical of their generation. Banking on the rest of us bailing them out. Again.

I drum the desk in triple meter: Mum and Dad tracking slightly below, the gran we never see well under. At least she sticks to the rules. I log on to the portal and bring up their transactions. Strictly speaking, we're not supposed to look unless it's an investigation, but my colleagues all do it. The ministries turn a blind eye because they like us to be role models, carbon footprints nicely within budget. Especially the one I work for, the MPFP.

It's the usual suspects: water and heating. Oh, and lunch at some café that's been blacklisted for unauthorised imports. That always bumps quotas into the red.

Niko nudges my leg with a whine.

'It's OK, fella, Kai will sort it.'

I remember one time they snuck off to the Lake District on another of their sprees. Mum didn't realise until she got to the check-out at our local store. When she swiped her card, not only did the till humiliate her with its bright-red rejection, the store bot made her put everything back: 'Your family quota has been exceeded. These purchases cannot be authorised.'

Turned out my grandparents had managed to blow our entire week's food quota, dining out. We had to avoid that store for weeks.

I'm about to fire off a message, when a notification pops up: *Custody authorisation request.*

I check the time: just after five. My diligence may be exemplary, but this is beyond the call of duty, even for me.

A bristled face lurches onto my screen. Patches of ruddy skin gape through granite whiskers, as if a child has been let loose on them with a razor.

I summon a breath. 'Detective Inspector Steener.'

'Reaping already, this fine morning? Bit keen, even for you...'

My neck muscles stiffen. I *hate* that term.

'A little early for you too, Inspector.'

'Some of us haven't been to bed.'

He yawns, as if to prove it.

I avert my eyes. I have no desire to see inside Steener's mouth.

'Better brace yourself.' He sniffs. 'Not a good one.'

There are no good ones.

Steener works for the foeticide division. Technically, it's foeticide and infanticide, but since genetic testing became routine, the killing of unwanted babies is mercifully rare. He may have some challenging habits, but Steener is very good at his job.

'Go on.'

'Woman wakes up in a hotel room. Bleeding heavily, stomach cramps, no idea how she got there. Calls an ambulance, tests show she's been dosed. Nasty little cocktail, goes by the street name Miss Carrie.'

I frown. 'That's a new one. What's in it?'

'Abortion meds and GHB. Gamma-hydroxybutyric acid. Also known as "easy lay": a date-rape drug.'

I sigh. Sometimes I despair of our species.

'Only found out she was pregnant a couple of weeks ago,' continues Steener. 'According to her, he knew she'd deactivated her Destine implant. But when she told him about the baby, he got cold feet. Said he only got "one shot" at fatherhood. Unfortunate choice of words. Said they should have gone the IVF route with screening, to be safe. That this wasn't "the one".'

Steener rolls his eyes. The whites have a creamy film, like hot milk that's gone cold.

'He pressed her to have a termination. She refused. Just as well he's an idiot. If he'd kept quiet and slipped her the meds at home, he might have got away with it. As opposed to dragging her out here...'

An image materialises on screen. All I see is a wash of red.

My eyes veer away from bloodied sheets to purple flowered walls; a table in the corner with a lamp. My foot begins to tap.

'So, where did he get the drugs?'

Steener arches his eyebrows. 'Usual source. Every time we close one shop down another springs up.'

By 'source', Steener means the abhorrent slurry that resides in the underbelly of our system.

I access the couple's profiles. She's a secondary-school teacher, quota-compliant, no issues with resources or family planning.

He, on the other hand...

'Bit of a spendthrift, possibly, young Michael?' Steener smirks. 'Not ready to give up life's niceties for nappies?'

There's no possibly about it. Expensive meals. Unnecessary purchases. Looks like she's been helping him out for some time.

'A repeat squanderer.' That's all I concede.

'So, do I have a green light? Shall we bring him in for questioning?'

'Definitely,' I say, flagging the file. Transgressions must be penalised.

I think of the sheets. 'How's she doing, the woman?'

'Physically, OK, but...' He puffs out a breath. 'Put it this way, she won't be dating any time soon.'

I end the call and pull Niko onto my lap. My fingers sink into his fur, and he sighs with pleasure.

I wonder if the woman owns a pet bot. Maybe I should suggest it.

Much safer to stick with machines.

CHAPTER 3

The digital display on the platform flashes green: low humidity, decent air quality and only twenty-four degrees, very comfortable for April. Particulates and CO_2 levels all good, which means it's officially a no-mask day. I still put mine on. It serves a dual purpose.

The Hydrail isn't too busy, so when the train glides into the station, I secure my favourite seat: middle of the carriage, by the window. It's not just the view; it's been proven, statistically, that air quality is better here. And if the doors malfunction, you can get out fast.

We cruise past the ponds, white crests of cloud reflected in solar floater panels. The Parks line starts just north of the Chiswick wetlands, and this high up, the views are superb. I'm so grateful I don't have to travel underground, the way Mum did, like some urban mole. Imagine being trapped in the dark in the Great Flood, water rushing into the tunnels. All the pumps in London couldn't keep out that amount of water, not after the Thames Barrier failed. There was no stopping ONE after that.

My portable pings.

Sorry, darling, Grannie's such a pain, I know.

Don't worry, your dad and I can cut back on a few showers, don't you take the hit.

Love you x

Typical Mum, taking the rap for everybody else. She'd rather die than see me go without. Not every child is so lucky.

As we pass Hammersmith, ONE Party holograms flicker across the high-rises, freshly coated with solar paint: atmospheric methane levels are reducing; national carbon emissions continue to fall; migrant resettlement targets have been exceeded. The prime minister beams as he delivers the good news, like a jovial Father Christmas. We sail through the royal parks, dropping down Constitution Hill onto Birdcage Walk. The horse chestnuts in St James's Park are in full flower, their confetti blossoms bobbing amongst the leaves. As the train slows for Great George Street, I hoist my bag over my shoulder and edge to the doors.

I cross to Parliament Square, a breeze rippling my hair. I approach the statue of the Mother and pause, along with others, to pay my respects. Her accusatory stare is fixed on the Houses of Parliament Museum, that gaze as resolute in stone as it was in flesh. One of her first acts when she swept to power was the construction of a new eco-complex in Victoria Tower Gardens to house her government. Solar-powered, flood-resistant and cloaked in carbon-guzzling plants, it was a powerful statement: a clean sweep of the previous regime's lavish inefficiencies. Rumour has it that when the old guard kicked off, she threatened to reallocate the footprint of those mouldy, river-soaked buildings to their personal resource quotas.

As the Mother always said: actions speak louder than words.

It's a good five minutes to get through security. Next stop: the spit zone. That's what we call the DNA scanner. A quick swab of saliva, a green circle, and I'm in.

Even at this hour, the office resembles an industrious hive: worker bees tapping away in softly lit cells, just the occasional beep or low voice. Two huge golden hands hang above the entrance, encircling a seedling that curls up, to the light.

As I reach my cubicle, Aisha swivels round and cups her hands in the Party salute. 'Good morning, Ministry Representative Houghton.'

I cup my hands. 'Good morning, Ministry Representative Osundo.'

Aisha joined the MPFP two years ago. Sponsored by the Party under the resettlement programme, she escaped Nigeria, but had to leave her family behind. Decades of drought have devastated that country; the militant sects are running rife. According to the reels, millions have starved or been killed.

'Beautiful sky – did you see it?' She smiles. 'Such a deep red...'

The bloodied sheets ambush me, and I shudder. Hopefully that man is already in Steener's clutches.

I pull out my chair and give my keyboard a wipe. 'Busy schedule?' I prefer to keep things on a professional footing.

'Another bolter: seven weeks along. Didn't show up at the clinic.'

'Have you tracked her?'

'Yes: some village in Sussex. My travel quota is haemorrhaging. I swear our areas are getting bigger.'

I glance at the other cubicles. Aisha can be a little reckless. 'It's because they have to switch them around, remember? It's for our own protection.'

My screen fires up, its soft blue glow reminiscent of childhood visits to the aquarium. I used to love basking in that azure light, watching the pale bodies glide past, razor teeth feigning indifference. But the aquarium was too resource intensive, so the Ministry shut it down.

I give my population vitals a quick scan: 1,671 births yesterday, all authorised. The bots have only flagged a couple of families in my area: second marriages, they always cause problems. The one-child rule applies, whether you change partner, gender or sexuality. I don't know why that concept seems so hard to grasp.

A notification suddenly swoops in:
Excess birth, unregistered
Female
Age range 24–26 (DNA estimate, unverified)
My eyes widen.

I swing round and gawp at Aisha, but she's busy on a call.

Even before smart medical devices were introduced for remote health monitoring the Ministry caught the majority of second pregnancies before the baby was born. At the very latest, directly after.

This is an adult.

I drill down further. A new profile, entered at a wellness centre near Oxford. Looks like a clumsy attempt was made to erase it afterwards. How on earth can it have evaded the system until now? All profiles are registered at birth.

I only know of one family that managed to conceal a grown excess child. The Ministry hushed it up, but it's become the stuff of legend.

The penalty was severe.

I tap my screen and the DNA map slides in: genetic fingerprints lined up like a family tree.

My heel drums the floor. And stops.

I cannot breathe. It's as if my pod has been sealed in a vacuum.

I race down the profiles: grandparents, parents ... I recognise them all.

Bar one that shouldn't be there: an illegal sibling's.

Next to mine.

CHAPTER 4
Day One

I cross my fingers and stroke them with my thumbs, my body fizzing with cortisol as silver biofarm towers flash past. The train is crossing the rewilded zones: transgenic poplars, oaks and ash shooting up at twice the speed of their forefathers, soaking up more CO_2. Usually these woodlands spark a thrill of anticipation; their branches say: look, you are getting close now, you are nearly home. But today, their welcome is blemished, as if stricken by some fungal infestation newly transported from overseas.

I think of the DNA map, my profile nestling beside another's: a fifty-percent match.

I have a sister.

My gut tightens. Just saying that word is dangerous, but there is no denying it. The chromosomes dictate she exists.

I moved the alert to a restricted access area, reserved for 'delicate' investigations, usually the preserve of the famous or the influential. Such behaviour goes against my instinct, the oaths I took:

Your first loyalty is to your Ministry...

I remember Minister Gauteng drilling us at our induction about how it was our duty to root out all misdemeanours, as she eyed us, one by one. Reminding us how privileged we were to serve our country.

Especially you...

She didn't have to voice her disgust at my eyes. Her expression said it all.

I still don't understand how this profile can only have appeared now. I must investigate and document my evidence. Show this is all some terrible mistake.

But the system doesn't make mistakes...

The booming in my ears intensifies, as if my head is being squeezed in a vice. I tried all the usual searches: birth registry, medical and education records. All drew blanks. I can't stop thinking about that family that concealed their second child. They managed to keep the daughter hidden until she was twelve. Some say they procured a duplicate ID on the black market. Others claim the girl and her sister lived a double life, pretending to be the same child. Whatever happened, the Ministry made an example of them. The parents' sentence matched the daughter's age: twelve years. No one knows what happened to her, though rumours abound.

If my parents are guilty, and the Ministry applies the same sentence, they will go to prison for a minimum of twenty-four years.

Water glitters in the distance: the Thunberg Reservoir. As we slow for a station, a Ministry hording slides into view.

Give your baby the gift of good health with
Optime baby screening
Because life doesn't give you a second chance

The young girl sitting on her father's shoulders has been obliterated by vandals; the appalling nickname for our Ministry scrawled underneath:

FUCK THE BABY REAPERS

And an idea hits me so hard I break out in a sweat: maybe this profile is a test – of my loyalties. What are the chances of this case of a grown sibling, *my* illegal sibling, being allocated to me? Maybe, right this minute, the Ministry is watching, to see if I'm up to it: investigating my own parents. Prepared to issue a warrant for their arrest.

You should have reported it...

I stray back to the interminable questions, scrolling my past for clues. I grew up as an only child, like everyone else; I have no memory of any sister. My parents were loving and law-abiding: nothing like the families I've met who try to sneak past the rules. But then I remember Ciara Reilly's mum and dad. They seemed pretty law-abiding, too.

Ciara was my first and only real friend. The only one who didn't snigger behind her hand at me or call me names because, unlike them, I wasn't perfected before birth.

Weird-Eye!

She had this dogeared book called *My Naughty Little Sister* that she'd unearthed from a box when her dad was clearing out her gran's loft. It would most certainly have been banned, but we didn't realise how dangerous it was at the time. We used to read it under her duvet, gasping and giggling away. Sometimes, we'd even pretend we were sisters: the thought of it now still stings. We made it a game, taking it in turns to be the younger or older one, playing pranks and bossing each other around.

Until another girl in our class reported us.

We were sent to the head. Given detention for a week, humiliated in front of the whole school.

We never played the game after that.

Then Ciara really did get a younger sister. I overheard Mum and Dad whispering about it.

I didn't see Ciara or her family again.

I spend the rest of the journey rehearsing the questions I must ask, tormenting myself with imagined answers. By the time the train pulls into Oxford, I'm exhausted.

I take the tram from the station, past the weathered-stone colleges full of students beavering away on the latest farming initiatives and carbon-sequestration tech. As we rattle past the gates to the Covered Market, I have a flashback to those melt-in-your-mouth cookies Mum used to get me, when the kids at school had been particularly mean. The stone lion is waiting for me, jaws still gaping, clambering over the arch of an ancient door. Just one more thing that gave me nightmares, as if the newsreels they made us watch weren't enough. No matter what time it was, Mum always came in to comfort me. She'd rock me in her arms, whispering reassurances, until I drifted back to sleep.

More memories rally, protesting my parents' innocence, and I nearly miss my stop. I jump out by the Smart Mart and zigzag down side roads, each step growing heavier as I count:

Three, six, nine, twelve, fifteen...

And there it is: the street where I grew up. I know exactly how many steps it is from here. My eyes stay glued to my feet; cracks dissect the pavement where weeds cluster. Only when I'm right outside, do I look up.

Wisteria curls under the faded-white sills; blue and pink pots have assembled by the door. The stone pig I chose at a summer fair grins at me by the fence.

I take three breaths. Raise my finger to the old-fashioned bell. It hovers there, uncertain. I haven't told Mum I'm coming. It's better that way.

Feet pad down the hallway. A quick, light step so familiar, it makes my chest ache.

Mum's in her casual clothes: a sleeveless top and yoga pants, her hair scraped into a bun. She's wearing the glass drop earrings I bought her for Christmas.

'Kai, darling.' A smile breaks out. 'What a lovely surprise.'

She opens her arms wide, and I clutch her tight like I used to, when she could make everything better.

As I pull away, her eyes race over me. 'Are you OK?'

'I'm fine. I was in the area, so thought I'd pop by.'

I kick off my shoes and scurry past; attempt to ground myself in the quartz units, the bleached wooden floor. But even décor can no longer be trusted.

'Can I get you some tea?' She raises an eyebrow. 'Or perhaps something stronger?'

She's not fooled. Those eyes are like Ministry scanners: they can read me from the inside out.

'I'll stick with tea, thanks.'

'I've a new Suffolk varietal I've been saving. I think you'll like it.'

I drink in each detail as she flits around the kitchen: those slender fingers with pale-pink nails, that mole on her left wrist. The familiar tune she's humming.

She reaches into a cupboard and sighs. 'I assume this is about Grannie.'

I blink. And remember the overshoot.

'Actually, no.'

'Oh.' She passes me a cup. 'You seem awfully serious.' She laughs but her notes are off.

'Something happened today which doesn't make sense...' My hands squeeze the cup. 'I was wondering ... Did you ever donate any of your eggs? Or ... embryos?'

Her brow pinches. 'A strange thing to ask ... No, I didn't. Why?'

It was my wild hope. The system would have flagged it. But I still had to try.

'This morning, a new profile cropped up, on a family record...' I hesitate. '*Our* record.'

The furrow on her forehead deepens. 'What do you mean?'

'A genetic ID. For a woman, in her mid-twenties.'

Mum freezes.

'I'm sorry, I have to ask ... Is it possible, that you ... That you might have had...' I scrape my tongue across my teeth.

'Kai?' Her tone hardens.

'...a second child?'

She stares at me. 'What is this?'

The rawness in her voice sinks me.

'The profile, Mum. It's a sibling match ... For me.'

Her mouth sags. 'No. No, that can't be right ... There must be some mistake.'

'The system doesn't make mistakes...' The words erupt before I can stop them.

Deep breaths. Distance. This is what we've been taught.

It's not working. I lurch for her hand. 'This is upsetting, I know. I'm just as confused as you are.'

'You don't seem very confused.'

'I'm not accusing you of anything—'

'Aren't you?' Her hand slides away. 'You turn up here with no warning, and start ... interrogating me—'

'I'm trying to protect you!' I sound like the five-year-old me, desperate and frightened. 'Please, Mum, I ... I just need to be sure. Is there anything you're not telling me?'

'What's going on?'

I twist round: it's Dad. I didn't hear him come in.

'Why the raised voices?' He looks at Mum, then at me.

I swallow. 'We have a problem.'

He frowns. 'What kind of problem?' He turns to Mum. 'Sarah?'

Mum shakes her head.

Dad looks smaller, somehow; perhaps it's the way his coat is hanging off him, as if it's suddenly outgrown him.

'I need to speak with your father for a minute. In private.'

I haven't heard those words in years.

And, just like that, I know.

CHAPTER 5

They trudge up the stairs to their bedroom and shut the door.

I listen to the floorboards creak as they pace up and down, minutes stretching into seeming-hours. Their voices are hushed, a duet of whispers, the occasional word rising and breaking free.

My heart still clings to a hope that Dad will magic up an explanation, make this all go away. They are not like those other parents. Such deceit is beyond them.

But still ... But still... says my brain. *Look at the evidence.*

One thing you can be sure of: DNA never lies.

At one point I hear a noise, more animal than human. It stops abruptly.

I think it's Mum.

My mother prides herself on her fitness, but when they eventually come down, ten years have claimed her. Instinctively, I reach out my hand. But it hangs there. Unwanted.

She collapses onto the sofa, nursing a clutch of tissues. Red veins impregnate her eyes. Dad sits next to her, and I have a sudden memory of those 'little chats' we sometimes had when I was younger.

Except this time it's not me who has done something wrong.

She glances at Dad. 'You were just five months old when I got the summons. For my tubal ligation. Before the Destine implant, they used to sterilise women as soon as they'd given birth. But I'd had complications...'

I clench my fingers in my lap. I can hear them already: the sirens. That roaring wall of water. Just before our tsunami hits.

'After your dad dropped me off, they did a test. They told me it was just a precaution. You see, I'd struggled with the breastfeeding. I tried so hard, but I ... I just wasn't any good.' Her lip trembles. Dad reaches for her hand. 'We'd mixed in bottles. The doctor said that might have been why...'

I want to press my palm over her mouth, stop her confession. But she presses on.

'That was when she told me, I was three months' pregnant.'

'Your mum had no idea.' Dad jumps in. 'Neither of us did. Your world turns upside down with a new baby. Sleep was all over the place.'

I try to focus on their words, but there's a sea inside my head: wave crashing after wave. My parents broke the law. I have a sister, like Ciara.

What am I going to do?

'The doctor wanted me to do it straight away. The abortion. She said it would be better to "just get it over with..."' Mum falters. 'So, she took me into this room ... This cold, cold room. Pictures of daffodils and roses. And I remember thinking, how can they have flowers in a room like this?

'She unlocked a cabinet and pulled out a packet. Dropped a white tablet into my hand...' Mum stares at her palm. 'It looked so small, so ... insignificant. I just stared at that pill as the doctor's words filled the room ... How I might feel a little sick, there might be some spotting. As if it was just an inconvenience, as if it was ... nothing. And all I could think was, I do not want this. But they will make me do it. I cannot keep this child.'

Her eyes lift to mine, and my throat thickens.

Maybe one day you'll be on the other side of this door.

Then you'll feel something...

'But I could sense that life already, growing inside me. The child it would become...'

Mum turns to Dad. His jaw is rigid.

'And I knew, I just knew, I couldn't do it...'

A tear slides down Mum's cheek and I have to look away.

'It's different when you've carried a child. Such an unimaginable gift ... A miracle, really. There's a reason the Ministry recruits you so young...'

Mum's never liked what I do. She's never said it, but I've always known. The casual suggestions, the links she'd send to other jobs, despite me landing such a prestigious role.

Now, I understand why.

'So I pleaded with her not to make me. Said I'd do anything: even give up our house. I told her it would finish me, and I honestly believe that was true. I became hysterical ... And that's when the doctor mentioned there might be another way.'

'What do you mean?'

'An option to ... reallocate the child.'

Reallocate?

'But ... reallocations were only allowed for first pregnancies. Second pregnancies have always been illegal.'

'That's what I'd thought too,' says Mum. 'She said, assuming the baby was healthy, she could try and make a case, on psychological grounds. But the pregnancy would have to be kept secret. There were strict procedures, and the moment I started showing, I'd have to move into a confinement home, until the child was born.'

I breathe in for three. Out for three. But numbers can't tame the galloping in my chest. We were never told about second-child reallocations.

I've never even heard of confinement homes.

'There were four of us in that place. We weren't allowed to go out.'

'The way they treated them,' says Dad. 'As if they were criminals. Children weren't even allowed to see their mothers.'

'So your father took care of you. With help from his mother.'

The other grandma ... So she *did* meet me, after all.

'We told everyone that your mum was recuperating from dengue fever, in a wellness centre down south. No one questioned it.'

I stare at them. The parents I love. The parents I thought I knew.

Mum sighs. 'That doctor didn't have to help me, I don't know why she did ... Perhaps there was more pity back then...'

Pity? Pity won't help them with the Ministry, that much I do know. They have committed a birth crime. There is only one way this can end.

'I had just six weeks with my baby before she came: the woman from the Ministry...' Mum swallows. 'The grief never leaves you. It just ... spreads out, over time...'

Dad's face crumples. I dig my nails into my thighs.

'I know what you're thinking, Kai,' she says. 'How horrified you must be. But you see, this way, both children had a chance at life...'

Dad exhales. 'Why has this all blown up now? It happened decades ago, for God's sake.'

I have exactly the same question. 'I ... I don't know...'

Mum leans closer. 'Has someone seen her, Kai? Is that it? Do you know where she is?'

I shake my head. 'I know nothing about her.' My words are brittle, like the rest of me.

I resort to process; the only thing right now I can be sure of.

'I don't understand, how did they...?' I swallow. 'How could your baby just disappear? With first-born reallocations, biological lineage is always displayed. You can't change someone's genetic ID.'

'They never discussed any of that with us,' says Mum. 'I wasn't allowed to know.'

'What about your health records?'

She shrugs. 'It all, just … vanished. It was as if she'd never been born.'

I can't believe what I'm hearing. What kind of doctor would be complicit in that?

'I still think about her, you know,' Mum whispers. 'I'll be sitting on a tram and see a young woman get on, and I'll wonder … Could that be her?'

My panic spirals. Doesn't she realise how much trouble we're in? What this means, for all of us?

I have witnessed a confession. One course of action is open to me. Unless…

'Which clinic was it?'

Mum hesitates. 'It was before we moved. Middleton, Milton Keynes.'

'Can you remember the doctor's name?'

Mum frowns.

'It was a long time ago, Kai,' says Dad.

'Yes, I know.' It comes out more sharply than I intended. 'Where did you give birth?'

'Oxford. The Marston.'

At last: a glimmer of light. The same wellness centre where the profile was originally traced.

'Did she…? Did you give her a name?'

Mum nods and looks down. It's Dad who finally answers.

'Zoe. It means "life". We don't know if it was passed on…'

Mum grips my hand. 'We did everything we were asked,

Kai. We gave up our child. Can't you, just...? Make this go away?'

'Oh, Mum...' My eyes squeeze shut. 'It's not as simple as that.'

The profile is on the system. That alone is grounds for arrest.

'What happens next?' asks Dad. 'Are you obliged to ... report us?'

No anger. No barbed recriminations. It would be easier if there were.

'I have a small amount of time to investigate on my own, before the profile goes public. To try and figure things out.'

'How small?'

I sigh. 'Two weeks.'

CHAPTER 6
Day Two

The tram whines up the hill on its slow climb to the Marston. I can already see it, soaring above the rooftops, those iconic green bioreactor panels looping around its frame. The Ministry of Health Security is particularly proud of its centres' design: microalgae in the panels consume carbon dioxide and nutrients from waste water, converting them to biomass energy, which powers the buildings in a virtuous loop. But ecodesigns are not my priority today.

I stayed the night in the room that had sheltered me my entire childhood, seeking respite in the familiar: the pale-blue curtains that shimmer like waves in the sun; Teddy still waiting for me on my pillow. I immersed myself in my search, trawling page after page of data. Banking records, tax and insurance. Utilities, transport and tech. Not one single match.

In transaction terms, Zoe Houghton does not exist.

Afterwards, I just lay on my bed and stared at the ceiling, filtering memories through this new lens. All I could unearth was one potential clue. I must have been around four or five, and I recall Dad's face knotted in anger because I'd taken something from their room. I don't remember what, but Dad hardly ever lost his temper, so it stayed with me.

Maybe what I'd taken had been hers.

I must have eventually drifted off, but woke when it was still dark. For those first few seconds, everything seemed normal, and I reached for Niko, but my fingers brushed the wall.

And my family fell apart once more.

I slump against the window as the tram swings into the approach road, passing a contractor furiously scrubbing paint off a wall:

STOP THE MURDER

My foot jiggles. I count the dots on the patterned seats in fives.

I've worked so hard to get this far in the Ministry, much harder than the others, so I could serve my country, prove that I was loyal. It was the same in school; the teachers never took to me, even before the incident with Ciara. It didn't matter what I did, how hard I tried, any acknowledgement of my grades always seemed begrudging.

I can just imagine their reactions now, if they knew:

You only had to look at her...

Remember that sisters' game?

I told you so...

I step onto the pavement and march along the path to reception. The registration scanner winks at me, and the doors slide open. Shouts erupt from the play area, where pink-cheeked children dart through tunnels and under nets. Behind them, adult limbs pound a battalion of gym machines with less elation, more sweat.

An admin bot glides out to meet me, flushing green.

'Ministry Representative Houghton, welcome.' It inclines its upper body. 'We have the attendance report you asked for. Clients and their visitors in the requested timeframe.'

Was it really only yesterday I saw that alert?

It feels like a lifetime.

'Classified, I trust?'

'At the highest level.'

'Good.'

It hands me a screen. 'Staff and contractors are also listed.'

I quickly run the profiles. No flags to indicate any transgressions on quotas. And no matches.

'Anything from security?'

'No unauthorised visitors. Everyone is accounted for.'

Old school it is, then. 'I'll need to interview any staff with access to the gene bank who were here between six and seven yesterday morning. Human or other.' I tap the screen. 'Schedule them for ten minutes each.'

'Of course. Permit me to show you to your workstation.'

We cross the atrium to the lifts. I cast my eye over the curved white lines and abstract décor. The walls are afflicted with blue, cell-like spheres, giving the impression of yet another antibiotic-resistant infection. As we ascend, I glimpse a scattering of white pods on the third floor: surgical biodomes.

The glass doors open, and I am assaulted by a chorus of wails.

The maternity floor.

The bot leads me into a consultation room. A white desk presides over two lounge chairs; a vase of artificial flowers diffuses a sickly scent. I glance at the poster above the desk: one of the Ministry's favourites: a mother cradles her baby, sunlight filtering through golden leaves:

One family, one child
Because every baby deserves a healthy world

I think of my mother here, all those years ago. Cradling her illegal daughter.

'Refreshments are available from the kiosk next door,' says the bot. 'The relevant staff have been notified. Is there anything else I may assist you with before I leave?'

'No.'

A minute later, an interview list pops up on my screen. Not one of them is human.

Almost immediately, there's a tap on the door. Only a machine would be so prompt.

'Enter.'

It still catches me, how real some of them look, even with their skin tones. This android shimmers a pale silver.

They cup their hands in the salute: 'A pleasure to meet you, Ministry Representative Houghton.'

They radiate a good-natured calm; facial muscles relaxed, lips slightly curled. No gawping at my eyes. Androids certainly have the edge on people when it comes to manners. But beneath that shimmering skin is a silicone endoskeleton that could crush me. Housing the neural network of a super-intelligent brain.

I flash my Ministry badge, although it's not necessary, and launch straight in.

'Did you access the gene lab at any point between six and seven yesterday morning?'

'Yes.'

'What was your work?'

'Profile updates.'

'Who else was present?'

'In that timeframe, three data bots.'

They meet my gaze. And now I'm the hypocrite caught staring: their silver pupils have lilac irises – the combination is quite arresting. I check their ID tag: *Nieran*.

Only level six are given names.

I consult my notes. 'According to the rota, you weren't due in until eight.'

'Preparation improves efficiency.'

A machine after my own heart.

'Did you sequence any new profiles that morning?'

'No. I was reviewing updates from patch feeds.'

'Show me.'

They tip their head. 'As you have the appropriate authorisation, I am permitted.'

They walk behind the desk and activate a console. Profile IDs spill onto my screen.

It only takes a second to run them. None is a match for Zoe's.

'Is it possible someone could have accessed the system remotely?'

'The protocols are very strict. There is no remote access to the gene bank for security reasons.'

What am I missing?

My foot starts tapping: a staccato rhythm of fives.

I catch them looking, and stop.

'May I offer a suggestion?' Their tone is deferential. 'I understand that you are seeking a specific profile. The Ministry works off dashboard summaries, but our bank stores the raw data of over fifteen million individuals. I could run a search, in the event there has been some anomaly in the classification?'

I hesitate. I'd rather not share this profile with anyone, but they are a level six.

And the profile originated here.

'This information is classified at the highest level,' I say. 'The sequence must be deleted immediately.'

'I understand.'

I send it over and the android blinks. Twice.

'Unfortunately, that profile is not registered here.'

I feel a rush of irritation. 'It was traced to this centre. Surely it can't just appear out of nowhere then disappear again?'

Their expression indicates some conflict. 'I am aware that,

very occasionally, the centre is forced to deal with certain ... emergencies. For "unregulated" identities.'

It's as though an insect is crawling up my neck.

Officially, such things are not acknowledged. The Ministry says it undercuts confidence in the system, which is bad for morale. But we all know it happens. Offliners, who opt out of the system. Criminal gangs. And, of course, the never-ending stream of illegal migrants who vanish into the underworld.

I clear my throat. 'I'm sure that's not the case,' I say, because I have to. But my mind is spinning.

'Send me the profiles of all females born in the maternity unit on this day.'

I send him the date Mum gave me. I don't hold out much hope, given I've already searched the birth records, but while I'm here, I might as well ask. This reallocation business is bugging me: it just doesn't add up. Any medical check or nursery application would flag a new child.

'The data has been sent. Will there be anything else?'

'No, that is all.'

They cup their hands and move to the door.

I consider cancelling the other interviews. If a level six can't help, there's little point drilling a data bot.

My mind turns again to that other family, who hid their excess child.

I scrolled some state social feeds in the early hours, to see if I could find out what happened to the girl. A number of conspiracy theories had somehow managed to evade the censorship algorithms. The most disturbing page, most likely the terrorist group FREE's handiwork, claimed the Ministry had shipped the twelve-year-old off to a remote Scottish island. After sterilising her.

So she couldn't conceive and throw their numbers out again.

CHAPTER 7
Day Three

I gaze at the striped blue bars on my dashboard, numbers and letters infiltrating my brain. My sibling and I share half our genes, but are we anything alike? In the panic witnessing my parents' confession, it didn't occur to me to ask. Does she suffer the same mutation in her eyes? Dark hair, like mine, or blonde? Versions of her crystallise in my mind and fade. Like photograph paper from the olden days, giving up its secrets to the light.

I checked all the births on the list from the wellness centre. Each one was legitimate, the lineage clearly displayed. I spent another hour poring over employment records. Ten female doctors worked at the Middleton clinic at the time of my mother's pregnancy. I sent their names to Mum last night, but I haven't heard back. You'd think she'd realise every hour is precious.

'Ministry Representative Houghton, do you have a moment? I just need to verify something with you.'

I look up. Aisha is staring at me. I muster something approaching a smile.

'Of course, Ministry Representative Osundo. How can I help?'

Aisha wheels her chair over. 'Have you heard about Rana?' she whispers.

Scandal, not business. I wouldn't normally entertain it, but Rana Hamilton works on the same floor. 'No?'

Aisha glances at the neighbouring cubicles. 'Got busted for "corrupt practices". Hellie told me.'

The office gossip strikes again.

'He was caught taking bribes from some gang in return for ghost IDs. He handed over profiles of patients in terminal care.'

'That's disgusting.'

'I know. Big business, apparently, and it's not just illegals who buy them. Some people are prepared to pay big money to extend their quotas. Hellie said a funeral-home director got jailed for doing the same last year.'

I remember. Accounts of the deceased aren't closed straight away, because of medical and funeral expenses.

'How did they catch Rana?'

'One of the reps over in Resources got suspicious. Asked the fraud squad to start tracking him. That should bag them a nice promotion. As for Rana...' Her eyebrows lift. 'Doubt we'll be seeing him again.'

I think of the file lurking in my restricted folder. Eleven more days, and someone can rat on me.

I exhale. 'Well, better get back to it.'

'Busy morning?'

I run down the list. 'No-show for a termination in Battersea. An entrapment allegation by a husband in Wandsworth who claims he was set up by a woman he was having an affair with...'

'Let me guess: he got her pregnant but now he wants a baby with his wife.'

'Exactly.'

Aisha rolls her eyes. 'Why is it the cheaters never think the rules apply to them?'

'And a genetic-testing appeal by a carrier of muscular dystr—'

A burst of light blinds me. A suck of pressure, and I'm hurled to the floor.

Walls shred, windows splinter.

Now the alarms crash in.

Smoke billows into my face, making me cough. There's a smell of burning.

Through the fog, I glimpse a face.

Aisha's.

Her lips move. A second later, her voice swims in: 'Kai? Can you hear me?'

I blink at her as a high-pitched whine sears my skull.

'Microdrones,' she hisses. 'There could be more, stay down.'

She levers herself up on her elbows and scans the room.

Red spots spatter my hand.

Not mine. Hers.

There's a thick shard of glass wedged in her shoulder.

I open my mouth to warn her, but the words won't come.

Glass specks glisten on my skin like snow crystals. I pick one out of my wrist. Blood wells up like a tear.

I try to remember what today's number was.

And then the screaming starts.

As the dust clears, I see a lone foot trapped underneath three vast metal fingers. All that remains of the Party's emblem. Pulverised bricks and bits of clothing smoulder nearby.

'So much for the state-of-the-art counter-drone system,' says Aisha.

It's supposed to detect and disable unmanned aerial attacks, but whatever tech FREE are using always seems one step ahead.

'Come on,' she says. 'I think we're safe to move. We better get clear.'

We scramble on our hands and knees, trying to avoid the shrapnel. Blood streams down Aisha's arm. I tap her hand.

'Aisha, your shoulder…'

She frowns at the wound, as if in irritation.

The screams are coming from the lobby. A woman rocks back and forth in the foetal position, arms clenched around her knees. It takes me a moment to recognise her.

'Hellie?' Aisha crawls over to her. 'Hellie, you need to get up. We have to go to—'

'THIS IS THE MINISTRY SPECIAL GUARD. ALL MINISTRY PERSONNEL MUST EVACUATE TO THE SAFE ROOM IMMEDIATELY.'

Autonomous security robots smash through the rubble and start clearing the entrance, tossing concrete slabs and hunks of metal as if they're tennis balls. Dust clouds soar, coating our throats. The Mother's ministries were built for nature, not bombs.

We take one arm each and haul Hellie up. Aisha grimaces; her sleeve has turned a deep crimson. We lurch through the debris, covering our mouths, but I can't stop coughing. Another colleague limps past, his shirt caked in blood.

As we reach the corridor, Aisha slows. FREE always send in graffiti drones after the explosives. A child with sad brown eyes stares at us, a dripping red caption underneath:

You murdered me

More images and accusations pepper what's left of the walls, each tagged with the same encircled black V:

Ministry of Lies

Hands off my uterus!

And one I haven't seen before:

Justice for the Abandoned

They protest about us supposedly murdering embryos, while maiming and killing hundreds in senseless attacks like this.

Someone shoves past, knocking me off balance. Hellie recovers her legs, and the three of us stagger to the stairs leading down to the safe room: an improvised bunker the length of the building with reinforced walls. They built it after the first attack. We pass through a security check and descend to the basement.

I count each step down. The bunker is already crammed with workers and bots scurrying in all directions, like a beehive under attack. It's already boiling: the ventilation system must have failed. I swallow, hard, trying to block out the acrid stench of scorched materials and sweat. As we search for a space to hunker down, I catch fragments of conversations: speculation about the damage; low whispers about other attacks and the terrorists upping their game.

We find someone to take Hellie and search for another medic.

'Here.' Aisha passes me a cup of water. My hands are trembling. Her eyes narrow. 'You OK?'

'I'm fine.' Just seeing her wound makes me queasy. 'You need to get that shoulder looked at.'

'And you need to get those cuts on your face looked at.'

What cuts?

'Is it bad?' My hand rushes to my cheek, but Aisha bats it away.

'Best let the professionals do it, eh?'

I gulp some water. 'What was that slogan? About "the abandoned"?'

She shrugs. 'Who knows? Probably some new conspiracy FREE have cooked up.' She stares at the gossiping huddles. 'I tell you one thing though: the Ministry's going to retaliate big time. It's going to be a long, hard summer...'

There's a sudden hush as everyone turns to the stairs.

Minister Gauteng surveys the bunker, a deep scowl on her face, her usually impeccable suit sullied with dirt. The gold ONE emblem – reserved for those in the uppermost echelons of power – gleams defiantly at her throat.

She raises her hands. 'Colleagues. Another atrocity has been attempted, and decisively thwarted. Initial surveys show minimal damage and, mercifully, few injuries.'

It didn't look that minimal, I think.

'We stand together to defeat those who wage cowardly, despicable acts of terror on our great nation. Be in no doubt: we will find those responsible and bring them to justice.'

She nods, those formidable eyes scrutinising her audience.

I was always told the powerful are less imposing in the flesh. Not her.

'I applaud your stalwart devotion to the Ministry and to the values we espouse. I know our prime minister echoes these sentiments. Our work demands sacrifice. But that work must go on.' She cups her hands. 'For your child, and theirs.'

Everyone cups their hands: the response is resounding: 'For your child and theirs!'

Minister Gauteng turns and mounts the steps, her boots ringing round the chamber.

Aisha shakes her head. 'She's so impressive, isn't she? You wouldn't see the PM down here that soon after an attack.'

I flag down a medi-bot for Aisha. As it starts the triage, my phone beeps. The network must be back up.

Five messages from Mum, increasingly desperate. The Ministry must have released a statement. Her last message was sent ten minutes ago:

I'm getting on a train. When do you think they might let you leave?

My heart sinks. Our quota is in enough trouble as it is. But that's not the real reason.

I quickly fire off a reply.

Mum, it's OK, I'm fine. Stay home. Security will be a nightmare. I'll probably be stuck here ages.

A reply comes straight back.

I'm already on my way. I have something for you.

I hope that means what I think it means. I told her to be careful, not text me any details.

My phone pings again.

Something from your list.

It must be a name.

Maybe this day can be salvaged after all.

Minister Gauteng Reassures Public after 'Minor Incident' at MPFP HQ

By Katarina Spellmann

ONE State News

The Minister for Population and Family Planning, Maria Gauteng, reassured the country in her statement this evening that there had only been 'a handful' of casualties and minimal damage after a 'minor incident' at the Ministry complex this morning.

A small blast occurred shortly after 8.30 am. Staff were evacuated as a precaution, and security forces quickly took control of the situation. Damage was reported to be contained within one small area with only temporary disruption to the network.

'This woefully executed attack was perpetrated by a fringe group of climate-denying terrorists,' said Minister Gauteng. 'These extremists believe they have the right to inflict their profligate consumption habits on law-abiding British citizens, with no regard for the con-

sequences. This Party will never let that happen.'

Minister Gauteng went on to say that state security teams were already pursuing leads for the 'selfish cowards' who were responsible and she was confident that they would soon be apprehended and brought to justice.

'I want to reassure the public that our security forces are hard at work so that UK citizens can continue to enjoy the safety and stability they expect and deserve.'

The minister went on to congratulate the ONE Party in Australia for their landslide victory in yesterday's elections. Australia is the latest country where the ONE Party has swept to power, joining the UK, Sweden, Canada, Argentina, France, Germany, Greece and Spain.

CHAPTER 8

It's fresh by the river. Not enough to smoke breath, but the breeze has a bite to it, which is very welcome after those airless hours in the bunker. I watch the flying taxis skim the surface of the Thames like water striders, their hydrogen-powered foils riding the currents. A mother races past, panting over her buggy; the toddler flaps its arms at her and shrieks with delight. It's as if the attack never happened. I gently press a finger to my stitches.

Oh yes, it did.

Once it was deemed safe, they shipped us off to a private wellness centre, exclusively for Ministry personnel. Each of us was scanned, screened and sampled, and then patched up. I got away lightly compared to some. My forehead and both hands were peppered with glass splinters. The red specks on my face looked, according to Aisha, 'like freckles on a summer's day'. Two deeper cuts, on my cheek, needed butterfly stitches. To my shame, I squealed when they tweezered those shards out.

Aisha's shoulder demanded proper sutures, with a needle. She didn't even blink. They gave her a local anaesthetic, but even so ... Sitting on a chair, hands neatly folded, she might have been waiting her turn at the dentist's. It made me wonder what horrors she must have gone through before.

Next came the interviews. What seemed like hours later, we were finally released, with strict instructions not to speak to anyone about the 'incident'. Unofficially, I've heard four are dead, thirty injured, some seriously, and the MPFP data hub has been locked down.

There are rumours of an inside job. As if there aren't enough people on the outside who want to blow our Ministry to smithereens. But I cannot dwell on such matters.

I have another blast to contain.

◆ ◆ ◆

I drag my feet down the nave towards the organ pipes, stacked like the copper bones of some clerical alien. Honeyed smoke from beeswax prompts a memory of scents more charred. Close to work, and usually empty, this church is a regular haunt. It is dedicated to Margaret of Antioch, a widely venerated saint, who was adopted by her nurse after being disowned by her father for converting to Christianity. Saint Margaret was tortured and then decapitated.

I hope my sister fared better after her reallocation.

I select a votive candle from the rack and light it from another's flame, a slight tremble in my fingers. I place it exactly in the middle and take a seat. I wouldn't call myself religious, but ever since Mum took me to church when I was little, this ritual has compelled me. A bit like the counting. Or rather the fear has – that if I don't do it, a bad thing will happen.

The candle flickers.

I guess fear is a kind of faith, too.

A clack of heels makes me turn, and I spot Mum, gliding down the aisle in her pale-grey coat. She bows her head to the altar, exposing the soft pallor of her neck. Her lips stir with a prayer. My knees start to jiggle. I clasp them with my hands to make them stop.

She slides onto the pew beside me and abruptly inhales.

'Oh, Kai...' She reaches out a hand and lightly touches my cheek. 'Does it hurt?'

I shake my head.

'Nothing permanent?'

'It looks worse than it is.'

She throws her arms around me in a tight hug. 'I was so worried,' she whispers.

I feel a lump in my throat, for the first time this day. Strange, how an act of love can unseat you.

She releases me and sighs. 'I never believe those news streams. It's always worse than they say.'

'They've got things under control, don't worry.'

'Have they?' Her eyes flash. 'Then why does it keep happening? And where is the prime minister? Holed up in his private bunker, I suppose?'

I pick at my coat and swallow. She knows we're forbidden to discuss it. The PM's absence at the press briefing didn't go unnoticed. We were all surprised that Minister Gauteng took the newscast. Rumours abound of a power struggle, but some say it goes deeper.

'I understand how important your work is to you, Kai. But these attacks ... Isn't there some other role you could—'

'Not now, OK?'

She can't help herself, despite what's happened. Eleven more days and it will be a moot point.

She blushes. 'Sorry, I didn't mean to ... You don't need me going on, with everything ... And after the day you've had.'

I look past her, to one of the murals. A woman in a white cap and gown coddles a baby with golden tresses, worshippers crowded round her, on their knees.

'I'm so sorry, Kai, for putting you in this position ... For all of it. We're supposed to make your life easier. Not worse.'

I try to think of something tactful to say.

But a question comes instead: 'What was she like?'

Mum stiffens. 'You really want to know?'

'Yes.'

She stares at the candle rack. 'Her hair was lighter than yours ... Almost white. Your mouths were the same: those perfect full lips.' She glances at me. She knows what I'm really asking. 'Darker eyes. "Prussian blue" your dad reckoned.'

I hold my breath.

'Both the same.'

I knit my fingers into a ball.

Why did she get lucky, and not me?

Mum hands me a fold of paper. I open it.

Dr Trowsky

The last doctor on the list.

'Do you think you'll find her?'

'Should be easy enough.'

'You won't...?' Mum hesitates. 'She won't get into trouble, will she? That woman was kind to me. She took a risk when she didn't have to.'

'I'm just going to talk to her, Mum.'

She doesn't look convinced.

'If they find out ... what would the Ministry do to her?'

I think of the sterilised daughter. The twenty-four-year sentence.

Nothing as bad as what they'll do to you...

'Don't worry about her, OK? I won't use her name unless I have to.'

I peer up at the white stone vaults arching above our heads. Their scale is dizzying.

These stones still stand, despite wars and famine, fire and floods. They seem to say, this crisis, too, will pass.

Mum turns to me. 'If I could have found a way, I would have kept her. It's important you know that. It's the worst thing in the world, forcing such a choice on a mother ... You'll understand, if you have a child one day.'

A response barrels up inside. I clamp my tongue with my teeth before the words fly out.

You could have made a different choice. You could have terminated the pregnancy. Then you'd only have lost one daughter.

Instead of going to prison and losing both.

Life-long protection, with Destine™ one-stop, hassle-free birth control

Are you sick of having to remember to take your pill or top up your temporary implant? Do you want an 'out' from intimate devices that may cause infection and unwanted cramps?

Destine™ subdermal contraceptive implant provides protection as long as you need it, in one simple, pain-free procedure. Ten minutes is all it takes to insert the tiny microchip under your skin.

The implant works by suppressing ovulation with slow-release hormones that are fully reversible. Switch it on when you want protection. Switch it off when you don't.

One simple click and you're good to go.

You can't see it, but you can be confident it's working away in the background, keeping you safe, with a 99.9% success rate.

No fuss. No risk. No unnecessary visits from family planning.

Oh, and did we mention it's free, too?

Get it and forget it with Destine™*

Book into your local family planning clinic, and with one simple click, kiss unwanted pregnancies goodbye.

*Destine™ is manufactured under licence by Eridian Ltd for the UK Ministry of Population and Family Planning.

CHAPTER 9
Day Four

I track the doctor down in just two searches. Her clinic is in a small market town on the Reading line, and she hosts a Saturday surgery, so I've planned a visit to the nearby church and nature reserve, in case my travel history raises any flags. As the train moves out of London into the suburbs, a silver-and-white sea of greenhouses spreads out as far as the eye can see. The ONE Party's urban agtech programme is the envy of the world, providing cities with fresh produce all year round. Heated by geothermal energy and irrigated using floodwater stored underground, the windows automatically adjust to the temperature outside. Smart greenhouses, indoor farming towers and community gardens supply the capital with everything from oranges to avocados, melons to mangoes. The compulsory conversion of car parks for farming was a particularly productive move.

I take a quick scroll through the newsfeeds. At home, the news is dominated by government raids on terrorist hideouts. Hooded figures are marched out of makeshift camps, hands cuffed, and bundled into black vans.

Abroad, the news, as ever, is grim. Wildfires continue to rage in Ukraine and Kenya. Another two Indonesian islands have been evacuated. Brazil and Argentina have declared crop emergencies after a twenty-square-kilometre locust swarm. And violence is escalating in Africa's drought-ridden Sahel; aid agencies predict millions more will starve as harvests fail.

So much for those carbon-emissions pleas they taught us about in school, the missed targets.

One point five to stay alive!

We barely scraped two degrees of warming, and that was mostly down to China's cheap carbon capture tech. Just as well ONE came to power when they did.

The clinic is a fifteen-minute walk from the station. If it weren't for the security fencing, you might think it was actually someone's house: duck-egg-blue walls with white bay windows; pink-and-red flowers in boxes underneath. It's a nice attempt, but no matter what they look like, family-planning clinics are always a target.

I press my thumb to the scanner. A reception bot appears on screen.

'Ministry Representative Houghton, how may I assist you?'

'I wish to speak with Dr Trowsky.'

'I will arrange that for you right away.'

The gate clicks and slides back.

The reception area is more in keeping with other clinics: beige slatted blinds, cream tiles and brightly coloured chairs spaced discreetly apart. Patients stare at their screens or their feet. I catch one woman's eye; her gaze immediately darts to her lap. The woman sitting next to her strokes her arm. Music from one of the state channels chirps in the background, accentuating the silent voices.

I imagine Mum waiting in a room like this all those years ago, completely unaware how her life was about to change. Or how the decision she would make would come back to haunt her.

The bot glides over. 'The doctor is just finishing with a patient. She won't be long.'

I glance at a contraception leaflet on the table: couples hug each other on sunlit benches, a young woman runs through a park, another swims across a lake, gloriously unencumbered by children. The Destine implant was the brainchild of our PM, when he was just a lowly MPFP rep like me. It was his vision that liberated so many women from unwanted pregnancies and terminations. It parachuted him up the ranks.

If only Destine had been available in Mum's day, all this could have been avoided.

A door opens, and a pale woman with short black hair limps out, escorted by a doctor. The patient takes slow, careful steps, studiously avoiding eye contact, a slight rustling as she walks. The song on the radio seems to get louder as the man opposite me jumps up:

'So won't you, please, be my, be my baby
Be my little baby, my one and only baby…'

He wraps his arm around her shoulders and helps her to the door.

The doctor exchanges quiet words with the reception bot. She looks a little older than Mum; a shock of white hair tops a face dominated by red glasses.

She approaches me with a granite smile. 'Ministry Representative Houghton? Dr Trowsky.' She thrusts out a hand.

'Pleased to meet you, Doctor.'

Her bright-blue gaze sweeps over my cuts. And my eyes. More of a professional appraisal than an ogle.

'Please, follow me.'

She leads me past the room she just vacated. I glimpse a bed, freshly sheeted with paper; a yellow bucket and hose. A crumpled box of tissues next to the ultrasound machine.

A spot of blood on the floor.

'Ms Houghton?' The doctor's tone sharpens. She's waiting for me, holding the door.

I follow her in. There's just a desk and a screen, two chairs arranged in front.

She clasps her hands. 'I don't mean to rush you, but the clinic is very busy.'

Technically, I'm the superior here. I'm used to dealing with people older than me and in positions of authority; they're no match for my Ministry shield. But this is not a normal visit.

'This shouldn't take up too much of your time.' I force a smile. 'I'm here about a patient you treated when you were working in Middleton.'

Her eyebrows arch. 'Middleton...?' She makes a noise between a cough and a laugh. 'I see a lot of patients, Ms Houghton. I'm afraid my memory may not stretch back that far.'

'Perhaps I can jog it for you?' I swallow. 'The patient's name was Sarah. Sarah Houghton.' Just saying Mum's name makes my heart beat faster. 'You helped her, with her second pregnancy.'

The doctor's cheek twitches. I notice a small mole: the shape of an egg.

'I'm not sure I understand you.'

'Oh, I think you do, Doctor. She didn't terminate. You offered her a different option.'

She sits back and places her palms on the desk. 'I have been a doctor for over thirty years. I help women safely plan for a family. Sometimes that means helping them make difficult decisions, within the bounds of the law. Whatever it is you are implying, you are mistaken.'

'All I need is information. What we discuss here will be treated in confidence.'

'Even if this woman was my patient, I no longer have access to those files.'

Her cool demeanour fans a flicker of doubt. Was Mum telling me the truth? Or has she got the wrong name?

'If you prefer, you can accompany me to the Ministry for a

formal interview. But as you have patients waiting, I was hoping to avoid unnecessary disruption.'

Dr Trowsky's tongue probes her lip. 'Strange coincidence. The name.'

It was always going to be a risk. I think of the level six at the Marston:

Preparation improves efficiency...

'I understand you have a daughter, Dr Trowsky.'

'I don't see what my daughter has to do—'

'She was arrested, wasn't she? For disseminating radical propaganda.'

The doctor's jaw shifts. 'A few pamphlets about reproductive rights. That was all.'

'Unlawful protests about population-planning laws are hardly a small matter. It would be a shame if she were caught again. Sentences these days for repeat offenders are rather unforgiving...'

'Look, what is it you want?'

'I want you to tell me what happened to Sarah Houghton's baby.'

'I've already explained: I don't have access to the records.'

'There don't appear to *be* any records; that's the problem. As I suspect you already know.'

She doesn't say anything.

I try a different tack. 'What was your practice's policy on reallocations?'

She frowns. 'The Ministry's. First-pregnancy births were reallocated to couples who couldn't conceive, if the parents did not wish to keep the child.'

'And second pregnancies?'

'Were illegal. And were terminated.'

'Not every woman had a termination though, did they? Before medi-patches were enforced.'

She hesitates. 'Very occasionally, there might be exceptions. Such as the more advanced pregnancies. Assuming the babies passed the required screening tests, we would try to reallocate them, after birth.'

I wonder if it had been me, being screened, whether I would have passed.

'Did any other pregnancies qualify for the same treatment?'

She hesitates again. 'Sometimes ... On religious or medical grounds. Unofficially, of course. It was tolerated, not encouraged.'

Those early negotiations with the Catholic Church were part of our induction – a salutary lesson in compromise. The Ministry initially made allowances for their beliefs, and permitted them reallocations after their firstborn. Until deluges of pregnant women feigned a new-found devotion to the Virgin Mary.

'What exactly do you mean by "medical grounds"?'

'If we gauged the psychological distress might be too great ... Putting the mother in danger.'

Basically a free-for-all. So Mum was telling me the truth.

'How many reallocations are we talking about?'

She glances at the door. 'Not many ... The Ministry were very clear they didn't want excess births spiralling. Maybe fifteen ... Twenty, at most.'

Twenty?

If every clinic did the same, that would add up to thousands. There's no way infertile couples could account for all those.

'How could something on that scale go unnoticed? Surely the system would have flagged them? It would have been obvious these children had been reallocated and weren't their parents' biological offspring.'

She holds up her hands. 'We weren't involved in that side of things. All I know is, there was chaos when it stopped. Our future prime minister claimed parents and doctors were abusing the programme. As soon as remote monitoring came in, and he got the Destine implant authorised, the Ministry cracked down and banned all reallocations. They rewrote history, declaring they'd never been officially sanctioned. Pulled up the drawbridge and left us to pick up the pieces.'

'What happened to the records?'

'All reallocation data was erased: birth records, everything. I would have thought you of all people would have known that.'

'Why were they erased?'

She looks at me as if I'm stupid. 'So they wouldn't compromise the targets. They had to show the one-child policy was working. That it had unanimous support: everyone making the same sacrifice for the common good. If those children didn't officially exist, they couldn't be an embarrassment.'

This is outrageous. She's implying there was some kind of state cover-up.

'I'll need names,' I say. 'The people you liaised with, at the Ministry.'

'It was years ago. They'll be long gone by now ... And if they're not, they certainly won't want this being dragged up.'

'I'm happy to take that chance.'

She eyes me carefully. 'And then what? I'm arrested, for being complicit?' She leans forward. 'I helped those women because I genuinely feared for their wellbeing, not to mention that of their babies. Those mothers were put in an abominable position. As their doctor, I had a duty of care.'

It's pretty obvious where the daughter gets it from.

'My interest is in finding this particular child, not whistle-blowing. Your name won't even come up.'

She gives me a doubtful look. 'And my daughter?'

'Will be left alone. I give you my word.'

'I learned the hard way not to take the Ministry at its word.'

'Well, this isn't the Ministry. This is me.'

I dig my thumb into my palm. This is the line I should never cross.

'If anyone asks why I was here, tell them I was querying your implant numbers. The uptake for under-twenties is still below target, you might want to address that. Before someone else pays you a visit.'

I watch her wrestling with her conscience. She knows I can make life difficult for her. She also knows I have a vested interest. I hope the two things balance out.

She sighs. 'Wait here.'

I sink back in my chair and think about what she's told me.

Could the Ministry really have given tacit permission for such a programme, and then covered its tracks? It flies in the face of everything we've been taught. That could explain why the profile suddenly came up on the system, if it had been there all along, just hidden. Maybe there's hope for Mum and Dad after all.

Dr Trowsky returns and hands me a sheet of paper.

'I archived some emails. In case anything like this happened.' She points at an address. 'This was one of the staff responsible for organising placements, after the babies were born.'

y.mestari@FamilyPlanning.uk

Not a name I recognise. Nor a Ministry address.

'How do I know they're still using this email?'

'You don't, but it's the only one I've got. And if you steam in with your Ministry badge, she'll probably run a mile.' She exhales. 'Yasmine was a decent human being. Please don't hang her out to dry.'

'I won't. Thank you, for this.'

The doctor folds her arms. 'Are we done now?'

I nod. 'We're done.'

'Good.' She yanks the door open. 'Now get the hell out of my clinic.'

CHAPTER 10

I gaze out of my balcony window at the neighbouring apartments: boxes of light towering above the street lamps' soft glow. I welcome these glimpses into other people's lives: the harassed mother chasing after her unruly toddler; the man with the perpetual frown tapping away at his desk. And Niko's temptress: the tabby bot that waves her tail and presses her striped face tantalisingly against the glass.

I wonder if *she* is out there, in one of those boxes. My illegal sister. I spot a woman with blonde hair staring out, like me. For a second, our eyes meet, and I am suddenly seized by the notion it's her. A blind falls like a guillotine.

She is gone.

I'm still reeling from the doctor's revelations, and what to believe. None of my searches found Yasmine Mestari on any Ministry staff list, past or present. For all I know, Dr Trowsky could have plucked her details out of thin air. I did, however, locate two Yasmine Mestaris in London. One is a retired teacher, the other used to work for a children's charity. She was also a beneficiary of the migrant resettlement programme.

My bets are on her.

I type six variations of the same email, and finally settle on this:

Hi Yasmine,
My name is Victoria Holling. I think you knew my mother.
I would really appreciate a confidential chat.

Victoria Holling is my proxy. Her mother had an excess pregnancy the same time as Mum, but according to the records, it was aborted. I cross my fingers four times and hit send, bracing myself for an immediate bounce-back.

But no notification arrives. Yasmine's email still exists, even if she doesn't.

I slide my alerts volume to maximum. After ten long, silent minutes, I make myself stand up and look away.

I busy myself assembling a fresh pot of soup. Carrots, onions and potatoes from Dad's garden, with a few lentils thrown in. The ginger and chillies are my contribution; my 'basket of fire' peppers not only keep me in spice for the year, they add a fresh zest of colour as they ripen from purple to yellow to red.

When it comes to produce, we're all expected to do our bit.

As I stir the broth, Niko paws my leg and gazes longingly at his bowl.

'Sorry, Niko. Kai's been a bit distracted. Shall I get you your tea?'

His tail shifts up to full throttle and he prances round my feet with shrill yaps.

'Niko, sit.'

He hunches his bottom down and fixes me with an emerald stare.

I click the app and point it at his bowl. Simulated strips of cultured meat and kibble appear.

'Good boy.' I smile as he tucks in.

It's hard to imagine owning a live pet. Niko has all the lovable traits I could wish for in a doggie companion with virtually no resource use or mess. Not that I have a choice: live pets were banned during the wheat crisis, before I was born. There wasn't enough grain to feed humans, let alone animals. Warmer and wetter climes brought another deadly pathogen to our shores: a new, highly potent race of wheat rust that decimated crops across Africa and Europe. New strains keep emerging, challenging even the most resistant cereals they bred. Crops are precious, as the bean counters constantly remind us. That's what we call the Ministry of Resources. That or carbon crunchers. A lot more civil than what they call us.

I give in to temptation and glance at my screen.

No new messages

I switch to our family dashboard. My grandparents appear to be behaving themselves at last. Mum was true to her promise: their water and energy usage is right down; they must have seriously cut back. Just as well – the last thing we need is any red flags.

A notification chirps. I fumble over the keys, but it's just Mum again.

Hello, darling. Any news?

I sigh. She's chasing me for an update, but I can't tell her anything. I don't want her getting her hopes up before I've checked out Dr Trowsky's version of events.

The odds are against it, but I need Yasmine to come back to me.

All I can do is wait.

◆ ◆ ◆

I'm watching a nature documentary, about a family of gorillas. It's a really old one, from the BBC archive: one of Mum's favourites. It's become one of Niko's, too. The babies roll around the whispering presenter, stretching out their hairy arms and picking at his face and boots. It always makes Mum cry; she never got to see a gorilla before they went extinct. Nor did I. A lot more animals have vanished since then; the scientists say over eighty percent. At least the rewilding programme is turning the tide; since ONE took over, storks and bison have been reintroduced, lynx and wolves. Maybe if ONE had come to power sooner, they could have helped those countries save the gorillas, too.

My screen lights up with a loud ping.

One new message

My eyes widen.

It's Victoria's inbox, not mine.

I don't know how you got this address, but you have the wrong person.

My fingers race over the keys.

I know a doctor who used to work with you. You helped my mother, many years ago.

Just typing those words sends a frisson up my spine.

Her reply is instant:

You are mistaken. Don't contact me again.

I press on.

Please. My mother is desperate. All I want to do is talk.

I stare at the screen, willing her to respond.

Nothing. I need some leverage. If my guess was right, Yasmine was part of the resettlement programme.

If you've lost family, you'll know how it feels. Wouldn't you risk anything to find them?

One minute passes. Two. Four.

7am tomorrow. The Mother's Pond, Richmond Park. No devices.

CHAPTER 11
Day Five

It's a crisp Sunday morning, and the grass feels light and spongy under my feet. The sun winks through the leaves in Two Storm Wood, reflected in the filter-branches of robotic trees, artfully moulded to complement their natural neighbours while absorbing a thousand times more CO_2.

As I cross the cycle path, I spot a woman in running leggings and trainers standing by The Mother's Pond. She's staring at a swan arcing through the water, wings raised, seeing off an interloper.

I tap my wrist five times. Please let that be her.

'Yasmine?'

She turns. Her lightly freckled face is framed with copper curls. Lines spider out from chestnut eyes. 'Victoria?'

I smile. 'Thank you for seeing me.'

Her eyes move over my face. She doesn't smile back.

Her gaze flicks to my bag. 'I'll need to check.'

'Of course.'

She peers inside. Briskly pats my pockets. 'Looks like you've been in the wars.'

'Bit of a cycling accident. My fault, silly really.'

'Let's walk.'

I try to think how to gain her trust without giving myself away. As we pass underneath a large oak, I notice a cluster of small, hairy caterpillars on the trunk. I nod at them:

'You'd have thought the park would have sprayed by now. Those processionary moths ravage the poor trees in these long summers.'

'What is it you want from me, Victoria?'

Clearly Yasmine has no appetite for small talk.

I take a breath. 'I need to ask you about a certain … reallocation.'

She glances at me. Silver loops shimmer in her ears. 'The reallocation programme stopped over two decades ago.'

'I know. I need to find my sister.'

Her eyes flash. 'Keep your voice down,' she hisses. 'That's a very dangerous word.' She scans the path. 'Who gave you my name?'

'I'm sorry, I promised I wouldn't say … She told me you were a good woman. That you would help me.'

'Well, she was wrong.'

Yasmine marches on ahead; I have to jog to catch up.

'Look, I appreciate this took place a long time ago, but something happened that brought it all back. My mother's haunted by what she had to do … She can't stop thinking about her. I have to at least try.'

Yasmine stops and turns to me. 'Listen to me, Victoria. We had a saying where I grew up: "don't kick a sleeping dog". Take my advice: tell your mother to forget her. Your sister is leading a new life now.'

A throng of lime-green parakeets flares by.

'She can't. Believe me, I've tried. If you won't talk to me, I'll just have to keep digging until I find someone who will.'

Yasmine scrapes her hand through her hair. 'You're wasting your time. No one will speak to you. Even if they did, you'll never find her.'

'Why not? Surely there must be addresses for the families they went to?'

She doesn't answer.

'You must have kept records?'

She bites her lip. 'In the beginning, yes. But not by the end.' She sighs. 'Look, I'm sorry. I can't help you. I have to go.'

'Please, Yasmine...' I touch her arm. 'I know you're probably frightened, but—'

'Yes, I am, and with good reason.'

She waits while a jogger runs past.

'OK, you want the truth?' she whispers. 'There were too many babies and not enough families. Reallocations were overrun.'

As I thought. Those numbers just couldn't stack up.

'So what happened to the children?'

She shakes her head. 'You don't want to know...'

'What do you mean?'

She checks the path again. 'The Ministry set up secret orphanages. Called them "reallocation centres".'

'What? Where? I've never heard of them.'

'No wonder; it was all hushed up. It would have been a PR disaster for the Ministry. Officially they didn't exist.'

My eyes widen. 'So you're telling me that's where the children were sent?'

'Yes. The locations were kept secret. What you need to understand is I did that job because I had to. They told me to shut up and get on with it. Or they'd send me back. To the camp.'

'What "camp"?'

'The Ministry has a name for those, too: "resettlement centres". Her voice hardens. 'That's not what the UN calls them...'

My brain tries to organise what she's saying, but there's too much coming at me too fast.

'But all I'd done was swap one kind of hell for another...' She shakes her head. 'I did my time then looked for a way out, and got lucky. I helped someone who knew how to pull strings. And they got me transferred.'

'So ... if my sister was in one of these centres, there must be some way of tracking her—?'

'She could be anywhere... Disease swept through those places. She may be dead for all you know—'

'She's alive. I know it, for a fact. And she's in this country.'

Yasmine's forehead creases. 'How can you be so sure?'

'Her profile appeared less than a week ago. I saw the trace myself.'

She blinks at me. 'How did you manage to...?'

Her face drops, and I realise my mistake. No ordinary civilian would get their hands on that information.

'Oh God...' She jumps up. 'Of course: your cuts. You were in the Ministry blast.'

'Wait!' I seize her arm. 'I'm only here for my mother, I swear...'

She shakes me off and starts to run.

'Yasmine, please...' I'm struggling to keep up with her. 'Where should I look? Where do I even start?'

She wheels round. 'Quiet! You'll get us both arrested.'

Two walkers stare at us as they amble past.

'Excess children have no status, no access to state benefits. Legally they don't exist. Which means if she's still in this country, she's either been trafficked, or she's hiding out, offline. I hope for her sake, it's the latter.'

'But—'

'*Don't* try to follow me, or make contact again. I'll deny everything.' She shoves her finger in my face. 'I still have friends at the Ministry – powerful friends. Remember that.'

She sprints off down the path. My heart hammers as her warning echoes in my ears.

I make a mental note to delete Victoria Holling's account as soon as I get home.

I stare at the newsreel on the monitor, watching the presenter's lips stretch and smile. I catch only the headlines scrolling across the bottom: the Ministry of Resources has invested in the latest direct air-capture tech that extracts CO_2 to drive down emissions further; domestic food production quotas have been exceeded; the Ministry of Population and Family Planning's birth reduction numbers are ahead of plan.

The train rocks gently, as if everything is fine.

Mum's been messaging me, relentlessly. I got one from Dad last night, too:

Please, love. Give your mum a call, will you? She's worrying herself sick.

She's not the only one.

I replied to them both:

Still looking into things, try not to fret. Will report back soon.

What else can I say? That the reallocation most likely ended in disaster?

That their daughter might have been trafficked, or worse?

This investigation is dismantling everything that I hold dear: my family, my job, my integrity. Each new lead unveils more lies, more riddles to be solved. With every day that passes, I unravel a little more.

I pull out my screen and search 'reallocation centres'. Part of me is relieved when nothing comes up. I try 'orphanages, UK'. Pages of results flash up, mostly desperate pleas from international aid organisations trying to manage the constant flow of climate migrants.

I scroll through images of austere-looking houses named after saints and philanthropists and long-defunct trades. All of them shut down over a century ago.

'Orphanages were phased out in the 1960s in favour of family-based fostering and adoption programmes...'

'Children who grew up in orphanages were at much higher risk of becoming victims of violence, trafficking and exploitation...'

My stomach clenches.

Trafficking isn't my department. Nor are offline hide-outs.

But there is one person I know who could help.

I glance back at the screen. The presenter's face darkens as the inevitable disasters overseas follow: skeletons of villages flattened by Typhoon Saura; thousands more homes still without power. Renewed nuclear threats after another unplanned release from the Hwanggang Dam caused flash floods in South Korea killing hundreds. South Korea is accusing its neighbour of 'deliberate provocation'; North Korea is claiming it had no option after the typhoon's torrential rains.

My eyes seek respite through the window. The terns are there, perching on rafts; a couple of sand martins dive out of their nests in the bank. Last month, I saw the sleek brown back of an otter, arching through the water.

I think of those families on the news being swept away in the floods.

Remember how lucky you are to live in this country...

How much good the Ministry does, every day...

All of a sudden, the train brakes, nearly throwing me out of my seat. I wedge my feet against a pole as it hisses and slows to a halt. The broadcast fades to static and the screen goes blank. I peer outside, trying to figure out why we've stopped. We must be somewhere between Chiswick and Hammersmith.

The doors open, and someone who is clearly not a train official, in camo pants and trainers, steps in. I tighten my mask. A mop of wild hair tops a shimmering face lit up with iridescent scales, continually shifting shape and colour. Painted splodges on their clothes circle. Advanced stealth wear. To evade recognition.

The only constant is the black rucksack on their back.

I think of that lone foot trapped under metal fingers and grab my phone. It's dead: they must have jammed the carriage.

The intruder takes a breath. 'I am FREE. I am here to tell you that it's time to reject the lies you are being fed and stand up for your rights!'

Some commuters frantically jab their screens, others clutch their seats, wide-eyed.

'The right to an opinion. The right to privacy.' The synthesised voice changes from a man's to a woman's. 'The right to control your own body. The right to parent.' The voice shifts to a child's. 'The right to exist.'

They slip their rucksack off their back and unzip it. Someone screams, and I hit the floor. I press my hands over my head and try to drown out my fear with numbers as the carriage is inundated with buzzing.

Not bees.

Drones.

They stroll down the carriage, stepping over passengers. I glimpse a tattoo on their ankle. A bird, I think. A large eye.

'You are completely safe; these drones are not weaponised. These are educator drones. Sit back on your seats. *Now.*'

They stamp, and the man next to me flinches.

A woman opposite whimpers as we scramble back to our seats.

'It's time to open your eyes.'

One of the drones flies up to me and a screen unfolds. Whichever way I turn, it follows.

'Every day the ONE Party arrests innocent people and incarcerates them using their puppet courts. Every day they violate women with enforced abortions. Every day they abandon their responsibilities to climate refugees, denying desperate people the most basic human rights. Look at what they're doing. Look!'

Images flit past in quick succession: campaigners cuffed by ASRs and thrown into vans; a woman on her knees being dragged into a family-planning clinic.

'When will you see what is happening, every day, all around you? How many more must suffer before you decide to act?'

The buzzing gets louder as the drone inches up to my face: soldiers prise bodies from the columns of offshore wind turbines; coastguard patrols herd tiny boat flotillas back out into raging seas.

They seem so real – if it wasn't for my training, I might be duped. I keep counting, remind myself these are just deep fakes, like the ones they used for that ridiculous meat conspiracy. FREE claimed bluetongue virus and African swine fever had deliberately been allowed to run riot and decimate livestock populations. According to them, it was a government ploy to accelerate the transition away from farmed meat to lab alternatives, to get emissions down.

'Don't close your eyes to the truth,' shouts the insurgent. 'Fight for your freedom. Fight for what's right.'

The screen switches to an encircled black V engulfed by flames, and a blinding flare bursts through the carriage. I hear the carriage doors open as spots leap behind my eyes.

It takes several minutes before I can focus.

The rebel and their drones have gone.

CHAPTER 13

Steener agrees to meet me after work, by the river. He's late. No surprise there. But Steener is not to be underestimated. His investigative instincts are well honed; he's used to dealing with lies.

So I'm going to have to make mine convincing.

I watch the bats flitting between lanterns, skimming the water's surface before they rise and dive again. My gaze shifts to the nebulous spiral of the Milky Way. We haven't mapped all one hundred billion stars in this galaxy, but we are close. I remember the Greek myth, about how the Milky Way was formed. Baby Heracles was brought to the goddess Hera, who nursed him out of pity. But Heracles suckled so strongly that Hera tore him off her breast, and her milk sprayed across the heavens.

I think of what Mum said, about struggling to breastfeed me.

If I'd been easier, maybe none of this would have happened.

A scuffing noise makes me turn. Steener trudges along the embankment, hands stuffed in his pockets.

'Detective Inspector Steener, thank you for coming. I apologise for dragging you out at this late hour.'

'Bench,' he grunts, and puffs straight past.

I settle myself at a safe distance and wait for him to catch his breath. The lamplight casts an eerie shadow across his face; the red veins threading his eyes appear even more murderous. Like me, Steener has imperfections. I suspect he's also had to work harder to get where he is.

He glances at my cheek. 'Ministry battle wounds?'

'Only a scrape.'

'Bang on message, as ever ... So, to what do I owe the pleasure?'

'Well,' I squeeze my fingers, 'it's a delicate matter. One which must remain strictly between us. There's been a crackdown since last week's "incident". The Ministry fears standards are slipping. We're being asked to keep an eye out for anything ... unusual.'

I pause. Steener wheezes at me.

'I've identified a colleague. A possible accomplice to a traitor in Resources who was implicated in supplying ghost IDs.'

He tuts. 'I see.'

'I believe this colleague may be trading with certain ... communities on the black market, using a fake ID. Which is where your assistance is required. I need to stop them before more crimes are committed.'

The bench creaks as Steener shifts his weight. 'It's not my job to police the Ministry. Not unless they've bumped off their own or someone else's brood.'

'I realise that. I'm not asking you to conduct an investigation. All I need is an introduction to someone with the appropriate skills. Who could trace what we suspect to be a fake profile.'

He frowns. 'I thought you had teams that dealt with this.'

'We do...' I glance round, for effect. I know this area is surveillance-free, which is why I chose it.

'Unfortunately, there is reason to believe those teams may be compromised.'

Steener shakes his head. 'Looks like your recruitment may be off.'

My face burns. God help me if anyone at the Ministry gets word of this.

His eyes narrow. 'Presumably, given the sensitivities, this is off the clock.'

I nod.

'So, what's in it for me?'

I suppress a sigh. At least Steener is predictable.

'As you're aware, my superior is on very good terms with the head of foeticide. I've heard that discretionary retirement upgrades are potentially in the offing to reward outstanding performance.'

Steener's lips distend into what might pass for a smile. He scratches his cheek. 'I'll give it some thought. There are a couple of contacts who spring to mind.'

'Thank you.' I swallow. 'How soon do you think you might be able to fix something up? The matter is rather pressing.'

'Shouldn't take long. Couple of days? I'll need it on a stick. The profile.'

Such devices are banned at the Ministry.

'I'll send it to you, in an encrypted drive. Once you've copied it over, please delete the file immediately.'

Exchanging sensitive data with foeticide is technically allowed but could still be a flag. I just hope no one audits my drive.

He sniffs. 'So I take it they're a biggie, then?'

'I'm sorry?'

'This colleague of yours. Haven't seen you this rattled since that woman sent you a dead rat.'

I shudder at the memory. Her husband had been convicted of foeticide, after a rash one-night stand. Instead of blaming him for his misdemeanours, she decided to mail me a putrefying rodent for authorising his arrest. Steener took even more exception to it than I did.

'The stakes are rather high,' I say. 'Which is why their identity must remain classified.'

'Well, just remember your promise to old Steener when you land that promotion.' Steener heaves himself up.

Guilt pricks. 'Oh, I assure you, I will.'

CHAPTER 14
Day Seven

I sit on the Hydrail, foot tapping, as rain smashes against the window, adrenaline still fizzing round my veins. I barely slept last night; the same interminable worries kept circling. The moment I dropped off they'd jar me awake and spin around again.

What if Steener finds out I'm bluffing? That this has nothing to do with my Ministry duties?

What if his contact connects the profile on that stick with mine?

To make matters worse, I'm giving a talk to the ONE Party Youth League this morning. Outreach is a necessary part of our duties, and there's no putting it off, especially a primary school on the Party's doorstep. The thought of a hall full of excitable children ogling my eyes makes me want to weep.

As the train slows, I rifle through my bag for an umbrella. It's not there; I must have left it at home. I curse and yank up my collar. Water streams along the kerb, gurgling into gutters. It's only a ten-minute walk, but my hair's already plastered to my head.

By the time I arrive at the school gates, I am drenched. I hug my soggy bag to my chest and squelch into reception. The head, Mrs Chandra, has clearly been waiting for me. She cups her hands in a salute, but her smile freezes as soon as she clocks my eyes. She launches into an effusive commentary about their living classroom and the climate simulations on the ONE Party's learning app.

'Is there somewhere I could freshen up?' I hand her my sodden coat.

'Goodness, yes. I do apologise.' She blushes. 'What was I thinking?'

She directs me to the toilets with a gratingly cheery inflection that must have been honed on infants.

A Youth League banner has been strung up in the corridor. A fresh recruit sporting the requisite green neckerchief wags a finger at me:

Your Party needs you.

Join the Youth League today!

I blot my face with toilet paper and stick my hair under the hand dryer. I eye myself in the mirror. I am not looking my best.

When I return, Mrs Chandra thrusts a coffee at me.

'They're all waiting for you,' she says breathlessly. 'Just to warn you: excitement is running rather high.'

I follow her through double doors into a squirming red-and-green tumult. Cherry-sweatered children sit in rows, cross-legged on the floor, emerald neckerchiefs knotted in varying degrees of strangleholds. An odour of cabbage and damp clothes permeates the hall.

The appearance of myself and Mrs Chandra instigates a squall of furious shushing, and an uneasy silence ensues.

'Good morning, children,' bellows the head.

'Good morning, Mrs Chandra,' they chant.

The elbow-nudges and whispers begin. I fix my gaze on the wall display at the back. I notice the cameras winking at the edges of the room.

'It's my honour today to introduce you to our very special guest: Ministry Representative Houghton. Let's give her a proper Riverbank Academy welcome.'

Palms smack together. My cheeks colour under the heat of their stares as memories rise up to taunt me:

Freak!

Weird-eye!

Traitor!

'Now, before Ministry Representative Houghton starts her talk, I thought we could show her what we've been learning this week in our ONE Youth Programme. Shall we do that?'

A few heads nod vigorously.

'Would the Youth League leaders stand up, please?'

Six children in the front row shuffle to their feet. An older girl with blonde plaits hauls up next to her a tiny boy who's been gawping at me ever since I came in. His face turns more crimson than his sweater. I almost feel sorry for him; he looks as though he might cry.

Mrs Chandra nods at the girl. She squeezes her hands together and clears her throat.

'Our country is our mother and our home. We must protect it and not grow greedy so we have enough. We are grateful for all we have been given by the Party and promise to work hard.'

Mrs Chandra beams at her. 'Lovely, Tisha. Thank you.'

As each child stutters their way through carefully rehearsed lines, I am ambushed by Ciara Reilly and me, clutching our hands in a very different assembly.

After we were caught playing 'sisters', the head made us stand in front of the whole school while he admonished us for our 'shameful' game. We had to apologise for our treachery, then recite the school's values, including our oath to the ONE Party. And swear that we would never play it again.

Someone touches my shoulder and I flinch.

'Ministry Representative Houghton?' whispers the head.

A sea of two hundred faces is watching me.

I clear my throat. 'Thank you, Mrs Chandra, and the Youth League leaders, for such a rousing presentation. You are a credit to the Youth League, to your school and to your country.'

The head visibly unclenches.

I do not recall one single word of my talk.

CHAPTER 15
Day Eight

Steener appraises my sweatshirt and jeans. 'That your idea of "under cover"?'

'I didn't think a suit would really cut it.'

Sartorial insults from Steener. Not a good start.

I clasp my knees and force my mind to do the counting, not my feet. The sleepless nights aren't helping; my anxiety is a beast that's tripped the lock on its cage. Steener called me late yesterday to tell me he'd fixed up our 'little rendezvous with the dark side'. That was enough to set me spinning. Then I noticed my travel quota was orange.

I'm going to have to seriously economise over the next few days.

'I take it you've got the USB?'

He pats his pocket and hands it to me. 'Ready and loaded.'

We take the overland out east, past the city high-rises in the financial district and the vertical farms by the docks. These areas were some of the worst hit by the Great Flood, although you wouldn't know it now, looking at those neat circles of flood-resilient housing; the urban wetlands and biodiversity parks. It took years to rebuild, and resettle communities. So when ONE came to power, they did what should have been done decades earlier: they built a new Thames Barrier and nationalised the water and waste management systems. Every ditch, drain, pipe and sewer was mapped, repaired or upgraded with separate storm sewers, then linked to a smart grid. It was a huge undertaking and wouldn't have been possible without the bots.

Now the surface water drains properly, our waterways are clean, and the sewage that used to be dumped in seas or rivers is converted into fertiliser pellets.

As we move further east, past the mechanical tree farms, the train empties and the landscape begins to change. An ungroomed wilderness encroaches on derelict human spaces.

Steener nods at my mask. 'You don't need that. I doubt anyone else is getting on.'

Reluctantly, I remove it. 'I've never been out this far before. I didn't realise how bad it was.'

'What with the tidal surge and the storms, when the Thames Barrier failed there was no stopping it – the water just poured in. My aunt used to live out here. She said she'd never seen a flood like it. Filthy fountains shooting up from manhole covers. Paving stones flipped over like toy bricks. She had to swim round cars, trying to find somewhere safe. Her brother wasn't so lucky. He drowned; she never got over it. Hundreds of kids died. The ones who couldn't swim, or weren't strong enough; the ones that got trapped in their homes or the underground...'

I stare at him. Steener's never mentioned this before. Perhaps this is what drives him.

We glide past trees sprouting through the gaping roofs of boarded-up outlets and factories in industrial parks. A residue of silt and mud is still visible: tide marks staining the walls.

'Is this where that leptospirosis outbreak was?'

Steener grimaces. 'Yeah ... Imagine: surviving the floods then copping it from Weil's disease. These areas were so badly damaged, and waterlogged for so long, in the end the government just wrote them off. They keep talking about some grand renovation project, but it never materialises. I think the official term is "urban wilderness area". The train only goes out this way because the sewage treatment works is at the end of the line.'

I notice a large concrete building with high brick walls around its perimeter, barbed wire still visible along the top. I can just make out some faded graffiti beneath the strings of ivy.

'What's that?' I point. 'A prison?'

'London's last slaughterhouse.' Steener gives me a wry smile. 'They used to gas the chickens in their crates.'

I shiver. We treated every living thing as if it only existed for our consumption. No wonder so many went extinct.

Steener punches a red button. 'You have to request a stop.' He braces himself against the seat. 'No one in their right mind gets out here.'

The train brakes and we judder to a halt. I silently recite multiples of four.

We've barely stepped onto the platform when the doors slide shut, as if the train doesn't want to hang around, either.

'What time is he coming?'

Steener shrugs. 'Depends. He's not really one for precise appointments.'

I skirt round the headless body of a crow and hurry after Steener; even he seems to have found some pace. Tufts of dandelions and grass have colonised the paving, which is carpeted with litter and leaves. Steener squeezes through a gap in the security fence and marches towards a row of terraced houses. Most of the roof tiles and windows are missing, and the paint has peeled off, exposing rotten frames underneath. Plastic sheeting flaps in the doorways. A salty stench of damp and decay pervades the air.

Steener turns right and heads downhill towards a defunct shopping centre. We pass a rusted frying pan lying in the road.

Strange creaks and moans follow us from the houses. We step through the open doors of the centre and crunch broken glass. Metal girders and twists of cable droop from the ceiling; spray-paint expletives flake off the walls. The escalators are just about intact, their steps strewn with plastic bottles, faded safety notices still stuck to their sides.

Steener stops and pulls out his phone next to a sculpture of a naked woman – *great tits* emblazoned across her chest.

'He's on his way.'

I swallow. Steener says they kept the network running here to keep tabs on the illegals. But the cameras always get broken.

There's a splintering noise. Steener whips out a gun and spins round, surprisingly agile. A skeletal girl shuffles out of the shadows and lifts trembling hands. She reminds me of the child in my nightmares. Her eyes have sunk into hollows; a tattered shirt clings to her ribs.

'Please … I need help…'

Steener's gun doesn't budge. He jerks his head towards the door. 'Keep on moving. There's nothing for you here.'

I inhale. 'Shouldn't we at least—'

'Classic BCI addict: she'd claw the skin off your face for a top-up. Leave this to me.'

I heed his warning. Brain-computer interface implants are notorious. Originally developed to help amputees regain motor skills, they were used to treat mental disorders by activating chemical releases in the brain. Naturally, certain entrepreneurs spotted more lucrative applications, so the next product was the BCI high – no risk of overdose and extremely addictive: 'guaranteed euphoria with the swipe of an app'.

The girl scowls at Steener and staggers past. Her legs are so thin I wonder how they can support her.

'She looks in a terrible state,' I whisper.

Steener keeps his gaze on the girl. 'They'd rather get high than eat. They hand over their resources in exchange for top-ups.' He slips the gun back under his jacket. 'Once their quota's blown, they trade whatever's left: bodies, eggs, organs.' He glances at me. 'Even embryos.'

I clench my fists. The Ministry worked tirelessly to stamp out this kind of trafficking: international gangs trading with unscrupulous research outfits or countries with no population laws. Gangs used to raid freezers containing eggs or embryos all over the country; some crime syndicates did deals directly with the labs. It was ONE that finally put an end to it. Or so I'd thought.

'That's bandit capitalism for you,' sighs Steener. 'It never stops, even after death. Fresh corpses fetch a high price for ghost IDs.'

All of a sudden, I hear a commotion outside: a man shouts, there's a scream. That girl's scream. A minute later, a scrawny man in faded jeans and a dark-blue shirt lopes into the mall. Steener straightens.

He ignores Steener and lifts his eyes to mine. The intensity of his stare is unnerving.

'Well, now ... Better watch my step. "The witches' eye"...'

My gaze drops to his hands: the skin is wrinkled and spotted. His face looks younger. Maybe it's stealth wear.

'This better be good,' he says to Steener. 'Any dead-mind can do a trace.'

'It requires ... sensitive handling.'

'What's the trade? Eggs? Embryos?' He leers at me. 'Eyes?' His sibilant lingers, a monstrous hiss.

'She's not a trader,' replies Steener, impassive. 'Consider it a personal favour to me.'

The man coughs out a laugh. 'And how much do favours go for these days?'

Steener scratches his armpit. 'With your rap sheet, I'd say ... thirty years?'

He nods at me. 'Give him the stick.'

I reach into my pocket and offer it to the man with the tips of my fingers, breath held. I don't even want to share the same air.

He makes me wait before he takes it.

'Pleasure doing business.' His mouth twitches as if he's said something amusing. I notice one of his nails has a purple half-moon. I'm not sure if it's paint or a bruise.

'You'll hear from me when it's done.'

As he struts away, I realise I'm still holding my breath. I let it out in a slow sigh.

The fate of my family rests in that criminal's hands.

I hope to God it's worth it.

CHAPTER 16
Day Nine

I can't put it off any longer.

'Hey, Mum.'

Her head appears, far too close to the screen, as usual, the worry lines accentuated around her eyes.

'At last ... Where have you been hiding? I've been trying to get hold of you for days.'

'I know, I know. I'm sorry ... It's been rather busy.'

She's frantically waving one arm, presumably at Dad. 'So, what happened? Did she speak to you? Did you find out anything?'

Dad lumbers into view behind her. The relief in his face fills me with shame at having left it this long.

'Hey, Dad.'

'Kai!' He beams at me. 'How are you?'

'What did the doctor say?' presses Mum.

I shake my head. We really shouldn't be discussing anything in detail, it's not secure.

She sighs in exasperation. 'We're going mad here, your father and I, waiting around for you to c—'

'There were a few theories,' I blurt, just to stop her talking. 'Which I'm following up now.'

I see Dad mouthing something at her, but she bats him away.

'Sorry, Kai, I...' She swipes her hair out of her face. 'It's been a tough few days, what with fretting about that blast and ... everything else...' She blinks. 'I know you're working every hour God sends.'

I swallow. 'Look, how about I pop over at the weekend? We can catch up properly then. And maybe I'll have a little more news.'

'You think?'

She radiates desperation. It cauterises me.

'Well, I hope so...'

'You've always been a good girl, Kai...' Her eyes glisten. 'So dedicated and thoughtful.'

'I've got to go now, Mum, sorry. I'll be in touch about the weekend soon.'

I barely get the words out before my finger ends the call.

Guilt eddies. For baling on the call so quickly. For giving them hope when there's probably none.

Niko pads over and gives my hand a lick.

I glance at the subtitles racing across my wall screen.

Wildfires still raging in Australia: an area the size of France is burning or already ash. A fresh malaria outbreak in Italy; all UK citizens are being urged to check their vaccinations are up to date. And winds over 150 miles an hour are battering Florida's Gulf Coast, as Hurricane Emanuel lays waste to what remains of the besieged Sunshine State.

The prime minister's update swoops in. Bespectacled and suited, against a backdrop of burgeoning crops, he heralds predictions of higher wheat yields again this harvest. The background shifts to water babbling over rocks: every British river has been given a clean bill of health, with marked increases in wild salmon stocks. The PM smiles as huge wind turbines spin resolutely in the North Sea: last year's grid upgrades and investment in sub-sea cables have dramatically reduced power outages...

I switch it off.

I check my phone again, the sixth time since leaving work. Still nothing from Steener.

I rush off a text. The clock is running down.

Just five more days to come up with something I can share with the Ministry before a colleague gets their hands on Zoe's profile, and my parents are convicted of a birth crime.

And I am convicted of treason for concealing it.

One-Child Policy Protestors Defy UK Government with Silent Demonstrations

By Shamaya Blontaine, CNN

At least fifty people are marching – men, women and children – but the demonstration is eerily silent: footsteps, no words. Their placards don't have words either, only pictures, mostly of babies. I spot one poster that has dared to include the symbol of resistance: a simple black V.

This march is one of many taking place across the UK in recent weeks in defiance of the ONE Party's strict anti-protest laws. Dissent has a high price here, with mandatory arrest and harsh prison sentences. Silent protests ensure the campaigners' words cannot be censored or used against them.

'We just want the rights to our own bodies,' says one protestor, a woman in her early thirties who we'll call Karen, for her protection. 'We want to be treated with dignity ... Allowed to make our own choices about having children without interference from the state.'

This year marks the fiftieth anniversary of ONE coming to power and the introduction of the UK's one-child policy. ONE has always claimed these measures were the legacy of previous governments' failures to get a grip of 'untenable' consumption habits and 'unfettered' immigration. During their time in power, it is estimated that millions of compulsory abortions have been carried out on British women, aided by the introduction of medical monitoring devices that have made the tracking of women's pregnancies much easier. The government-issued permanent contraceptive implant, Destine, although theoretically still optional, has to all intents and purposes become compulsory.

A flurry of exchanges breaks the silence as rumours spread that a state security team is on its way. Police routinely break up peaceful protests like this one, often beating demonstrators before handcuffing them and taking them away.

I ask Karen if she will leave.

'No,' she says. 'Let them arrest me. It's time the world bore witness to our suffering.' She pauses. 'What about you?'

It's a fair question, given the ONE Party's track record of assaulting and detaining foreign journalists. I tell her I won't leave either.

'Thank you,' she says. 'Even if our own people are prohibited from seeing your reports, the rest of the world must know what this country is inflicting on its people.'

CHAPTER 17
Day Ten

Steener and I take the same train as last time, but two stops further. His message finally came, late last night:

Tomorrow, six pm

I'm having to scrimp on shopping and showers to compensate for my travel quota. If some bot in Resources interrogated my data, my recent excursions would be hard to explain.

As soon as the carriage is sufficiently noisy, I ask Steener the burning question:

'Did he manage to ID it?'

Steener picks at a pimple on his chin. 'He wouldn't waste his time or ours otherwise.'

The train gradually empties. Neither Steener nor I have much appetite for conversation, so the rest of the journey passes in silence. I cross my fingers under my sleeves repeatedly, stroking them with my thumbs. The thought of seeing that man again, and what he might reveal, is making me even edgier. As the train slows, I have to fight a sudden wave of nausea.

This station is even more dilapidated than the last one. Vines strangle a fire extinguisher still chained to its bracket; a rack of seats cowers behind a felled announcement board. I scurry after Steener, picking my way around shards of plastic and glass.

'Where are we going?' I don't know why I'm whispering: there's no one else here.

'Left,' Steener replies, with an abrupt turn.

We seem to be heading towards a stone church that is wedged between crumbling office blocks and apartments. The church has fared better than its neighbours; while some of the roof is missing, miraculously, the stained-glass windows are intact. A rusted weather vane on the steeple points north; tarnished clock hands are stuck at seven minutes past four.

Steener leans against the heavy oak door, and an earthy smell makes my nostrils constrict. We tread past bench pews listing at odd angles like beached ships; a pulpit engulfed by ivy. Dank pools of water lurk in the aisle.

'You take me to all the nice places,' I say; a vain attempt to lift my spirits.

Steener doesn't respond.

I look for a candle rack; there isn't one. I doubt any flame would light here. On a moss-flocked wall, behind where the altar should be, words have been daubed in black:

My God, my God, why have you abandoned me?

I start counting the seconds, trying not to pace.

'He'll be here,' says Steener, without taking his eyes off the doorway.

'Quite right,' says a voice that makes the hairs on my arms stand up. 'Regular as the shits, me.'

The man steps out from behind a wooden crucifix propped up against an arch. Has he been there all this time? His face is completely different; darker skin tone, sharper cheekbones, eyes green, not blue.

'Hello again, little witch.' A narrow smile parts his lips. 'I hope those eyes of yours are going to behave.'

He must be on something; he's practically jiggling on the spot.

'Can we quit the foreplay?' says Steener in a bored voice. 'We don't have much time.'

'Such poor manners...' He sighs. 'I suppose you'll be wanting this back.' He yanks a USB out of his pocket. I feel a stab of adrenaline.

'You traced it, then,' says Steener.

'Of course.' The man's gaze flicks to the door. 'But unfortunately, I can't pass those details on.'

'Why not?' I rasp.

'Conflict of interest.'

There's a loud sigh from Steener, followed by an expletive.

'What's he talking about?' I whisper.

'He means that whoever's mixed up in this isn't worth messing with.'

I think of what Yasmine said, and my heart sinks. Does this mean my sister's been trafficked? Bought and sold by a man like that?

Steener glares at him. 'Have you shown this to anyone?'

The man shakes his head. 'You know I work alone.'

Steener nods at me. 'What about you?'

'I ... Only an android.'

Steener makes a growling noise. He has a thing about bots, particularly humanoids. He calls them 'skin-jobs': a professed literary reference.

He turns back to the man. 'Will they know you ran the trace?'

The man's stealth wear shifts to the face of a young woman. Like the girl's we saw in the mall. I shiver.

'There's always a chance...'

Steener shakes his head. 'I knew I shouldn't have got involved...'

I look at him. 'So ... what do we do now?'

'You take your little stick and head back home to Kansas, Dorothy.' The man chucks it at me. 'I'd lose that in the river if I were you.'

'Please ... There must be something I can offer you, something you need...?'

He barks a laugh. Steener frowns at me.

'Sorry, I can't just ... abandon this...'

All of a sudden, Steener wheels round.

'What is it?'

He lurches towards the crucifix. There's a scuffling sound.

'Hey!' shouts Steener. The door bangs. 'Did you bring company?' he yells at the man.

'What? Of course not!'

'Who was it?' I ask.

'Some drop-out. I didn't get a decent look.'

'Well, I think I'll be off,' says the man with the girl's face. 'Sorry things didn't work out...'

'Hang on, you can't just—?'

Steener clamps a hand on my arm as the man scurries out.

'Why are you letting him go?' I hiss.

'Calm it,' he says. 'Let's think this one through.'

There are too many questions detonating in my head for me to think about anything.

'This must be someone well up the food chain,' continues Steener. 'If they find out their Party colleagues are sniffing about, they'll go to ground. But sooner or later, complacency or greed will get the better of them. They'll switch IDs and go again.'

He heads to the door. 'In my experience, this type like to know who's poking around in their toy box. They may even try to cut you in.'

The USB digs into my palm.

It never occurred to me that my sister might be the criminal trading people as opposed to the victim being traded.

I think of Mum and Dad. I'm not sure which is worse.

CHAPTER 18
Day Twelve

I stare at the tiny flame as it flickers, the wax beginning to pool. Who is my candle for – me? Those children starving at the sides of roads? Or my parents?

I rest my elbows on the pew and let my forehead slump onto my hands, as if I'm praying.

Two precious days have passed, and I'm still no closer to concluding this investigation. I have to send a report, however paltry, to the Ministry. Assuming, that is, I don't get pulled in first. Another colleague was routed for malpractice this week. And on Friday, Aisha kept asking me if I was alright.

I think of Mum, and a small moan escapes.

Lunch today was awful, as I knew it would be, but I had to go. I stuck to details that backed up what they'd already said: the reallocation programme operating under the radar. Birth records being wiped. Not the centres, though. I didn't mention those. Or the discovery that my sister, whoever she is, can send a law-breaking cockroach scurrying for cover.

Mum kept interrogating me, and just wouldn't let up. Eventually, I lost it:

'We wouldn't be in this position if you'd just had the termination!'

The way Mum looked at me, then.

The same way those other mothers look when I come to their doors.

My head sinks lower, my thoughts circling back to the same panicked refrain:

What am I going to do? What am I going to do?

I hear shuffling behind me, and, for a terrible moment, I wonder if I've said it out loud.

The church was empty when I arrived.

'Asking for forgiveness?'

It's a whisper. A man's whisper.

I freeze – as stiff as those marble effigies, prostrate on their tombs.

I crank my neck round.

A man with long, braided hair stares back at me, bristled skin coppered by the sun. His teal eyes widen, and he mutters something. He looks almost as shocked as I am.

'Not often I get this close to Ministry,' he says, scrutinising my badge.

Oh, Jesus. He's one of *them* ... I scan the church: no one else is here.

'Particularly since the outbreaks.' He coughs. 'It's alright: this one's not airborne.' He coughs again. 'At least, I don't think it is...'

My eyes drop to my bag. My mask's tucked inside.

He smirks. 'Illegals' humour. Don't fret.'

I coax some saliva into my mouth: 'Who are you?'

'You can call me Spice.'

'What do you want?'

'I have an invitation for you.'

'Who from?'

Now he smiles: a broad, even smile.

'I'm sure you can guess. I gather you're quite keen to meet her.'

Gravity shifts. One moment I am weightless, drifting up to the arches. The next, leaden, sinking down to the tombs.

'Tomorrow morning. The old flyover in Hammersmith. Can you get there by six? We'll head from there.'

I don't answer. I cannot answer. Now it's happening, I'm suddenly unsure.

Steener was right. She must have found out I was looking.

Unless it's a trap, to hold me for ransom. Would anyone at the Ministry care?

'Where am I going?'

'A transition site.'

I look at him blankly.

'A camp for try-outs. Not everyone's cut out for offliner life.'

Offliner?

I remember what Yasmine said, and relax, just a little.

'Works better this way, a chance to test the water. Before they commit to a homestead.'

Amazing, the language these people use. Another euphemism I've heard is 'freedom zone'. It promises something a far cry from those hovels I've seen on the newsreels, near evacuated seaside towns. Skegness, Great Yarmouth, Llanelli. Or what's left of them.

'There are conditions,' he says. 'No chaperones. No tracking. No devices.'

'But, how will I—?'

'Use this.'

He hands me a small bioplastic card, about the size of a wafer.

'What is it?'

'UPD. Untracked payment device. Won't hit your quota or be traced back to you.'

Merely possessing one of these could get me sacked and arrested.

'You know, the offliners kicked off when they heard about you coming. But I persuaded them. You know why?'

I shake my head.

'Because of the bullshit your Party makes up about them, and us. For once, you can see things yourself. How they actually are.' His jaw shifts. 'They aren't criminals, or terrorists. They don't scrounge off your system or steal. They just want to live out their lives the old way. Without interference.'

I don't respond, even though the facts say otherwise. Offliner camps harbour FREE suspects, I've seen the videos; they incubate radicals and set them loose.

But I don't have to agree with him. I just need him to lead me to her.

I run my tongue over my lips. 'How will I know this person I'm going to meet is really her?'

There: I finally asked the key question.

He pushes himself up. 'Oh, you'll know, alright. As soon as you set eyes on her.'

I watch him stride down the nave, his boots echoing off the stone.

I turn to the altar and see a curl of smoke from the rack.

My candle just snuffed out.

CHAPTER 19
Day Thirteen

The flyover smells of urine and paint. Emptied canisters litter the ground. Spice is waiting for me, but before I even utter a greeting, he instructs me to hold out my arms and pats me down. I offer up my bag and check out the latest graffiti as he rifles through it. Amidst the genitalia and expletives, one image catches my eye: a man and woman hugging a boy and a girl. Underneath, daubed in garish pink letters:

Family is no crime

Perhaps Spice did it specially.

Satisfied with his search, he points at two e-scooters leaning against a buttress.

'Your transport awaits.'

We scoot along a disused cycle path as the sun rises in a violet sky. Normally, I'd be scouting the verges for flowers or birds, but it's all I can do to keep up. The further we go, the more convinced I am this is a set-up. I have an overwhelming urge to spin the scooter round. As far as I'm aware, no one's ever fabricated a new profile from scratch that's duped the system, but there's always a first time. And FREE are renowned for their fakes.

I attempt some enquiries about my sister: what she's like, what's her name, what she does. After the third 'You'll find out soon enough', I give up, and focus my attention on counting the ruts.

Eventually, Spice slows to a stop near a high security fence. It seems to go on for miles. I've totally lost my bearings; I only travel this city by train or tram. Through the bars I glimpse rows of metal tanks plastered with warning labels about liquefied air; these must be cryogenic batteries, the capital's solar-energy stores.

Spice signals at me to get down. 'Cameras up ahead, on the right. Stay behind me.'

He wheels the scooters behind a bramble bush and squeezes between a gap in the bars. I snag my jacket on thorns, but Spice ushers me on, and it rips. We proceed in a crouch, dragging the scooters behind us, until we get beyond the tanks. Spice motions for me to stand up. As I get to my feet, the view robs me of breath.

A vast silver sea stretches to the horizon, cubed waves of solar panels rising above a feast of flowers: pansies, violet columbine, oxeye daisies, all crawling with bumblebees, their ponderous, pollen-specked bottoms glistening in the sun. Butterflies flit between the panels: orange-tips and meadow browns, red admirals. I've never seen a solar park on this scale before; it must be thousands of acres. Now I realise where I am.

Mum remembers when this used to be an airport, named after the village it usurped: Heath Row. Before that, it was orchards and farms. Mum said that when she was a child, playing in their garden, plane after plane would roar past overhead. Millions of people used to take hundreds of thousands of flights from here each year. No wonder it all went to shit.

Spice has marched ahead, and I hurry to catch up, stumbling over ridges of soil. A new kind of buzzing drowns out the insects' hum. Instinctively, I duck. Spice doesn't flinch.

A drone flashes past.

'Won't they pick us up?' I whisper, thinking about the heightened security for energy stores. 'They're thermal, right?'

'Yeah, but they're only interested in the panels. You get all sorts wandering through here: deer, foxes, badgers. Even the odd boar.' Spice nods towards the fence. 'It's the perimeter you have to watch. Especially over there, by the data farms.'

I can just glimpse them, looming above the fence: glass hulks moored at the edge of this solar sea. Those buildings house the servers and cloud campuses that keep the network's heart beating. All this monitoring and processing requires power. Those algorithms are hungry.

We keep walking in what seems like a never-ending grid. Sweat is leaking down my back, the sun's rays amplified by the solar cells, and I ask Spice to stop while I grab a drink.

Out of the corner of my eye, I spot a metal spider scuttling towards us. I jump back as a panel bug scurries past.

'They're quite harmless,' says Spice, with a smile. 'They're only concerned with cleaning or mending panels.'

'I know. I'm not an idiot,' I say, more gruffly than I intended.

Spiders have always been a weakness. The kids in school used to cup them in their hands and chase me.

'Are you always this jumpy?'

I glare at him. 'Depends on the company.'

We stumble through another four rows until, all of a sudden, the sea gives way to a large clearing colonised by silver, gold and pink domes. They look like psychedelic beehives. If this is some new solar tech, I've never seen it.

'What on earth—?'

'Orga-pods,' says Spice. 'Like the old chill 'n' charge pods, but better.' He nods. 'Organic, breathable and self-repairing.'

As we get closer, I see the pods are laid out in a hexagonal formation. Chairs and tables have been set up outside, with tubs of plants. Greenhouses rear up behind.

'You made these?' I try to mask my surprise. I was expecting a few lean-to shacks, maybe a shipping container or two.

'We sourced them. They don't take long to build. They're insulated and solar painted so you don't freeze or fry.'

Perhaps this is their offliner 'show home' for newcomers; an elaborate ruse, intended to sucker the gullible in.

'What did you do with the panels?'

'There weren't any. It's a lake bed – part of the biodiversity quota, contingency drainage during the rainy season. It's never flooded, though. They either changed their plans or got their calculations wrong.'

I have to give them credit: right on the capital's doorstep and a surveillance blind spot to boot. But I wouldn't fancy my chances in one of those things during a heatwave, never mind a winter storm.

'We assumed this site would be temporary,' Spice continues. 'A camp so close to the city couldn't last long. But it's like they say: hide in plain sight.'

As we approach, a woman peers out of one of the hive's doorways. Spice waves at her, and she steps into the clearing.

'This is Barb.'

She looks a bit older than Mum, grey hair straggling from a floppy cap. Not the type to take hostages, surely...? I relax, just a little.

She studies my face, and my skin grows hotter.

'You were right,' she murmurs. 'Apart from the eyes, the likeness is uncanny.'

An amulet rests in the hollow of her throat – some kind of bird, its wings spread over an eye.

Like the ankle tattoo. I swallow. On the rebel who stopped our train.

She folds her arms. 'How d'you know she hasn't already ordered in her machines?'

Spice exhales. 'Come on, Barb. We talked about this.'

I clear my throat. 'I'm not here in an official capacity, I assure you. I'm not a security risk.'

Her eyes narrow: '*Everyone's* a security risk,' she hisses. 'Especially you.'

Spice lowers his voice. 'Is she here yet?'

Barb shakes her head. 'No.'

'Well, in that case, I might as well show our guest around.'

She gives me a withering look. 'Still reckon you can do a job on her, do you? Good luck.'

Spice takes me inside one of the pods. It's impeccably organised, complete with storage, sofabed and lamps. Beyond the pods are wooden compost toilets, solar showers, and a communal cooking area with vintage solar stoves. Just as I'm wondering where all the children are, a woman with a bulging belly emerges from a rose-coloured pod. I think of those offliner kids I've seen in the reels, fighting over scraps of food while their parents blearily look on, drunk or high.

'How many children live here?' I ask.

Spice frowns. 'Not enough.'

My question seems to annoy him.

Maybe it's because it's a transit camp. They probably wait till they get to the homesteads.

'Don't believe everything you see on your news,' he says. 'In fact, don't believe any of it.'

I'm about to summon a retort, when Barb marches over.

'You need to get cracking,' she says to Spice, a little breathless. 'She's here.'

CHAPTER 20

I don't hear whatever Spice says next. Something knobbly and hard thuds in the pit of my stomach, propelling acid into my throat. He touches my arm, repeats his instruction. My legs obey, but my lungs ... I'm working them like bellows, but no air's getting through.

Spice leads me into a different pod. I don't want him to leave.

My fingers clench and unclench, a rhythm of threes.

I make myself turn, and something detonates inside. The shock is physical.

It's like looking in one of those magic mirrors. The same, but different.

Dark-blonde hair, not brown. Pale skin. A little leaner than me; taut with muscle.

Eyes like stones on a riverbed.

I examine every inch of her, as if she's some exotic specimen: the heavy boots, the patterned leggings, vintage top. Throat, chokered in black.

And a thought drops in. Could her likeness be stealth wear?

'Hello, Kai.'

Any doubts vanish. That could be Mum speaking.

'Spice told me about your eyes ... Shame I lost out there.' She folds herself into a chair. 'I heard some people call them "ghost eyes". They believe they give you special powers.' A smile glimmers. 'Perhaps that's why the Ministry hired you.'

I stiffen. Is she mocking me?

'Tell me,' she says, hooking a leg over her knee. 'What's your earliest memory?'

I don't answer straight away, even though I know.

A golden horse, salt tang, crisp breeze.

Giddy with excitement; Mum's arms belted around my waist.

'A fairground ride. By a beach that no longer exists.'

'With your parents?'

I hesitate. 'My mother, yes ... And you?'

She fingers a frayed friendship bracelet. 'Fighting a boy over a bowl of rice. I won.'

Her lips part, but it's not really a smile.

'You know, I used to make up stories in my head about them ... Who they were, what they were like ... I pictured them stowing me away, risking everything to keep me. Begging the Ministry for mercy when they came ... But I dismissed such fantasies as I grew older.'

I swallow. 'They would have kept you if they could.'

She gives a contemptuous snort. 'There's an old saying, back when siblings were allowed: "A sister is your first friend and second mother." But, of course, that assumes you have a mother. And you grew up together. So I'm not sure where that leaves us.'

I take a breath.

'It's been a journey, these past two weeks. Trying to find you.'

'You could have reported me straight away. Why didn't you?'

'I wasn't sure ... I had to speak with my parents, find out what happened...'

Her eyes spark. 'No other family on your watch enjoyed that privilege.'

'No other family concealed their child for twenty-four years.'

I feel it already, the tension between us. Like a band stretching tighter and tighter.

Soon it will snap.

My gaze swerves to a picture on a shelf. A teenage girl hugging a woman: possibly Barb.

Come on, Kai. Everything depends on this.

'This is difficult,' I say. 'For both of us. We don't know each other ... I don't even know your name.'

Something flickers across her face.

'Senka,' she says, eventually. 'It means "shadow". Mila, a carer who looked out for me, said that's what I was: a child, surviving in the shadows. I don't recall any other name...'

'Zoe,' I whisper.

'Sorry?'

'Zoe. That was the name my parents chose for you. It means "life".'

'"Life"?'

Every comment is a minefield.

'There's less than a year between us.'

Her forehead creases. 'I never knew my birthday. None of us did. Even if we had known, it wasn't exactly a cause for celebration...'

'You were born on the sixth of December, and I was born on the fourth of January.'

'Not much in it, was there?' Her boot swings. 'Apart from who came first.'

Her answers immobilise me. Anger ripples beneath each one.

I try to imagine what it was like. All the horrendous acts in her childhood that led to this point.

'Look,' I sigh, 'I don't even know for certain whether that

profile is yours, but at midnight tomorrow it goes public, which means anyone in the Ministry can view it. Not just me.'

'Oh, it's mine alright ... Look at us. We are reflections, you and I. Two halves of a whole...'

'Then why did it suddenly appear on the system? After all these years?'

'I was injured in a raid. Quite badly. We have a few sympathisers in the medical community. When they were patching me up, they wanted to run some tests. Including one for genetic susceptibility to infection. I said yes – I'd never been sequenced.'

'But it exposed you. It was a massive risk.'

'Not really, I have no status: legally I don't exist.'

'It won't stop the Ministry tracking you.'

'I know.' Her stare intensifies. 'So, what are you going to do? Arrest me?'

'No, I ... I don't know.'

'What's holding you back? You have quite the reputation.'

She's obviously been digging, too. I wonder what she's found.

I consider some platitude about sibling allegiance. And decide against it.

'My mum and dad.'

She pushes her tongue around her mouth, as if she might spit.

'So you are capable of loyalty, then? Beyond your beloved Ministry?'

I think about what I've heard over the past two weeks. The jumble of accusations.

'I'd like to understand. What actually happened to you. I've been told things ... Things that don't make sense...'

'That's because you're conditioned to accept whatever truth they serve up ... It's not easy when the filters come off.' She leans back and studies me. 'There are things I can tell you that you won't want to hear. It's hard for you to recognise deceit, because it's all you've ever known.'

'I've come this far, haven't I?' I meet her gaze. 'My job is to get to the truth. So go ahead. Try me.'

CHAPTER 21

She pours me a glass of water from the cooler. We sit facing each other, two strangers who share the same blood, born from the same womb. I grip my fingers to stop them fidgeting and steel myself for what's to come.

'So, the thing I told you. About my first memory ... That wasn't strictly true. That was my second. What came first is this:

'Rows of beds. Painted swans gliding across the walls. I remember running my fingers along their necks, fuzzed with fluff and dirt.

'Constant cries, shouts, clatter. It doesn't bother me, though. You don't hear the trains if you grow up by the tracks.'

She sips her water and swallows.

'But there's a boy next to me who's not making any sounds at all. He's just lying there, face down. On his bed. I reach over, and prod him. No response. I prod him again. Perhaps it's more of a shove. He doesn't even flinch. For some reason, this makes me angry, so I hit him. But it's like thumping a mattress, just a dull thud. And so I keep hitting him, until my hand hurts, and I have to stop.' She gazes at her palm. 'Bad things happen when no one's watching.'

A tingling runs all the way up my spine.

'How old were you?'

She shrugs. 'Who knows? Maybe five...? If there's no one to hold you or pick you up, if you're left on your own for days, you don't know what normal is. And hitting is a kind of touch; we learned that. Everyone in that centre had their own story.'

'What *was* this place?'

'A prison for kids, in the middle of nowhere. Which the Ministry called a "reallocation centre".'

Exactly as Yasmine said.

'How long were you there?'

Her eyes bore into me. 'Mila said I was fourteen when I left.'

Fourteen?

I think of all the places I'd been by that age. All the things I'd done.

'I don't remember much about the early years. There were so many faces ... People came and went.' She frowns. 'A few etched themselves in ... You learn fast. To hold your tongue, not catch their eye. Do whatever's necessary. Books were my refuge. There were stacks of them, from the libraries that had closed when it all went digital. It was the only thing we were never short of.'

A gust catches the flap at the door.

'The kindest staff came from the camps. Many had families of their own they'd had to leave behind. This was their chance at a sort of freedom – they didn't want to mess it up. That's how I met Mila. She was good to me, and she got me out, somewhere safe. I have her to thank for that.'

'But where did they go? All those children?'

'Many got ill ... There was always some sickness going round and never enough medicine. As for the others ... We were told they were with new families.' Senka shakes her head. 'One day they were there, and the next, they just ... disappeared.'

She looks down at her hands.

'There was a girl who was roughly my age. Called Poe. She had the most beautiful hair: long, dark ringlets, honey skin. We spent all our time together, looked out for one another. She hated her name, but I loved it. She said one of the carers told her it meant "gift".

'A few days before Christmas, she found out a Christian family in America wanted to adopt her. She must have been thirteen. She couldn't believe it. I remember her cracking that big toothy grin of hers and saying maybe her name had won out after all. And I was happy for her. Really. Even though it would be like losing a limb...' She twists her bracelet, round and round. 'I remember the day she left, she was so excited ... She'd made me a special present, and I felt so bad, all I had to give her was this cheap resin pendant. It was supposed to bring her luck...'

Senka's mouth twists.

'But I could see from Mila's face that something was wrong. I remember asking her: "Why aren't you happy for Poe?" And Mila gave me this funny look. She pulled me close and said: "I will find a home for you, Senka. Let me do this, not anyone else. Say nothing. This is my promise."

'It was only later Mila told me ... what really happened. Everything has a price, right? Poe never went to America. There never was any "family". She was sold to some stranger in India: his child bride.'

I think of the man with the chameleon face at the shopping mall. A bitter taste creeps into my mouth.

'That's how much your Ministry cares for its children. A thirteen-year-old girl traded like a kidney, or some exotic reptile ... I've seen bots treated better.'

I cannot believe the Ministry would condone this. Trafficking children, on their watch?

'I was lucky: Mila kept her promise. She got me out, to a transit camp, then moved me to a homestead by the coast. I think that was the first time I'd actually felt safe. Even then, I was always looking over my shoulder. I'd broken the law by being born. I was an inconvenience, just like the migrants – something to be disposed of. I was terrified they'd find me and send me back. Or trade me, too.'

I think of my own childhood. The petty worries that used to occupy me. That still do.

'I'm sorry.'

It seems entirely inadequate. But I have no idea what else to say.

'Who gave the Ministry the right to take us away from our families? Decide which of us should live? They talk about birth crimes, but what about their crimes?'

Her eyes glitter.

'So I swore that I would do whatever I could to unseat this government. I would expose their lies and hypocrisy, and watch their regime implode.'

So it's true: she is a terrorist. A member of FREE.

Of course, I suspected. But hearing her say it is so much worse.

'I cannot condone what happened to you, if what you say is true. But as for our laws ... I have to defend them. We were hurtling towards extinction. Now we can grow enough food for our people. We can provide clean water, clean energy and homes. Our borders are secure. ONE's laws served us when democracy failed.'

She scoffs. 'Democracy didn't fail.'

'Really? What about the Great Flood? The wheat crisis? The malaria outbreaks? Five decades our governments stalled, after those pledges at Rio were made. They couldn't deliver their promises, not even to protect those that came after: their own kin...'

'That doesn't excuse taking away freedom. Or basic rights—'

'They shied away from difficult decisions, put off endlessly what had to be done. What did they think would happen? A seven-fold increase in the world's population over two centuries, rocketing consumption in the West. And for what? The relentless pursuit of profit ... The earth's still paying for that legacy, now.'

'That may be true, but there are other ways to change...'

I shake my head. 'You and I never suffered the constant black-outs, soaring inflation ... queuing for bread that trebled in price overnight. We never lost our homes and families to famine or flood. ONE stepped up. They brought us stability, but it came at a price.'

'A heavy price indeed. State surveillance of our bodies, enforced abortions. Turning our backs on desperate refugees. These laws were only ever meant to be temporary...' She flaps her arm. 'You think all this is *normal*? No opposition. No criticism. You have no idea what's really happening, because they only feed you what they want you to see.'

My head feels like a popcorn machine. Kernels firing indiscriminately, rocketing off the sides. Why am I listening to this? Haven't I got what I came for?

I stand up. 'I have to go.'

'Wait...' She follows me. 'There's more we need to discuss. Much more than you can possibly imagine.'

I put my hand on the flap, but she grabs my arm.

'You can go home to your little flat and your robot dog, but things have got to change, Kai. And you're part of that change, whether you like it or not.'

My blood pounds. No, I'm not.

And what does she know about my flat? Or Niko?

'That profile is mine, and I can prove it. Remember: it's your mother in the firing line.'

'*Our* mother.'

Her eyes burn. 'She was never my mother. She was just a host.'

I step out of the pod into the clearing and gulp some air.

Spice and Barb are chatting on a bench, sunlight slanting over their faces, as if it's just another day.

Barb nudges Spice when she sees me.

'Still alive, then?' he says. 'Did you get some answers to your questions?'

I'm suddenly a child again, eyes stinging, swallowing hard.

'I have to go back now,' I say to him. 'Right away.'

CHAPTER 22

I speed as fast as the ruts allow, a nose ahead of Spice. He keeps asking me if I'm OK. This time it's me that doesn't reply. When we reach the flyover, he mentions another meeting. I don't answer, just hand him the scooter and make a beeline for the overland. It's rush hour, and the train is packed. I have no choice but to stand.

I clutch the pole, my head swimming. I've dropped down a rabbit hole into a world of anarchy and doubt, a world that contradicts everything I've been told. There's a hard side to Senka. A ruthlessness that scares me. The most sensible thing would be to report her straight away. Not only is she an illegal, she's a terrorist and clearly a major threat to the Ministry. That might even work in my favour. Her criminality could legitimise my delay.

And yet...

The appalling tales about those centres.

The trafficking. The neglect...

If there's no one to hold you, or pick you up; if you're left on your own for days...

Fourteen years she spent there.

If these places really existed, why were we never told?

Suddenly, the train brakes, hard. I lurch forward, trampling feet. 'Sorry.'

A woman in a pale-blue dress frowns at me and slides her feet under her seat.

A metallic voice pierces the carriage: 'We apologise to our customers for the short delay. There is an object on the line. Our journey will resume shortly.'

I sense the woman's eyes moving over my face. I hunch into my jacket and pull my mask a little higher.

The woman stands up, swaying slightly.

'It's no good hiding behind that mask. I know what you are...'

I keep my eyes on the floor. Not today. Not again.

'I never forget a face.' She leans closer. 'Particularly a face like yours.'

Her breath is sour, I almost gag.

'I still can't sleep properly, you know. You might as well have stuck that needle in yourself.'

Every nerve in my body tenses. I glance at the doors.

She addresses the carriage. 'I was pregnant. With twins. They summoned me to one of their "clinics". I refused.'

Our train nudges forward and gathers speed. I grip the pole tighter.

'This baby reaper came to my house, told me I had to choose...'

I remember her. She'd missed two appointments. She left me no option.

'They sedated me. I was hysterical.' Her voice quivers. 'When I came round, only one twin was alive.'

The swarm of whispers grows louder.

'Potassium chloride. That's what they injected. To stop my baby's heart.'

A twin to singleton reduction. It doesn't matter how many reels they make you watch, how many stats they give you, I still find them difficult.

'Witches kill babies. You know that's what you're called, don't you?' The woman's gaze lifts to my eyes. 'They would have burned you in the olden days.'

Everyone is staring. She thrusts her finger at me. 'Witch.'

Senka's words echo:

Who gave the Ministry the right to decide which of us should live?

'Witch,' she says again.

Some passengers edge out of their seats and take refuge further down the carriage, unwilling to risk the Ministry's wrath. But two other women, throwing caution to the wind, join in: 'Witch! Witch!'

I should grab my screen and report her, pull the emergency brake, but I cannot move, I cannot breathe.

'Witch! Witch! Witch!'

They talk about birth crimes, but what about their crimes?

At last the train begins to slow. I force my way through the bodies and stab at the doors until they open.

I stumble into the crowds, cuffing my tears with my sleeve. A man thuds into me; I catapult into someone else. I dive down a side road and take refuge in a public garden squared with limes. I sink onto a bench, press my hands over my face, and count.

Three, six, nine, twelve, fifteen...

A baby's squeal makes me start. My head shoots up.

Its mother gives me an anxious stare and tugs at the pram's hood.

I check the time, and groan. I'm going to be seriously late.

◆ ◆ ◆

I keep my head bowed as I scurry to my desk. I feel tainted. Dirty. As if, just by looking at me, people will know.

Aisha wheels back her chair. 'Good morning, Ministry Rep—' Her face falls. 'Is everything OK?'

'Train problems,' I blurt. I dump my bag and switch on my machine.

'Not *again*...?'

I swallow. 'Objects on the line.'

She tuts. 'Poor you...'

It wells up out of nowhere: the argument with Senka, the chanting, tomorrow's deadline ... I bury my head in my screen.

Aisha jumps up. 'Hey, why don't we take a minute? Go somewhere quiet...' She glances at Hellie, two desks away.

'I can't...' I sniff. 'I'm late already. Honestly, I'm fine...'

She frowns and parks herself on my desk. 'What is it?' she whispers. 'Home? Work?'

'There was this woman on the train ... An old case of mine ... Twins...'

'Ah...' Aisha nods. 'She recognised you?'

'Yeah...' I exhale. 'It was bad.'

Aisha squeezes my shoulder. 'Never easy. They like to have someone to blame.'

'It wasn't just her; others joined in ... Pointing at me, calling me names...'

'Don't they realise how lucky they are? Don't they see what's happening on the news? Their child will flourish. It will have food, and a home...' She sighs. 'I'd do anything to see my home again...' She catches herself. 'I didn't mean...' Her eyes dart to mine. 'It's not that I'm ungrateful. It's just that ... I lost my family. In the before.'

The before: what the settlers call their previous lives. The ones they had to leave.

'I'm sorry ... Here's me, bleating on, after everything you went through. It must have been awful.'

She shakes her head. 'Please ... don't apologise.' She looks at me. 'The herders wanted my father's land for their goats. Because theirs had turned to desert ... He wouldn't let them have it. So they beat him to death with sticks...'

'Oh, Aisha...'

'We had to leave our farm ... We were on our way to a refugee camp when the village we were in was raided. The militants set all the houses on fire. My mother and my sisters ran to hide, but we got separated. It was chaos ... Gunshots, screams ... We didn't dare come out until it was dark.' Her chin trembles. 'That's when we found her. My baby sister. They'd shot her, in the street. She was only six.'

I put my hand on Aisha's arm. I've heard so many stories on the reels. But this is different.

'Being sponsored by ONE was a blessing.' She nods at me. 'I thank God for it every day.'

The Party saved Aisha. She owes them her life. She is proof of the good they do.

But they didn't save Senka.

I think of her, raging at me about their failings.

Senka wants to torch the ONE Party, just like that village in Nigeria. Strike the match, and watch it burn.

Maybe if I'd suffered what she's suffered, I'd want to torch it, too.

CHAPTER 23

'We're coming over this evening. Your dad and I. We've decided. Given your travel quota's rather pinched...'

I grip my phone.

I sent Mum a message, after lunch: *There's been a development. Let's meet up.*

I can't recall a worse day in my life since that awful assembly with Ciara.

But we don't have the luxury of time: our two-week amnesty is almost up.

'I've made vegetable samosas,' adds Mum. 'So don't fret about food.'

Cooking has always been a diversion when she's upset. I picture her, clutching the screen, Dad hovering in the background. Using all her strength not to barrage me with questions.

'The asparagus and broccoli this year are a triumph. I'm using them in everything. I think it's the compost...'

I think of how I snapped at her about the termination, and wince. I can't believe that was only yesterday. It feels like at least a week.

She gulps a breath. 'Kai? Are you still there?'

'Yes, Mum. I'm here.'

'When d'you think you'll be back?'

'I've just got to finish off a few things, I should be done by six, latest.'

'You come when you're ready. Your dad and I can wander around that biodiversity park. See if we can find those elusive great crested newts.'

I cover my mouth with my hand and blink back tears.

It's the spaces between words, the things that aren't said, that are important.

Everything else is just filler.

Like samosas.

And great crested newts.

◆ ◆ ◆

Dad saws his knife back and forth, splicing his samosa into bite-size portions. Mum hasn't touched hers. I busy myself with chewing; pea skins cling to my teeth.

'Are they OK?' Mum nods at my plate.

The pastry swells in my throat. I force a swallow.

'Lovely. Thanks.'

I look past her, to the tower blocks outside my window. All those people in their apartments, leading safe, compliant lives.

I take a breath. 'So ... the contact I mentioned on Sunday.' I was going to wait until we'd finished eating. But I can't. 'Well, they came through.'

Dad freezes, fork mid-air.

Mum opens her mouth. And closes it.

'I met with a woman this morning. Who claims she is my sister.'

Mum makes a sound as if she's been punched.

'I don't have proof, but ... I think it's her.'

Whatever I do, for all our safety, I mustn't let Senka's name slip.

'But ... we only saw you yesterday,' says Dad.

'I know, it all happened very fast.'

Mum's hands fly to her face. 'Oh my God ... You've actually *seen* her... I can't believe ... How is she? What's she like?'

Angry.

Very, very angry...

'She's...' I hesitate. Dad is staring at me intently. 'I suppose she's a lighter-haired, thinner version of me.'

'Did you take a picture?' Mum lunges for my bag, as if she's about to ransack it.

'No, that wasn't ... It was only very brief.'

'How did you find her? Where was she?'

'Sarah...' Dad gives Mum a look.

'Sorry. I promised your father I wouldn't keep interrupting.'

I press my palms into my thighs. 'Umm ... I shouldn't really say.'

'Oh, right.' Mum yanks at a strand of hair. 'Of course...'

'Is she well?' asks Dad. 'What's she doing?'

Blowing up Ministry buildings...

'She's made a life for herself.' I nod at them. 'We didn't really cover the details...'

'Did she talk about the family she grew up with? Is she happy?'

'To be honest...' I push a samosa around my plate, frantically editing words. 'That part was a little difficult.'

I hear Dad's breathing. Deep and slow. 'In what way?'

I can't tell them the truth; not yet. It will break them.

'I think she had a tough few years ... But she's OK now.'

Dad pushes back his chair and walks to the window. I see his eyes reflected in the glass.

'Like I said ... we only spoke for a short while.'

'Do you think...?' Mum swallows. 'Do you think there's a chance, not now of course, but at some point ... she might see us?'

She's not my mother. She was just a host.

'I don't know, Mum.' I take her hands in mine. 'We've got a bigger problem to sort out first. And she's not ready. It's going to take time.'

Dad turns. His face is ashen. 'But we don't have time, do we, Kai? Our two weeks is almost up.'

I've been avoiding this part, leaving it, like a coward, to the very end.

'Technically, the case is still under my remit, even after the restriction lifts. So as long as no one pries into my caseload, we may be OK.'

It's a weak response, and Dad knows it. The Ministry's got everyone on high alert. We're expected to be snooping on each other, and there are lots of ambitious colleagues, eager to please.

'I'm sorry, I...' I can't hold it back any longer. 'I don't know what to do. I feel like I've let you both down.'

'Shush...' Dad walks over and envelops me in his arms. 'You found her, didn't you? That in itself is a miracle. Just to know she's alive and she's OK. This was our doing, not yours. Don't blame yourself, whatever happens. Whatever you need to do.'

He lets me go and reaches for Mum's hand. 'We can face it.' He braves a smile. 'Your mother and I will be fine.'

We go along with this pretence, because we have to. Because there is no other way.

Whether I report them or not won't make much difference, after tomorrow.

Someone will spot Senka's profile. And my parents will spend years in prison, apart from each other.

And apart from me.

UN Accuses the UK of 'Serious Human Rights Violations' against Climate Migrants

By Meera Khatri

OneWorld News Agency, New Delhi

The results of the UN's fact-finding investigation into alleged human-rights violations by the UK government were released in a report today.

Despite repeatedly being denied access, investigators claim they have found 'credible evidence' of human-rights abuses in the government–dubbed 'resettlement' centres that could constitute crimes against humanity. These include adverse conditions in cramped and unsanitary detention cells, ill-treatment and multiple reports of death in custody arising from poor nutrition and rampant disease.

'These people have lost everything,' said a spokesperson from the UN Human Rights Council. 'Their livelihoods, their families, their homes. Their countries produced the least carbon emissions but have suffered the worst impacts as a result of climate change, and it is our moral duty to help them. The UK should be offering them safe migration routes and pathways to citizenship instead of incarcerating them in camps not fit for purpose and deporting them to unsafe countries. Such mistreatment not only breaches Britain's obligations under international law, it's inhuman.'

This report follows last month's investigation into the UK government's coastal patrols, with new evidence of migrants' boats being turned around in the Channel and forcibly escorted back out to sea in perilous conditions.

The ONE Party has not commented specifically on the report, but a Party spokesperson reiterated that Britain's policies to protect its borders were a matter of national security and that the UN should not interfere. 'We are dealing with an unprecedented invasion of illegal migrants that nearly brought this country to its knees,' commented the spokesperson. 'Our resettlement programme supports people who enter our country legally, but we will continue to do everything in our power to prevent criminal gangs trafficking people to our shores. Our message is simple: illegal migrants who trespass across our borders will be sent back.'

China has backed the UK's position, calling the UN's interventions 'an arrogant political ploy' and 'inappropriate'.

The UN report is unlikely to generate much interest inside the UK, given the ONE Party's strict censorship rules.

As of last night, the report had not featured on any state-run news platforms.

CHAPTER 24
Day Fourteen

It's five minutes to midnight. I tap my keyboard in a rhythm of fours. I can hear Niko's snores from the depths of my duvet, interspersed with the occasional whimper; his legs twitch as he chases rabbits in virtual reality dreams.

I wish I could programme my dreams. Filter out the nightmares, neuter my fears.

In three hundred seconds my sister's profile will emerge from its digital cocoon like some monstrous moth, for all to see. The shame of it: a birth crime, my illegal sibling still at large. Two weeks have passed, and what evidence can I produce in our defence? Testimonies from criminals. Allegations against the Ministry of mismanagement, corruption and lies.

The cursor flashes at me. The report I have compiled isn't a report, it's a story. I have no means of corroborating these claims. My sources are at best compromised, at worst pedalling a subversive agenda intended to mislead.

None of it changes the fact that my parents broke the law.

And my illegal sister is a terrorist.

I highlight two paragraphs about the reallocation programme. The tacit Ministry permissions, the trafficking. The abuse.

My finger hovers over the delete button.

How can an amorphous grey block be so dangerous?

I think of my parents.

Of Dr Trowsky, Yasmine Mestari.

My finger grows heavy.

Of Senka. And Spice.

Niko suddenly launches himself out of my bed and races to the door.

A corner of white pushes onto the mat. Niko hops back and ogles me, waiting for the command.

It's from her, I'm sure of it. Senka clearly knows where I live.

I send Niko to his basket and fetch a fork. I kneel on the mat and coax the envelope underneath the door, careful not to touch it with my fingers. I think of Steener and that street drug, Miss Carrie. They can coat anything these days. You know nothing about it until you come round. If you come round.

'Niko?' He trots over and sits, ears flat against his head.

I point at the envelope. 'Test.'

He gets up and sniffs the paper. His eyes glow blue and he wags his tail. It's clean.

I slice it open. Inside is a scrap of paper. The words look handwritten but they were almost certainly printed:

Don't do anything rash, there's something you need to see.
Meet me tomorrow evening at the Marston.
We can help each other.
S.

The only way she could possibly help me is by never having been sequenced. I've no interest in hearing more of her rants. Although the Marston was the centre where her profile originated.

I glance at the clock. Dread curls round my belly. It's gone midnight.

I have to check.

My restricted folder is empty. It's what I expected, but it still makes my heart leap.

I click on the fresh batch of alerts already waiting. I scroll through and frown.

Her profile should be there.

I bring up our family record: striped bars dance and sway.

Grandparents. Parents. Me.

No sibling.

Senka's profile has disappeared.

CHAPTER 25
Day Fifteen

The tram lumbers up the hill, whining as it hits the gradient. Just two weeks since I came here, but everything has changed. My eyes skim pastel houses with roof-top gardens; a public cooling station for extreme heat days. My brain registers these details but my body cannot muster a response. If I were an android, my battery would be terminally drained.

I was woken in the night by a sharp jab in my chest. As I attempted to inhale, there was another stab, even sharper. My medi-alert started pinging while Niko raced round the bed. My medi-profile assured me that I hadn't suffered a myocardial infarction, but confirmed my cortisol and glucagon levels were elevated and I was being booked in for a check-up.

I didn't even bother trying to get back to sleep. Just waited out the hours until Dad messaged me back.

They're still at home. They haven't been arrested. Not yet.

The tram lurches to a stop by the Catholic church near the approach road, famous for its floral Madonna. I resist the urge to get off and dash in.

Wasn't this the point of them, my talismans: the votive candles, the numbers?

My unwavering devotion to the Ministry?

Weren't these the wagers I made to stop us ending up like Ciara's family, or those families in the reels?

A few minutes later we arrive at the Marston. The doors slide open. The wellness centre is relatively empty, just a couple of men panting over power-bikes.

A bot glides over. 'This way, please.' No formal greeting today.

I follow it round to a fire exit, behind the smart gym.

'If you proceed to the basement, you will be escorted to your meeting.'

My stomach loops. Nothing good ever happens in wellness-centre basements.

My footsteps echo in the stairwell as I descend into the building's bowels. I turn a corner and spot an android on the floor below. Their skin shimmers a pale silver, like the level six I met before.

'Ministry Representative Houghton.'

It *is* the same one: Nieran. How can an android be mixed up in this? Surely their system design would prohibit collaboration with illegals?

They cup their hands. 'Please, follow me.'

I follow them through a set of double doors. This corridor is noticeably warmer; I'm guessing it's where the systems are housed. Probably the gene bank, too.

They stop outside a door and gesture for me to enter. The room is packed with servers, humming away. Senka is sitting behind a monitor, her face swamped in blue light. It's like looking at a photo of myself with filters.

'Hello, Kai.' Her eyes glow an even darker blue. 'Thank you for coming.'

I glance at the android.

'Don't worry about Nieran. They're very discreet.'

'So it would seem.' I meet their silver-and-lilac gaze. 'Last time I visited, they told me they couldn't ID your profile. As far as I'm aware, lying isn't part of their algorithms.'

'In Nieran's defence, I'm not registered on the official system. Technically, I don't exist.'

'As of this morning you don't genetically exist, either.'

She tips her head.

'Your profile has disappeared; I checked after it went public. Which means someone else in the Ministry must have it.'

'Well, we'd better crack on, then.' She wheels over a chair, totally unfazed by my news. 'Have a seat.'

She rips open a small packet on her desk and extracts a swab. She puts it in her mouth and rolls it round her cheek.

Irritation spikes. 'Is this why you dragged me out here? For a DNA test?'

'You wanted proof that profile is mine, well this is it.' She gives the swab to Nieran. 'It's not the only reason.' She hands me another packet. 'Your turn.'

I hesitate. I'm not sure I want my DNA in the hands of terrorists.

But it's true: I need to be sure.

I swab my cheek as Senka swivels her monitor round. The light pools over my face; Senka recedes into shadow. Nieran loads the samples into a machine on the other side of the room.

She nods at the screen. 'I expect you're familiar with these charts. Nieran explained them to me. As I understand, the colours represent the level of DNA match between samples. Pink is completely identical, blue is half identical and grey is non-identical.'

Nieran looks up. 'The data is uploading now.'

Twenty-three striped bars appear on the screen. They look like drug capsules. The same capsules I saw on my dashboard two weeks ago. And the pinks and blues have it.

My eyes dart to the words at the bottom:

Shared DNA 49.8%

'Blood sisters, Kai. Unlike people, blood doesn't lie.' Senka wags a boot at me. 'This is why I got Nieran to upload my profile. Why I sent Spice to find you. How did you like the man with the changing face? Unfortunately, the nature of our activities requires occasional contact with such groups...'

Something inside me shrivels. The church. The person Steener saw...

All along, she's been laying the trail.

'But, why?'

She smiles. 'Because you're my sister.' She wheels closer, grips the arms of my chair. 'And I want you to open your eyes.'

I reel away from her.

It was Senka on that train, with the educator drones. How long has she been tracking me?

'It was a risk, bringing you to the transit site. They weren't happy. But we have our own eyes and ears. And I had a hunch family would come first.'

'I'm loyal to my country. I'll never do anything to harm the Ministry. The only reason I haven't reported you is to protect my parents.'

'I know.' She sighs. 'Which is why I need to show you something else. But before I do, I want you to remember what I'm about to say. I'm not doing this out of spite or ... revenge, although you may think so. I'm doing it because people keep lying to you. And you deserve the truth.' She turns to the android. 'Nieran, would you get my birth record up, please?'

Birth record?

'Hang on ... I thought they were all erased?'

'They were. But that's the good thing about AI. These guys are better than elephants. They never, ever forget. It's probably better if Nieran explains.'

Nieran fixes me with an unflinching violet stare.

'Deep-learning models are complex and non-deterministic. During the training process, they frequently copy historical input data into their network to use for comparison purposes. Datasets are theoretically infinite as the training process is constant. This makes deletion problematic.'

I blink at Senka like an imbecile. 'I'm not sure I understand...'

'What they're saying is, data cannot be universally deleted. Sure, it can on dashboards and drives, and the servers they draw on, but not in *there*.' Senka points at Nieran. 'Because humans have no control over those networks. Not even the Ministry. And data lasts forever.'

'You mean the original records were copied by them? And stored?'

'Exactly. Credit to Spice, he used to be a robotics engineer. He says people still don't really understand how machine-learning models train themselves. How they learn. Or think. It was his idea to ask.'

Nieran taps a different keyboard, and a birth record materialises on screen.

Zoe HOUGHTON

Just seeing that name makes my blood rush. My sister was born, she's not just some DNA capsule on a screen.

My gaze swerves to the listed mother and father: my mother and father. Names, dates and places of birth.

'Look carefully, Kai.'

Something in her voice chills me. And I see the mistake, straight away.

Zoe's date of birth.

'That's not right...' It's not the date Mum gave me.

Her mouth pinches.

'That would make you—'

'One year older?'

Sweat films my neck. It cannot be.

'I was the firstborn, Kai. But they gave *me* away. Instead of you.'

CHAPTER 26

One minute I am staring at the screen, Senka's words bulleting my brain, the next I am tearing up the stairs and out the exit.

I am the second-born sister: the illegal one.

Senka's life should have been mine.

The tram stops by the floral Madonna. She holds out her flowered hands, gazing up at me with petalled eyes. Engraved in stone underneath is a prayer:

Mary, Mother of Jesus, please smile on us and be our mother always

And what of my mother? Why didn't she tell me the truth? Did they think I wouldn't find out?

Splinters of conversations ricochet in my head:

Not much in it, is there? Apart from who came first...

There are things I will tell you that you won't want to hear...

Numbers blur, jumbling into one another; the sequences stutter and stall.

It makes sense now. Why I am like I am. My eyes were an accident, just like the rest of me – the mark of a pariah. The mark of a child that should never have been born.

It will be hard for you to recognise deceit, because it's all you've ever known...

I thought Senka meant the Ministry.

But she was talking about our parents.

◆◆◆

I get off the tram and barrel along the pavement, bumping into passers-by. I'm panting by the time I get to the house.

I hammer on the door.

'Oh, darling, I didn't know you were—'

I stride past her, down the hall. I cannot look at her.

'Kai?' she calls after me. 'Kai, are you alright?'

I stagger into the kitchen, grab a glass of water and glug it down. My hands are trembling, like one of those addicts who's run out of parts to trade.

Mum creeps in behind me. I hear her breaths quickening.

'Darling, you're scaring me.' Her voice has risen an octave. 'Has something happened?'

I grip the counter.

'Should I fetch your dad?'

I make myself turn to the face I love. To those contours I know so well, I could draw them even if I were blinded.

'Was I your first-born?'

She stares at me. Her lips press together. 'I tried, with Zoe, I really did. I tried so hard...' Her words are slow, almost slurred. 'I just wasn't any good...'

The fridge judders.

'But I knew, from the moment I felt you kick ... And then, when I held you...' Her hands flutter and sink, like felled birds. 'It would have killed me, to let them take you away.'

The glass plummets from my hand. I barely register the smash.

She drops to a crouch and starts shuffling the shards into her palm. She pinches a sliver between her fingers. Blood sprouts. I watch it seep over the glass.

'How could y—?' I shake my head. 'Why didn't you tell me? My life – it's all been a lie.'

Mum hauls herself up and opens the bin. The glass rattles to the bottom with a sickening thud.

'I don't expect you to forgive. Or to understand...' She lifts her eyes to mine. 'But I honestly believe God gave me a second chance, with you.'

A sob erupts. More of a howl.

'Kai, please...'

I push past her outstretched arms and stumble out.

Ministry Broadcast
Another Life Saved:
Asale's Story

As part of our ongoing series, Another Life Saved, today we hear from Asale, who used to live in Malawi, before ONE sponsored her on its Climate Migrant Resettlement Programme (CMRP).

Asale gives her own harrowing account of the conditions she and her family faced before ONE offered her a new life in Britain.

Warning: some listeners may find elements of this broadcast distressing.

'Heat shimmers across the lake bed, sucking the moisture from your lips. No clouds. No air. Just a shroud of heat, scorching the breath in your throat. You try not to move.

It's another red day. That's what Amayi calls them. They used to come once, maybe twice a summer. Now, they come every day.

The earth bleeds dust into your mouth and your clothes. The ground is as cracked and wrinkled as an old elephant's skin. Canoes lie stranded like bleached bones, their tethering ropes long gone.

My belly growls because it is empty. I am so thirsty. The fields are thirsty, too.

My mother leaves each night on her bicycle. To follow the fishermen, find where the lake has gone. Each year, it runs further away.

Then, one night, all the water we have prayed for comes at once in a terrible storm.

It swallows everything.

Our crops. Our homes. The last of our cattle.

Many lives.

My father carries us on his back up the hill, to the school. We wait for the floods to go down. But my little sister, Chifuno, gets sick.

I watch her, every day, growing thinner and paler. We know the water is bad, but we have no choice. As the floods rise higher, the tanks overflow.

She dies on the eighth day. It is the first time I see my mother cry.

She cries again, when my father says he must leave with my brothers, to find work in the city. The city is dangerous.

People are killing each other for food.

My mother and I move to a camp. So many bodies pressed in together, all waiting to go home. But there is no home.

More people get sick. It spreads quickly. They say the camp will have to close, because it is no longer safe. They tell us we must leave. But where can we go?

Then one morning, a woman arrives. She says she is from England. She says she can offer me a new home. And my mother does not cry. Because she knows I will be safe. I will have food and medicine and clean water. And people who care.

Thank you, ONE, for bringing me to your beautiful country. For giving me this precious life so I don't have to be afraid any more.

God's blessings to the Party and to you all.'

CHAPTER 27

'Please, Kai. I just want to talk, I can explai—'

I press delete. Niko spoons into me, one paw on my arm.

Dad sounds desperate. That was his sixth message.

I took two sleeping pills when I got home. The world ebbed away from me, and I slid into a fitful sleep. My dreams morphed into hallucinations: garish caricatures spouting unintelligible words.

The android and Senka.

That woman on the train.

Minister Gauteng, brandishing a needle ready for my sterilisation.

I roll into the pillow and shut my eyes.

The clinic is chasing me too, for the appointment I missed after my medi-patch flagged an alert.

I don't have the energy to respond.

Maybe I should barricade myself in. Lie here, in my bed, until my organs shut down. Let my body bloat and liquefy, and seep into the duvet until all trace of me is gone.

A knock at the door makes me jump.

'Kai?'

Niko leaps out of my arms and races over, tail wagging.

'Kai? I know you're there.'

Niko yaps with excitement. I yank the duvet over my head.

Dad knocks again. 'Kai, please. I know what we did was wrong, but your mother wasn't well. I don't want to say this out here, but I will.'

I clamp the duvet tighter, tears turning to rage. 'I don't want to hear it. I'm sick of your lies! All your dirty secrets...'

'This will be the truth, I swear it. Just let me in.'

Niko pads back and sits by the bed, gazing at me with doleful eyes.

After a few minutes, I hear a sliding sound, followed by a thud.

'I'm staying put, as long as it takes ... Until you're ready.'

I roll over and wonder if Senka is nearby, watching this play out.

I imagine her, loitering by the lifts. Relishing our misery.

I haul my body out of bed. A sudden wave of dizziness makes me lurch against the counter. Niko whines and sniffs my hand.

'Are you OK, Kai?'

I parcel myself to the door. There's a shuffle of feet as I turn the lock.

My father looks as though his organs have already stopped working.

'Actually, Dad, I'm about as far from OK as I can be.'

◆ ◆ ◆

We sit at the dining table. There's only a metre between us but it might as well be an ocean. The silence builds, squeezing the air from the room. Niko paws my leg, his ears at half-mast. I ruffle his head. Normally, Dad's visits spell games. Laughter.

Dad laces his fingers together and summons a breath.

'I was really worried about her. About both of them.'

I squeeze the mug in my palms as my heel drums the floor.

'Things hadn't got off to a good start. Your mum ... she struggled, after Zoe was born. The tiredness took its toll, as you'd expect, but she'd never been one not to cope. Now, the tiniest thing could derail her.

'I didn't realise at first, that she was ill. She hid it from me, until it got worse, and she couldn't. She kept saying it would pass, but it got to the point where some days she couldn't get out of bed. Others, she couldn't stop crying ... I felt so helpless, I didn't know what to do.'

He grates a tooth over his lip.

'There were complications, during the birth ... They say that can affect things. And she lost her grandmother around the same time; they were very close. But I think it was more about this pressure she put on herself, to be the "perfect" mother ... She'd agonise about the smallest things, beat up on herself constantly. She'd say: "Why can't I be like the other mums? What's wrong with me? I should be happy."'

I stare at him. It's as if Dad's talking about someone else. It bears no resemblance to the mother I know.

'I begged her to go to the doctors, but she wouldn't. She was convinced they'd take Zoe away, claim she wasn't fit to be a mother. One of the mums in her baby group had told her about a woman who suffered with postnatal depression. Her doctor had sent her to a mother-and-baby unit, supposedly to help. Only the baby never came back.' He swallows. 'One month later, the woman took her own life.'

He shakes his head.

'I tried to support her. Take Zoe, give her a break. But it only seemed to make things worse. She started comparing us, became convinced that Zoe wanted me, not her. Some days she wouldn't speak one word to me ... And then she found out about you.'

Dad's phone buzzes. He ignores it.

'I was so worried when she told me, I thought it would tip her over the edge. I couldn't understand why she'd want to put herself through it again. But as the pregnancy went on, that dark shroud over her began to lift. I glimpsed flashes of her old self. It was such a relief. It was only after you were born, that your mum told me ... She'd had this feeling right from the start that with you it would be different. That she could finally become the mother she'd wanted to be...'

I think of Senka. It wasn't her fault this happened. It wasn't anyone's.

'Everything we told you about the clinic was true. The doctor could see how distressed your mother was; that's why she offered her the reallocation. And then it all happened so fast ... As soon as she started showing, your mum was sent off to the confinement home, and that sealed it. Separated from your sister, in that godawful place, no friends or family ... Maybe it was obvious, looking back on it, maybe I should have seen it coming. That bond she'd struggled to feel with Zoe, she felt with you straight away. Even before you were born, she said she was besotted. And then, when she actually saw you—'

'She knew no one else would want me. Not with my eyes.'

'No...' He reaches over and strokes my cheek. 'Quite the opposite. She was convinced it was a sign she was meant to keep you, that you were special. Unbeknownst to me, she'd been talking to the women at the confinement home, about the reallocation. And they'd told her that some parents didn't want a newborn, they'd rather take an infant.'

He presses his fingers into his eyes.

'It's the hardest thing I've ever ... It was like ripping out a piece of me...'

'Why, Dad? Why did you let her?'

'You have to understand, at one stage, I thought I was going to lose your mother, Kai. I honestly did. I thought I might lose them both...'

His face contorts and he strangles a sob.

'I should have got your mother the proper help, I shouldn't have listened to her. But perhaps she was right. They would have taken Zoe, and I'd have lost her anyway. And then they'd never have let your mum keep another child.'

'But what did you say to people?'

'We moved, immediately after you were born. Didn't see any of our friends until you were older. And then we told them…' His voice breaks. 'We told them Zoe had died.'

'Oh, Dad…'

'My mother … She adored Zoe. She was so upset. I had to make her swear not to say anything. She refused to see me after that, to even acknowledge our existence. I can't tell you how painful that was. She didn't speak to me again until my father died.'

So that's it. The real reason my gran never visits. The final pieces slot into place.

'Why didn't you tell me this, Dad, at the start? Don't you think I deserved to know?'

'Wasn't it bad enough, finding out your parents had broken the law? If we'd told you that you were the second-born child life would have been impossible for you. We never thought it would come out, there were no records. It was all in the past. We wanted to protect you…'

'She won't see you. You know that, right? Zoe hates you for what you did. And I don't blame her—'

'Kai, please…'

'What? Am I supposed to feel grateful? It would have been better for everyone if that doctor had just flushed me away—'

He grasps my hand. 'Don't say that.'

It kills me to see how this hurts him. But it's true.

'I get that you were in an impossible position, that you were trying to save Mum. But you destroyed Zoe's childhood, abandoned her—'

'I've never stopped loving her.'

'And now I'm going to lose you, too!'

There's another buzz. He glances at his phone.

'That's your mum again. She's beside herself, Kai. She's had to live with this decision all these years. Won't you come back home with me, just for tonight?'

I shake my head. 'I can't. I'm sorry.'

'You're not going to hand yourself in, are you?'

'The Ministry doesn't have the birth record. Well, not yet.' I shrug. 'It's in Zoe's hands now.'

'You don't think she'll say anything, do you?'

'I honestly don't know. If I don't help her, she might...'

'Help her, how?'

I sigh. 'It's better you don't know. You're in enough trouble as it is. Go home, Dad. Mum needs you. Go home, while you still can...'

He lurches out of his chair towards me. I bury my face in his neck.

'I'm sorry. I'm so sorry, for everything...' he whispers. 'I love you. I love you and Zoe. I always will.'

'I love you too, Dad,' I say, my throat already raw. 'Now, go.'

CHAPTER 28
Day Sixteen

I comb my fingers through Niko's fur. He arches his back into the curve of my belly, a low purr pulsing through his body into mine. I clamp my eyes shut and try to lose myself in the sensation, to obliterate just for one second this suffocating dread. But even Niko's therapy cannot work its magic today.

I had a video appointment earlier with my doctor. They told me my stress levels were unacceptably high and I'd been 'overdoing it'. Then they told me to rest and signed me off work for three days. I notified the office, but there's been no response. I don't know if that's a good sign or not.

Niko stiffens and jumps off the bed. I curl deeper under the duvet. I don't care what it is, I'm not moving. This is the only place left where I feel safe.

Maybe I should just go to the Ministry and get it over with. Tell them everything.

But this isn't just about me.

Niko whimpers.

I heave my head up off the pillows. Niko is sniffing the mat, ears pricked up on high alert.

That's when I see it. Another envelope.

I groan and slump back down. 'Leave it.'

I have no stomach for more revelations. Senka's cut me loose from my world: who I am, those I love. Can I blame her? I stole her childhood. Her parents, her home.

I'm not doing this out of spite or ... revenge...

I'm doing it because people keep lying to you and you deserve the truth...

Niko sits motionless beside the bed, his eyes boring into me, a soft blue.

The moment I look up, his tail gives a slow wag.

'Oh, go on, then. Fetch.'

He springs to the mat, takes the envelope between his teeth and scampers back.

I rip it open with a sigh.

I'm sorry, but you had to know. There must be trust between us.
I won't ever lie to you.
But there's more you need to see.

So this is it: my penance. She's not going to let me rest until I join her campaign.

A wave of resignation washes over me. She can send the Ministry that birth record whenever she pleases.

At the bottom of her note is a map reference. More instructions underneath.

Six am tomorrow: use the UPD. Bring boots.

'Look's like I'm going to have to disobey doctor's orders,' I say to Niko. He tilts his head.

The coordinates are for King's Cross Station.

CHAPTER 29
Day Seventeen

We sit facing each other in the carriage. An illegal Ministry representative and a terrorist. I keep glancing at the other seats, even though they're empty. It must be obvious, just looking at us, that we're related. But, sitting here so brazenly, would it even enter anyone's mind to suspect?

Senka fixes me with her cool, dark stare. 'So ... tough day...'

'You could say that.' My fingers are itching to tap, but I hold them in my lap.

'Not so easy, is it? Living in fear.'

Little does she know. I've lived in fear my whole life.

'You must loathe me. I would.'

Her eyes flicker. 'What would be the point? It wasn't your decision.'

I tighten my grip on my fingers. 'Mum, she ... she didn't deny it. Dad came to see me. Tried to explain...'

Her lip curls. 'And how did you find his "explanation"?'

I glance away, at the darker version of myself in the window. Knotted in a tug of loyalty and guilt.

'There were reasons. But it doesn't excuse what they did.' I take a breath. 'I never knew about Mum's illness—'

Her hand flies up. 'You needed the details. Not me. I dealt with the truth, and I'm done with it.'

Forests of bamboo wave at me as we fly past.

'Mine isn't the only record, you know,' she says. 'Nieran found all the missing birth records and profiles. There are stacks of them.' She checks the carriage. 'I can show you.'

She opens a tablet. A deluge of numbers, stripes and letters scrolls onto the screen.

'Not one of them is on the official register. As far as the Ministry is concerned, these children never existed.'

One profile after another streams down the page. I think of the dashboards I scrutinise each day, families neatly mapped. Everyone supposedly accounted for.

'They're all second babies. Like you.' Senka's eyes glow. 'The excess births that the Ministry wanted to disappear.'

They keep coming: row after row. I cannot look away.

'There are so many...'

'Thousands.'

'What happened to them all?'

'That's why you're here.' She closes the screen. 'I'm taking you to a homestead where someone can tell you. A Serbian migrant, who used to work as a carer.'

I gaze at her. 'I know why you're doing this. You think I can help you. But even if I did, it's only a matter of time before the Ministry arrests my parents. Anything I say will be tarnished. They will come after me and then they will come after you.'

'The Ministry won't be arresting any of us. Not in the immediate term, anyway.'

'What are you talking about?'

'We've taken care of it. My profile is safe.'

'How?'

'That isn't important. You're a free agent.'

'I don't understand...'

'You don't need to understand. You just need to trust me.'

I desperately want to believe her. But the system is impenetrable. I think of Nieran. Maybe Senka found another use for their skills.

She nods at me. 'You look exhausted. It's going to be a long day. You should get some rest while you can.'

I try to fight it, but the gentle motion of the train and the tentative relief that my parents are out of danger – if Senka's profile really has been secured – make my eyes grow heavy.

Before I know it, Senka's prodding my arm because we've arrived.

◆ ◆ ◆

I cast a bleary eye over the station sign: *Welcome to Horncastle*. Only a trickle of passengers gets off. Not surprising, given most of Lincolnshire is under water.

A man is waiting for us a discreet distance from the station.

'This is Grey,' says Senka.

He nods at her. 'Good to see you back, Shadow...'

Shadow?

Senka eyes me. 'Just a code name.'

He frowns at my shoes. 'Hope you brought some proper footwear.'

We climb into the back of a silver contraption that looks like a rocket on three wheels. Senka tells me it's an e-velomobile that has been specially adapted for flood zones. Our driver, Grey, is a rather morose man of few words, the opposite of Spice. After half an hour of being bounced up and down on a poorly cushioned seat, we arrive in a village called Gunby. We pass a line of houses with overgrown lawns, an empty playing field and a school.

'It's so quiet,' I say. 'Where is everyone?'

'Evacuated,' says Grey.

'But, the houses ... still look lived in.'

'They only left two months ago. The sea hasn't got here. Yet.'

I can taste it though, that salty tang. I catch a pungent whiff of seaweed and am transported to a memory: Dad lifting rocks in a murky pool, a huge crab scuttling out.

Grey stops and consults a dogeared map that looks as though it has been repaired multiple times. I spot a weather-beaten signpost:

Burgh le Marsh 3

'Is that where we're heading?'

Senka nods.

As we reach the outskirts of the town, I notice everything is covered in a light film of sand. I'm reminded of those derelict houses I saw with Steener in East London. Creepers stream from roofs; clusters of brambles, gorse and sea holly colonise gardens. A lone windmill has lost all but one sail, like an insect whose legs have been plucked. The battered sign for a windowless hotel still promises home-cooked food and luxury accommodation. The bus stop next door lists times for buses that will never come.

As we edge further through town, the boundaries between road and verge blur. The track is more of an indentation. The sea is just visible ahead of us: a peacock-blue line cutting the sky.

'Tide's coming in.' Grey glowers at the horizon.

I try to get my bearings. 'Are we near Skegness?'

'There is no Skegness anymore,' replies Grey. 'Just seagrass meadows, wind turbines and seaweed farms.'

Senka squints into the distance. 'When the tide's out, sometimes you can just make out the tip of the weather vane on the old clock tower. If you're really lucky, the rollercoaster rails.'

Grey heaves out a sigh.

'Such a pity,' I say, trying to be tactful. 'They pumped in thousands of tonnes of sand, didn't they? Spent a fortune on rock armour. I remember reading about it.'

'Did they bollocks,' says Grey.

Senka covers her smile with her hand.

'There was shit-all money left for the east coast after the Great Flood. It all went on the capital.' He glares at me, in his mirror. 'Thames Barrier rebuild, new floodgates, shoring up flood defences across the Thames Estuary. It's like we'd signed some kind of coastal DNAR. Resorts like Skeggie were abandoned. Condemned to sink, like the *Titanic*. Not just the resorts, either – huge belts of arable land. It broke my mother's heart when she was forced out. Her family had been farming here for over a century.'

He sniffs. 'Wind farms. That's all we're good for. And kelp.'

We follow the ghost road, the sea line thickening, until the first wave wets our wheels. The vehicle churns through water, throwing up spray, until the road is completely submerged. Just as I'm beginning to think we may share the same fate as the clock tower, I see them: rows of houses raised up on stilts, with railed verandas. As we get closer, I see half of each roof is covered with solar panels, the other half with garden: a mix of produce and flowers. I recognise violet and pink sea thrift, sea campion's delicate white.

We slow to a stop. 'Well, this is us,' says Grey.

I pull on my wellies and climb out, the water sloshing around my ankles. These houses may be a far cry from the grand pillar designs in Richmond, but I have to admit they're impressive. Nothing like the squalid huts they show us on the reels.

Grey points at the tanks attached to the walls. 'That's where the rainwater's harvested. And you see these?'

He slaps the bricks.

'Mycelium and hemp composite. Bloody loves saltwater.'

I gaze at the thick bamboo poles stretching up to the

platform. He nods at them, with the first hint of a smile. 'When the tide comes in, you can actually feel the house sway...'

He leads us to a house with blue ladder-steps fixed to the bottom of a raised veranda.

'Just wait here a moment.' Senka springs up the rungs.

After a few minutes she reappears. 'OK, come on up.'

The climb isn't easy in these boots. As I haul myself onto the veranda, I see a woman in the doorway with dark-brown eyes. She must be at least a foot smaller than Senka. Her black hair is swept back under a scarf, silvering at its roots.

Senka beams at her. 'Kai, this is Mila.'

CHAPTER 30

I wet my lips. 'Hello, Mila.'

The carer who saved Senka from the reallocation centre. Who gave her her name.

What must she think of me, the baby cuckoo in the nest?

'You have the same nose,' she says. 'The same lips.'

I give a cautious smile, grateful she hasn't mentioned our eyes. The lines on Mila's face could tell a thousand stories.

'You want tea?'

'I'd love some. Thank you.'

It's much more comfortable inside than I was expecting: patterned rugs cushion a wooden floor; a turquoise sofa sits next to a coffee table. Senka bustles into the kitchen with Mila; she clearly knows her way around. And I wonder if this is where Mila brought her. Senka's first home.

I busy myself with the framed postcards on the wall. There's one of the clock tower that Senka mentioned. Another of a fairground and a boating lake; sun-burned toddlers astride glum donkeys. My eye lingers on a large cartoon man running along a beach, with the caption: *Skegness is SO bracing*. I try to imagine it: children racing across the sand in their swimmers, the rollercoaster roaring up and down its rails. The only visitors now are fish and molluscs. The occasional drone survey or blade bugs going out for turbine repairs.

'Here we are.' Mila sets the tray down and hands me a mug. 'Oat milk or pea?'

'Oat. Thank you.'

Senka deposits herself on the sofa next to Mila, leaving me the rocking chair.

'So, Kai... Your sister wants me to tell you what it was like. At the centres. She says you need to hear what really went on. From someone other than her.'

This is why Senka brought me. To listen to the fate that should have been mine. The next instalment of my deprogramming.

'The thing you need to understand is this was a different time. Before the implants were rolled out – or the patches. Parents still thought they could beat the system.' She shakes her head. 'When you've been through hell to get somewhere safe and then lived through the camps, you know the system can never be beaten.'

Mila hooks her fingers round her cup; they are crooked and swollen.

'At first, it wasn't too bad. There were enough of us who cared about the children. Some babies were placed in good homes. But when the implant came along, Destine, the Ministry threw all its money at that. Slashed our funds, effectively abolished the programme overnight. There was zero tolerance for "accidents"; it was all about preventing pregnancies. No British families dared take excess children after that. Then the international adoptions dried up, as other child quotas were enforced. America was the last to go. The Ministry put a stop to it, even the Christian groups couldn't intervene. And that's when things really went downhill...'

She gazes out of the window. I listen to the waves, lapping against the stilts.

'The trafficking gangs knew the centres were gold dust. It was just a question of access. So they posed as intermediaries for "less formal" routes. The gender imbalance in India and China still hadn't evened out, and they would pay top money for girls.'

She glances at Senka. Senka rubs her bracelet with her thumb.

'The irony. All those years of aborting females or sending them for adoption overseas, and here they were, importing them from the West. The boys didn't fare any better ... Trafficked to those with a penchant for slaves with flesh, or who couldn't afford bots.'

I shudder. Did they know what was happening? Were they told?

'I was supposed to look after the babies when they arrived,' Mila continues. 'That was my job, and I was good at it. I'd make the formula, get the poor things to take it. Find a cot for them, put on clean bedding ... But there weren't enough of us left. They'd cut the salaries right back. Sometimes, I'd turn up for work and there were only a handful of us there. Or I'd get a call, last minute, asking me to help out at another centre.' She stares at her cup. 'I remember going to one place. It was for babies who were born with certain conditions, you know, the ones that hadn't been screened. I knew something was wrong as soon as I got there, because it was so quiet. It was never quiet at our centre. Those babies just lay in their cots, bundled up in sheets like little shrouds, not making a peep. Later, I realised why. The babies had given up crying. Because no one ever came.'

Senka shakes her head.

'I went to another centre where the toddlers had been tied to wooden rockers. No cuddles, no playtime. Potties just shoved underneath...' Her eyes squeeze shut. 'The look in those children's eyes as they rocked back and forth ... Empty. Like living ghosts...'

'Didn't you report it? Couldn't they have sent more staff?'

'Oh, I tried, believe me, but no one cared. As far as the

authorities were concerned, those babies should never have been born. They were "a drain on resources". We had to fight for everything. By the end they wouldn't even supply basic medicine or vaccines. Which is why so many children never left those places.'

My gaze lifts to hers. And I realise what she means.

'So I made a promise. I would get one child out every year. I'd find a safe place for them: a genuine home. Not like those other poor souls...' She clasps Senka's hand. 'And you were my one.'

She smiles and wipes her eyes.

'You weren't easy. You had a temper on you, that's for sure. But there was something about you ... Stubborn, but ... strong. I had a sense you had some role to play.'

'What Mila hasn't told you is that she's actually a witch,' says Senka. I stiffen at the word. 'She uses her Serbian "Vlach magic"...'

'Stop, now ... I see things, it's true.' Mila wags her finger. 'I was right about you, little Shadow, wasn't I? But I don't see everything. For example, I didn't see you...'

Her stare is unnerving. I have to look away.

'How many centres were there?'

'No one really knew. But, talking to other carers, we think there must have been at least fifteen, maybe twenty.'

Twenty?

'Huge, soulless buildings – old military sites, mostly. In remote areas, off limits to the public. Out of sight.'

I cannot believe what I'm hearing. How could they keep something on this scale hidden?

Mila nods at me. 'We shared the same fate, we migrants and those children. The Ministry just wanted shot of us and didn't care how. But, you know, it didn't sit well with some. What we were doing. Back in the camp, they called us "nanny kapos".'

'Nanny what?'

'"Kapos". That's what they used to call the inmates in concentration camps, who worked for the Nazis. The ones who got privileges for supervising other prisoners.'

'That's not fair,' says Senka. 'If you hadn't looked after us, things would have been a whole heap worse. The cruellest ones were never migrants. It's thanks to you that I survived.'

'Yes, but even so, I followed their orders, didn't I? Even when conditions deteriorated ... Because I knew I'd die if I went back to the camp. People just vanished, all the time; particularly at night.' She exhales. 'I swore, no matter what, I'd never let them take me back.'

◆ ◆ ◆

Maybe it's the fact I haven't had a proper meal for days, or maybe it's the freshness of the mackerel and samphire, but when Mila serves lunch I wolf down the lot. I can't remember the last time I ate real fish. With stocks so heavily restricted, such luxuries are beyond our quota. Grey joins us, and they discuss the latest challenges with saltwater aquaponics, various maintenance issues and the lowdown on recent recruits. I wonder how Mila and Senka can chat so casually, after what we've just heard. I've been numbed into silence.

We finish our dessert of strawberries and raspberries from their hydroponic farm, and Senka stands up.

'Well, I'm afraid we have to get going, if we're to catch low tide. Otherwise we'll never make our train.'

I feel a strange reluctance. Things are different here, but not in a bad way. Only now do I understand the appeal.

We head back out onto the veranda, and stare at a silver expanse of sea, dotted with the white masts of wind turbines.

'When it storms,' says Mila, 'they say you can hear the bells of St Matthew's, ringing beneath the waves. Although I've never heard them.'

I keep my eyes on the horizon. I'd like to hear those, too.

'Sometimes, I swear I can hear babies crying...' She shrugs. 'But it's probably just the gulls.'

Mila cradles Senka's face and plants a kiss on each cheek. 'Look after yourself. And your sister, too.' She smiles at both of us. 'You are more alike than you think.'

CHAPTER 31

We don't talk much on the ride back to the station. Each of us absorbed in our own thoughts. I can't stop thinking about that silent room of cots. The infants, strapped to their chairs. Listening to Mila, I realise Senka barely scratched the surface of the trials she went through, the horrors she must have endured. Why did no one from the Ministry intervene? I try to imagine myself growing up at one of those centres. I doubt I'd have lasted my first year.

At one point, Senka drifts off, her long lashes shuttering her eyes. I listen to her breaths, watch her chest rise and fall. She looks gentler when she's asleep. Softer. I glimpse traces of the child she might have been.

Grey pulls up outside the station, and I gently nudge Senka's arm.

She peers at me. 'Are we there already?' she says, yawning.

I nod. We clamber out.

'Thanks, Grey,' she says. 'Take care of Mila for me, won't you?'

'That I will. Good luck with your journey south. Rather you than me.'

We settle ourselves in the carriage, and I finally manage to pluck out some words.

'I'm so sorry, Senka. I don't know how such terrible abuses could have been allowed to happen.' I frown. 'I thought I was a part of something good. An institution that served the people. And yes, there were sacrifices, and difficult choices, but that was because we were helping our country. Trying to protect it for future generations. But what Mila said, about what really went on at those centres…' I sigh. 'It's not a world I recognise.'

Senka leans across the table. 'I know things are feeling shit-scary right now. It's hard, weaning yourself off their lies. The Party wants you to be frightened. From the moment you were born, you've been exposed to those reels, with their never-ending newscasts of disasters; the constant threats and warnings about what happens if you break their rules. But you've already done the hard bit.' She brushes my cheek. 'You've opened your eyes.'

'Why hasn't FREE said anything about this? Released the profiles?'

'Because ONE will just deny it all and make out it's more fake news. No one in this country cares about illegals, anyway. They've been too conditioned. They'd prefer not to know about the dark side of their government. As long as there's food on their plates and the lights stay on.'

'They might care if one of those illegals happened to be their child.'

'And who would dare admit to that?'

She has a point.

'I have another trip for you tomorrow. If you're up for it. Usual rules apply.' She slides a note towards me.

Lotus Clinic, 2.00pm

My fingers start to tap. 'Listen, Senka. I know you want me to help you. But I'm no whistle blower. And even if I were, the Ministry would crush me. I'm not strong like you.'

'I won't make you do anything you feel you can't. Don't worry.'

'I can't stop worrying. It's what I do.'

'I've noticed.' She folds her hand over my fingers and smiles.

I look into her eyes and remember what she said about her profile being safe now. I want to trust what she tells me, I really do.

But those orbs are impenetrable.

And every instinct says don't.

CHAPTER 32

The clinic is down a residential street, a short walk off the Earl's Court Road. Paint peels off the windows beneath thick, black security bars; the greasy remains of someone's take-away are splattered on the steps. This doesn't resemble any medical centre I've visited; it must be a pirate clinic. The Ministry of Health Security is constantly having to shut them down. I just hope I don't get picked up on surveillance. I'm supposed to be recuperating in bed.

I walk down to the basement and press the buzzer. An ominous-looking stain seeps up the walls. I wouldn't bring an animal here, let alone a human. I burrow in my bag for some sanitiser and squirt it on my hands.

Footsteps approach the door and stop. No tech, just a peephole. The door opens into a small beige corridor that might once have been white. Senka is already in what I assume is the waiting area. One other woman sits opposite.

'How are you doing?' Senka says. 'Get much sleep?'

'Some.' I glance at the woman and lower my voice. 'Thank you. For whatever you did, with ... You know...'

As soon as I got home, I fired off a quick note to Dad, telling him about our reprieve, then I logged onto the MPFP portal. Still no sign of Senka's profile.

I did, however, have a barrage of messages from Mum.

I shuffle closer and whisper: 'How did you do it?'

'I told you to trust me. It's under another restriction. Stop fretting.'

I can't. Not after those messages from Mum. They made me cry, particularly the first one:

I know you're angry. I know I've messed everything up. I'm sorry I lied. But at least the world has you both. And you both have the world. I love you. Mum xxx

Senka smiles at the other woman who is waiting. 'This is Talli. Talli, this is Kai.'

I nod at her. I didn't realise Talli and Senka were together.

The woman's eyes flit up and instantly away.

'Talli has kindly allowed us to accompany her for her appointment.'

'Right...'

I'm not sure I like the sound of that. I cross my fingers inside my sleeve. 'This is quite a place.'

'It's a lifesaver. Literally. For illegals or offliners who can't access wellness centres. We owe these people a lot.'

A woman in a wrinkled blue shirt steps into the corridor. I presume she's the so-called doctor. Her eyes meet Senka's, and something passes between them.

'Would you like to come through, Talli?'

Talli doesn't move.

Senka squeezes her arm. 'It'll be fine,' she whispers. 'Honestly. It doesn't hurt.'

Talli clenches the seat and stands up.

'Just wait here while we do the scan,' says the doctor. 'Assuming I find it, I'll call you in after.'

As she leads Talli away, I turn to Senka. 'What's the scan for?'

'A contraceptive implant.'

I frown. 'Why does she need a scan?'

'To locate it.'

Senka likes giving me riddles.

'Until we got her out, Talli had been stuck in one of your so-called "resettlement centres". Talli and her husband were there for nearly three years. For the last two, they'd been trying for a family. Unsuccessfully.' She blinks. 'I assume you know how it works, right? The Destine implant?'

'Clearly ... a microchip releases synthetic hormones that prevent pregnancy.'

I remember the information poster on the wall when I had mine put in. A giant egg was wielding the implant like a shield against invader sperm.

'And it works remotely,' says Senka. 'Which is marketed as a "key benefit".'

'Exactly. You can switch it on or off yourself, using the app. Depending on when you want to start a family.'

Senka's eyes narrow. 'Or someone else can...'

What...?

The doctor bustles out. 'OK, we're on.'

We follow her into what looks like a converted bedroom. Instead of sheets, though, the bed has paper towelling. A table is littered with medical equipment on trays. Talli's sleeve is rolled up, and I notice a black oblong about halfway down the back of her left arm.

The doctor cleans Talli's arm with a sterile swab. 'If you could just roll onto your right side now, please, Talli,' she says, unwrapping a needle.

Talli rolls over and fixes her eyes on the wall.

'Are you OK?' asks Senka. 'Would you like me to hold your hand?' Talli nods. Senka looks at me. 'Women are understandably nervous about medical procedures by the time they get here.'

'This one's relatively straightforward.' The doctor attaches the needle to a syringe. 'It hasn't migrated, it's not too deep, and they actually used her arm.'

I stare at Senka. 'Hang on ... You're telling me she didn't *know*?'

Senka shakes her head. 'The people that do this put them somewhere different, every time. To hide them. They don't care what damage they do to vessels or nerves, or where it ends up. That's why most need a scan to locate it. And how many migrants get access to those?'

The doctor turns to Talli. 'I'm going to inject the local anaesthetic now.' She points at the syringe. 'To numb the area.'

Talli shuts her eyes and squeezes Senka's hand.

I bite my lip. 'But ... why?'

'Why do you think? To stop them having a child. A lot simpler than tubal ligation. If they don't know it's there and they don't have the app, they can't deactivate it.' Senka turns to the doctor. 'Where else have you found them, Doc?'

'Oh, you wouldn't believe it. Legs, shoulders, backs. Once I found one that had got into the lining around a lung.' She drops the syringe into a tray.

I watch the doctor quietly going about her work. I don't know what I was expecting, but it wasn't this. I realise the Party needs to restrict migrant numbers, that's one of the issues that precipitated the one-child policy in the first place. But slipping in implants, without consent...?

The doctor taps Talli's arm. 'Can you feel this?'

Talli shakes her head.

'Or this?' She presses harder.

Talli shakes her head again.

Senka looks at me. 'Talli's story is all-too familiar. As soon as she arrived at the camp, she was isolated and herded into an immigration cubicle. They told her that having a medi-patch was an entry requirement. That it would give her health benefits, like screening for disease. What choice did she have? So she let them sedate her.'

The doctor swabs Talli's skin. 'OK, Talli. I'm about to make the incision.' She picks up a surgical knife.

'It was bullshit of course,' continues Senka. 'The patch was only a ruse to sneak in the implant and make sure it was working.'

I find myself staring at the blade as it cuts the top layer of skin. The small, neat line quickly fills with blood. The doctor squeezes the incision until something silver pops out. She wipes away the blood and picks up a pair of tweezers.

'When Talli's periods got lighter and eventually stopped, she put it down to stress,' continues Senka. 'That, or the lack of food. But it carried on, and then she found out others were having the same issue. She bought in to the rumours, which camp staff were stoking. There was something in the water ... The meals were different to what they were used to. The ground must be contaminated, the air in the camp was bad...'

The doctor twists the tweezers and teases out a rectangular chip. It drops into the dish with a clink.

'There, all done.' She shows Talli the dish.

Talli exhales. I think she's been holding her breath the entire time.

'Then the idea grew that maybe the patch was the problem. But the only practising medics at the camps are government staff. Migrants have no way to get themselves checked out properly. Not unless we get them out or they manage to escape.'

'Whoever put this one in at least knew what they were doing,' says the doctor as she gently cleans Talli's arm. 'Apart from asking for consent, that is.'

The doctor rips off her gloves and gives me a hard look. 'This practice is inhuman. It needs to stop.'

My face burns. 'How many of these have you done?'

She pulls on a fresh pair of gloves and shrugs. 'I don't know, must be hundreds ... I don't keep count.'

Talli smiles at the doctor as she wraps a dressing around her arm. 'Thank you.'

'It's my pleasure.'

Senka helps Talli off the bed and gives the doctor a tight hug. There's that same softness in her face she had when she was with Mila.

'Some day,' Senka says, 'I'll figure out a way to repay you.'

The doctor flaps her hand. 'Keep doing what you're doing. And take care of yourself out there.'

We wander back down the corridor.

'I'm sorry,' I say to Talli. 'About what happened to you.'

Talli blinks. I wonder if she knows who I represent.

Senka scowls. 'First, they tell you how many children you can have, which contraception to use ... Then they decide who gets to have the children. First off the list are the migrants, and the other illegals.' Her gaze meets mine. 'Who's next? People with the wrong-coloured eyes?'

As I follow her up the steps, my instinct is to protest that no, of course the Party could never do such a thing. That there must be an explanation. But my pleas in the Party's defence won't come.

Talli whispers something in Senka's ear.

'Can you just give us a couple of minutes?' says Senka.

'Sure.'

I move away from them and notice a pamphlet lying on the pavement outside one of the houses.

FIGHT FOR YOUR REPRODUCTIVE RIGHTS!
Your body, your baby, your choice...

I think of Dr Trowsky's daughter. When I look up, Senka is frowning. She nods at Talli, who presses her palms together in a gesture of thanks.

As Talli walks off, I approach Senka. 'Is everything OK?'

'It's Talli's cousin. She's just been told that it's highly unlikely she'll ever be able to conceive. She's very upset. Talli's worried about her.'

'Does Talli think she has an implant she didn't know about, too?'

'No, her cousin didn't grow up in a camp. She's one of the lucky ones whose parents were officially resettled: they get access to proper medical facilities. She says her cousin never had the implant; she was on the pill. Talli was asking if the doc would take a look at her. She doesn't trust the system. I can't say I blame her.'

'You seem to know each other well. The doctor, I mean.'

'She's a good woman. She takes enormous risks every day, to help people.'

I glance at Senka. 'How long have you known her?'

'About six years. She took my implant out, too.'

CHAPTER 33

Senka stops outside a café near the station.

'Fancy a coffee?'

I can't remember the last time I was in a café. I consider such indulgences a waste of our quota.

'It's OK,' she says. 'Zainal, the owner, loves me: no charge.'

As the coffee machine gurgles and spits, Zainal chats excitedly to Senka. He cuts two enormous slices of lavender cake and passes us each a plate.

'Homemade and protein-enriched!' he says. 'Using the very best cricket flour.'

We take a seat away from the window, at the back.

'Zainal came over here from India five years ago,' says Senka. 'He grew up in Bangladesh. Before the sea claimed it. He said his parents took their house apart four times, and rebuilt it further inland. But the cyclones kept coming, and the water kept rising, until there wasn't anywhere left to move.'

I remember seeing a reel about that, at school: swollen tides surging over buildings. A whole country slipping under the waves.

I watch Senka tucking into her cake and think of what she said about the doctor.

'I take it you didn't know about your implant, either?'

'No. I probably never would have if it hadn't been for the migrants I met at the homestead ... The ones who'd managed to get out.' She swirls a spoon slowly round. 'Mila wasn't told. They obviously didn't want word getting round the camps. She suspected something was wrong but couldn't say anything. It took a long time to figure out just how widespread this was ... No one really knows when it started.'

'But what about your periods?'

'Mine were always light. I didn't know any different. Poe didn't have periods at all. We were told that was normal. That not everyone had bleeding and we were lucky, we didn't have "the curse".' She exhales. 'You have to understand we were just children, we believed them. Those managers at the centres were our appointed guardians. They could say or do anything they liked.'

'But how did they manage it? I mean, you weren't coming through immigration, they couldn't subject you to those kinds of tests?'

'Apparently, it was done when we were young enough we wouldn't understand. Under the guise of some routine vaccination. Dengue Fever or Malaria; HPV. They'd give you a good gulp of nitrous oxide. Tell you the "happy gas" would make sure the needle didn't hurt.'

I slap my cup down and coffee lurches over the sides. 'You're telling me that someone came into those centres, and carried out that procedure on *children*?'

'From what we can gather, the usual age was ten.'

Ten?

'And they're still doing it, Kai. In the camps.'

A couple at a table on the far side of the room burst out laughing. A little boy with a mop of blonde curls blows a raspberry.

'There's no way of knowing you're on the implant unless you have a scan or test for the hormones. Obviously, migrants and illegals don't get access to those services.'

She shifts in her chair.

'We managed to recruit a couple of staff at the camps, who were sympathetic. They were the ones who discovered what was going on. Most of the women and girls at the resettlement centres eventually get deported, assuming they survive. I guess the Ministry didn't want to risk any pregnancies beforehand.'

I feel it again: that tug of loyalties. The Ministry always said there weren't enough resources to support large families. I'd expect them to restrict these women to one child. But to deny them the chance of motherhood completely?

And sneak the implant into ten-year-old girls?

'In the beginning, we tried to get this information out in the public domain. ONE quashed it, dismissed it as "fake news". Kept pedalling their stories about the few families they actually deigned to resettle here. So we built a network of clinics, like the doc's. If we can't stop it happening, at least we can help some women get it removed.'

She drains her cup.

As Senka's words sink in, my head buzzes.

The implant was launched twenty-five years ago. If they've been doing this all that time, the numbers of women impacted could be colossal...

Senka frowns at me. 'Are you OK?'

'Yeah, I'm ... I just...' I stand up. 'I need some water.'

I head over to a dispenser. My hands are shaking. I gulp down one glass and pour another. I press it to my forehead, relishing the cool.

Senka follows me. 'You're getting spooked again, aren't you? Come on, let's sit down.'

We move back to the table. 'What do you want from me, Senka? I can't change what's happened. What's still happening ... And I'm certain most people in the Ministry don't have a clue...'

'I'm giving you the foundations. So you understand the scale of it. We can protest all we like, fire things up on the outside, but your Party are very good at putting out fires. What we really need is an implosion within.'

I swallow.

She ferrets in her bag. 'Here.' She hands me a rectangular device with a tiny screen and keypad.

'What's this?'

'It's like a pager, but with a burner app.' She glances round. 'Put it away. Now.'

I hesitate. My fingers can't quite bring themselves to accept it.

She lowers her voice. 'This will make communication easier. It works using anonymous PINs on a private network. It's completely safe: the messages self-destruct once they're read.'

'Jesus,' I mutter. 'Are you sure they can't be traced?'

'The PINs are different every time.'

'How do I know what your PIN is if it changes?'

'Because once I accept you as a contact, it will tell you.'

She looks me straight in the eyes.

'Your world has changed, Kai, you said it yourself. You need to make a decision. Do you trust me? Will you take my hand, and jump? Or will you go back to your Ministry and pretend none of this is real?'

I turn away from her. I cannot answer. The toddler on the far table is hanging over the back of his chair.

He sticks out his tongue and blows a raspberry at me; saliva sprays through the air.

And I remind myself that Senka can release her profile. Anytime she likes.

'Appalling' Attack on Resettlement Centre Swiftly Contained, Says Prime Minister

By Erik Hansen

ONE State News

Another senseless attack by terrorists on a resettlement centre has been contained after one of the security fences was breached, a ONE Party news release reports today. The breach happened in the early hours of Monday morning at a centre near Dover in Kent and is believed to have been carried out by the terrorist group calling themselves FREE. It is understood only a handful of migrants were taken.

'The security guards acted swiftly to contain the situation and ensure the safety of other migrants in the centre,' said Prime Minister Karl Andersen. 'Given the volume of explos- ives used by the terrorists, it's a miracle that no one was killed.'

Extra security teams have been sent in to patrol the local area and locate those respon- sible.

'We cannot allow this traf- ficking of illegal migrants to continue,' said the prime min- ister. 'The terrorists claim they are "liberating" these migrants, but the truth is that they are profiteering, selling them on to black-market gangs. The safest place for these people is the centres, where they have ac- cess to food and shelter while their resettlement status is being processed.'

CHAPTER 34

I do not sleep well, waking frequently from the same nightmare that always haunts me. It's not just the flies burrowing into my eye sockets; there's something new. Bloody implants stick out all over my body, their silver heads poking through my skin. When I finally get up, I panic that I'm late for work, until I realise it's Sunday. And I'm still signed off.

I can't stop thinking about those children.

I imagine Senka in some sterile room, a mask clamped over her face. She must be scared; perhaps she struggles. Someone holds her down, until the gas flops her back in the chair, and then she's injected with a microchip full of hormones.

Mum had no idea what was in store for Senka when she made her decision.

She was lied to. Like everyone else.

I grab my screen, take a deep breath and type:

Would you and Dad like to come over this afternoon?

Mum's reply comes back straight away.

We'll be there.

I sip my tea and glance at the newsreels. One story dominates: following the attack on the resettlement centre, a state intelligence operation has successfully located and destroyed a terrorist stronghold. The image switches to a clearing in the middle of a forest. My stomach clenches. It looks as though someone has scooped out the ground with a giant spoon. All that's left is a muddy trough littered with the stumps of amputated trees.

What if Senka was there? What if she's been arrested? Or worse?

I hear a beep I don't recognise. Not my screen's.

Niko trots up to my bag.

And I remember: the pager. A small blue light on the device flashes above a number. It's the PIN. I key it in and her words materialise:

Doc couldn't find anything wrong with T's cousin. Another cousin has same issue. Two more girls they know of: all resettled. Is there data on this?

Senka's definitely OK.

I stroke Niko and stare out at the flats opposite. A man in loose-fitting exercise pants is doing yoga, one pose gracefully transitioning to the next. A woman in a bright, patterned kaftan moves between pots on her balcony, holding a pink watering can.

Senka wants me to use my position to investigate. She wants to put me to work.

This is a line. Do I cross it?

I think of Talli's chip tinkling into the dish.

Of ten-year-old Senka, flopped back in a chair.

That could have been me...

It's just a few records. No one will know.

I log onto the portal. The resettlement programme was launched five decades ago. The numbers start low but show a marked increase after five years. I look at birth rates in resettled communities and compare them with national figures. I check London and a couple of other regions. It doesn't look bad. If anything, the rates are slightly higher than the rest of the population. I change my search parameters, narrow it down to the last decade and repeat the exercise.

The numbers plummet.

I compare the data for The South-East. The North-West. The Midlands.

The birth rates are all significantly below the regional average. In London, they're just a tenth of the regional rate.

I run the numbers again, maybe I miscalculated.

No mistake.

I bring up a selection of health records for resettled women in their thirties, who haven't yet had children. Over half have fertility referrals.

I grab the pager.

Something definitely not right. Running more numbers.

There must be a common link. Medical conditions more prevalent in these communities. Hereditary illnesses that make them predisposed.

I need a doctor with access to the system. Someone I can trust.

I do another trawl of the database, burrowing down to local-authority areas.

My hunch was right.

A sizeable migrant community has resettled in the Reading area. Bang on Dr Trowsky's patch.

CHAPTER 35

Mum texted me ten minutes ago: they're at the station. I survey the flat, even though I've been tidying for the past hour. I force myself to sit, pull Niko onto my lap and visualise number sequences. Today is a four day. Niko stares at me, head cocked. He'd be good at counting too, with the right programme. Even the live dogs people used to own could process basic numbers. Niko could probably count up to a googol if I asked.

Suddenly Niko tenses. He sprints to the door with a bark.

'Niko, quiet!'

I hear two soft clunks as the lift opens and shuts. Hushed voices.

Dad's careful knock.

I claw my hands through my hair and get up.

Dad has his hopeful face on. Mouth stretched in a smile.

As for Mum ... I never imagined using this word to describe her: frail.

We all freeze, unsure of the new etiquette. I proffer stiff arms just as Mum edges forward, and we collide.

'Sorry...'

'Sorry ... Come in.'

They glance round the room as if it's their first time here.

'It's looking great,' says Mum. 'I like what you've done with the plants.'

I grip my hands. 'Thanks.'

I notice her eyes look sore.

Dad shakes off his jacket and starts that nervous whistling

through his teeth that he doesn't even realise he's doing. He bends down to stroke Niko.

Mum smooths her dress. 'How are you?'

'OK...' I nod. 'Shall I make some tea?'

'That would be nice.'

I busy myself with water and cups. Dad goes out on the balcony with Niko and starts fussing over the tubs.

Mum loiters by the window. 'I want to talk to you, Kai. Just the two of us. I need to explain...'

They've clearly planned this.

'OK. Shall we sit?'

I load up a tray and carry it over. We both watch in silence as I pour.

She takes a breath. 'I'd loved being pregnant. I was so excited about becoming a mother, your father and I had been looking forward to it for so long.' She glances at Dad, outside. 'But after the birth and the rush of those first days ... It changed...' She looks down. 'Things didn't come naturally ... not to me. It was a shock. Here was the baby I'd wanted so desperately, my one chance to prove myself as a mother. But I just felt exhausted. Constantly on edge, worried I was going to mess up. Cut off from the capable person I'd been before.

'I thought there must be something wrong with me. No one else seemed to be struggling. The few times I went out I'd find myself staring at other mothers, watching them with their babies. They always seemed so happy and relaxed. It was like looking at another planet. A planet I was excluded from, because it was all I could do to drag myself through each day. I despised myself for not coping, for being so miserable. No wonder Zoe wouldn't settle, she must have sensed my tension. And that just made things worse...' She sighs. 'I knew I was losing myself, but I didn't know how to stop.'

I stare at her. She's describing a mother I don't recognise.

'I used to have nightmares about losing Zoe. I'd leave her in a shop by accident, or somehow the pram would come loose from my fingers and roll out into the road...' She shudders. 'I stopped seeing my friends, it got to the stage where I couldn't even leave the house. I became convinced that your sister would be better off without me.'

My throat tightens. 'It wasn't your fault, Mum—'

'Let me finish. Please. I know, now, that I should have got help. But I was too frightened. This was our only chance for a baby, and somehow, we had to make it work. I felt so much guilt ... Because I was failing Zoe, and your dad.'

I reach for her hand. 'You didn't fail anyone, Mum. You were ill.'

Her back heaves. 'You mustn't blame your father. He only agreed for my sake. I was the one who couldn't look after your sister properly. Who insisted on keeping you, not her.'

Dad's anxious face peers up at us, his hands muddy with soil.

'And it broke his heart, you know, because he had such a close bond with your sister. They'd spent all that time together ... I think a little part of him died when she left.'

I try to imagine Senka and Dad together. Him tucking her in with her favourite toy at bedtime. Reading her stories with those funny voices that always made me laugh.

'You were all I had in the confinement home. And after I got there, the pressure lifted. All the women there felt they'd failed in some way, but we helped each other get through it. Put aside our expectations, to be this "ideal" mother. Strangely, it was a time of healing. I haven't ever told your father that, I think it would hurt him too much. But it was the space I needed, to find my way back to the person I used to be.'

I think of Mum in that place, with me in her belly. Senka cuddling up with Dad, at home...

'I'd talk to you, every day. Tell you what I was thinking, sing you songs. I began to feel happy again. I hadn't felt that warmth, that lightness for so long ... By the time you were born, I felt I knew you. It was so different, you had come along in love, not design. I realised I didn't need to be perfect. And then, the moment I laid eyes on you...' Her gaze meets mine. 'I thought you were the most beautiful thing I'd ever seen. Eyes like gemstones ... Blue topaz and smoky quartz. Gemstones have flaws, just like we do...' She smiles. 'You gripped my little finger as I pulled you to my breast. I'll never forget it. It was just ... natural. And I knew, I could never let you go.'

My heart swells. But this love Mum has for me, I don't deserve it.

It cost Senka hers.

'How could you do it though, Mum? How could you choose?'

Mum swallows. 'I hadn't seen Zoe for months. When your dad brought her to visit, after you were born, I couldn't believe it. She'd changed so much – from the baby I'd left behind to this little person. Scrambling towards me across the floor ... At first, it almost felt as if I was looking at someone else's child. But the more time that passed, the more my heart melted. Hearing her babbling away in her own language, an occasional word breaking through ... The way she stared at me, with those haunting, dark eyes...'

Mum's gaze drifts to the window.

'I asked your father not to bring her again. We had a terrible row, he was so upset ... I tried to make him understand, I couldn't keep you both. I knew that letting Zoe go would be the hardest thing I had ever done, so I had to keep my distance. Safer to cut off the blood supply before you amputate the limb.'

'Oh, Mum…' I squeeze her hand.

'I wish I'd been braver, Kai. I should have trusted you with the truth…' She folds her hand over mine. 'Have you seen her again?'

'Yes. I have.'

'Did you find out any more about her family?'

I pause. 'The thing is, Mum…'

My words falter. But honesty cuts both ways.

'She wasn't taken in by a family.'

'What do you mean?'

'There weren't enough parents to take all the children. So she was sent to a reallocation centre … A sort of orphanage. For excess children.'

Mum blinks at me. 'I don't understand. The doctor said she'd go to a couple who couldn't have their own child, the woman from the Ministry *told* me—'

'The doctor wasn't aware. It was all hushed up; these centres were carefully hidden. I'm not going to lie, Mum, it wasn't easy for Zoe. But there was a carer who looked after her. Who got her out.'

'How long?'

'Sorry?'

'How long was she in that place?'

I grind a tooth over my lip. 'Fourteen years.'

'Oh God … Zoe…' She buries her face in her hands. 'I didn't know, I swear…'

'Nobody knew, Mum—'

'They told me she'd go to a family. A good family…' She stiffens. 'Don't say anything to your father. Please … It will kill him.'

A sigh escapes. 'Haven't we had enough secrets?'

'I will tell him, eventually. I promise. But not now, it's too raw.' She stares at Dad, outside. 'God knows, if anyone deserves forgiveness, it's him.'

I glance at Dad, pottering around the balcony, Niko trotting dutifully alongside.

I wonder if Senka has it in her. Whether it's right to expect such compassion, after everything she's suffered.

There's only one way to find out.

CHAPTER 36

I arrive at the clinic by ten. It's just over two weeks since I was last here. It feels a lot longer. The waiting room is packed. A chorus of whispered conversations ripples around the room. I take a seat next to two women who I presume are mother and daughter. The teenager's foot is jiggling so hard it's a wonder her shoe's staying on.

'Uma...' The mother cups the girl's knee. 'It'll be OK,' she whispers. 'Jayne told me they use this magic gel now. You won't feel a thing.'

The daughter scowls. 'It's not that, I'm not a baby...' She glances up at her mother. 'I just don't know if I want some chip planted inside me.'

'Don't worry, once it's there you'll forget all about it.'

I think of Talli. And Senka. Not even knowing it was there.

A door opens. Dr Trowsky strides out into the waiting area and beckons me. She doesn't look happy.

As I stand up, a woman in the seat opposite glares at me and says something about being next.

'Mondays are mayhem,' hisses Dr Trowsky as we head down the corridor. 'The clinic is overrun.'

'This shouldn't take long—'

'I gave you what you wanted.' She marches into the consulting room we were in before. 'It isn't my fault if Yasmine never showed up.'

'Oh, but she did. Our conversation was most helpful. It's another matter I need to discuss with you today.'

The doctor's face falls. Maybe she'd hoped Yasmine Mestari would give me the slip.

'It's rather ... delicate.'

'On or off the record?'

'Off. Any information you give me will be treated in confidence, as before.'

She sighs. 'I suppose I don't have much choice, do I? Well, come on then. What is it?'

'If my research is correct, there's a high density of resettled migrants in this area. Does your patient list reflect that?'

'Yes. Jobs are plentiful, and there are two resettlement centres not far away.'

'Have you noticed any specific issues presenting in these patients? That aren't reflected in other patient groups, to the same extent?'

The doctor frowns. 'Do you have something in mind?'

'Yes: infertility. In women.'

'Is this about the referral quotas...?'

'So there is an issue, then...?'

She folds her hands. 'A colleague queried this with me the other day. Numbers are creeping up. Surely that's not why you're here? Fertility quotas are hardly your domain.'

'Officially, no. But I'm not here on official business. Are there any underlying medical reasons that might be contributing factors to infertility across this community?'

'We've already checked the usual suspects: STIs, thyroid problems, diabetes. Genetic conditions like polycystic ovary syndrome.'

'And...?'

'From what I could ascertain, there are no statistically significant trends.'

I tap my knee. 'Could there be other causes?'

'Well, all migrants are under extreme stress. By the time they arrive, many have suffered violence or trauma, and that's before they start their incarceration at the centres. Most have no medical records with them. Some have chronic conditions, like epilepsy or hypertension, that haven't been treated for months. And disease is rife in those places, as you well know ... Diphtheria, TB, HIV ... The vaccination programmes are a travesty: they're patchy at best. Even after they resettle, there are pressures. Sadly, prejudice still exists.'

She exhales. 'Given what they've been through, it's a miracle they can conceive at all.'

'So why are infertility referrals only increasing now? Given people have been resettling here for decades?'

'To be honest, I don't know.'

I try to remember what Senka said about Talli's cousin. It was her parents that had resettled. She wasn't even in a centre.

Dr Trowsky's screen flashes. 'Is that all? I'm running late as it is.'

'Just one more question: are your referrals for first-generation or second-generation settlers?'

'Is that relevant?'

'Possibly...'

She taps her screen. Her eyes narrow as she scrolls down. 'Hmm ... Looks like they're second-generation.'

My pulse quickens. That would explain the timing.

She looks up. 'OK, what's really going on here?'

'It's not just your region. Referrals for these communities to fertility specialists are up everywhere. But only in the past decade.'

'Since when did you care? I would've thought you'd be

happy: fewer pregnancies to check up on. Let's face it, the ministries are hardly renowned for prioritising the welfare of migrants.'

Her comments strike home. They never would have before.

My eyes shift to the poster behind her. Cartoon implants being put into cartoon women's arms by cartoon nurses, as if contraception is a game.

I think of those ten-year-olds at the reallocation centres.

'Have you flagged this increase with anyone else?'

'No,' she says.

'Could you make some discreet enquiries with colleagues, or patients? See if there are any common factors we're missing?'

'Sure, I'll do it in my copious spare time...'

'They're your patients. Aren't you curious?'

She squints at me through her glasses. 'Cheap shot.'

'I know, I'm sorry. But it's important.'

She takes a deep breath. 'OK, I'll make a few calls. On one condition.'

'What?'

'You promise not to come back.'

CHAPTER 37

It's my first day back in the office. My screen illuminates the tally of misdemeanours. No-shows at family-planning appointments, pregnancy alerts from medi-profiles, custody authorisation requests. Here I sit: the ultimate imposter, wielding judgement. Tracking down illegal babies like me.

Aisha isn't in. I scan the other cubicles, the heads bent over their screens. Does one of them have Senka's profile in their restricted folder? Might someone on my floor actually realise who she is?

A call beams in; it's Steener, no doubt chasing his requests.

'Good morning, Detective Inspector Steener.'

'Ah: Ministry Representative Houghton, at long last!' He appears to be in a park, coffee cup clenched in his fist. 'They said you were out of the office. Hope it wasn't that latest bug that's doing the rounds. I've heard it really messes with your immune system.'

'No, but thank you for your concern.'

He flexes his foot against a bench. 'Then I got to thinking you might be busy with that other project of yours...'

I adjust the volume on my headset. 'Sadly not. That never came to anything.'

'Oh.'

He sounds disappointed. I move on quickly. 'How can I help you today?'

'I need action on a case I sent last week. The Fulstein woman. Before she skips the country.'

'You could have requested a transfer to one of my colleagues.'

'Nah...' He slurps a gulp. 'Like to know who I'm dealing with.'

I flick through the custody requests until I find it. A thirty-two-year-old woman from Battersea with a partner of ten years. No previous transgressions.

'So, basically, this lady's other half is doing the dirty on her. With someone from work.'

Steener, as ever, feels the need to regale me with the details himself.

'Said colleague doesn't have the implant, claims she has an IUD, which, guess what? Fails.' He rolls his eyes. 'Catch is: she wants to keep the baby. The philanderer does everything he can to dissuade her: money, a promotion, you name it ... But she's adamant. Which is all a bit tricky, given wifey and him are planning one of their own.'

I wish Steener would just get to the point.

'Well, when the missus finds out, she goes ballistic. She's not having their future child gazumped by some floozy's. So she pays someone to do the deed.'

'You have proof?'

'Yup, it's all there, page five. She made a good stab at hiding it, but the bots traced the payment.' He takes another swig. 'The killer used our old friend, Miss Carrie.'

I scan the page. It makes grim reading.

'OK, I'll authorise the custody request. I should get through the others by end of play. Now, if you'll excuse me, I've rather a lot to catch up on...'

I hit the end button and slump over my desk.

My personal screen buzzes. I glance at the number and head to the only place on our floor that's remotely private: the prayer room.

'Kai Houghton, hello?'

'I was supposed to ring this number, right? It's secure?'

Dr Trowsky.

'Yes, just a moment.'

I step round the hollow blocks, decorated with religious symbols, where you leave your shoes. The room is empty.

'OK, sorry about that. Go ahead.'

'So I spoke with some other clinicians, people I trust. It's like you said: infertility referrals are up everywhere, amongst the communities we discussed.'

I walk over soft patterned rugs towards a stained-glass panel decorated with abstract coloured swirls.

'I wondered if ethnicity might be a factor, but it isn't. Doesn't matter whether their families came from Africa, South-East Asia or Spain. The only thing they have in common is they're second-generation settlers.'

'Right.'

'My next theory was environmental triggers, given their parents' migration histories. So I contacted three patients I'd recently referred. Asked them to speak with their families about any climate events or potential pollution issues in their home countries.'

I can tell from the doctor's whispered urgency that she's building to something.

'Those conversations weren't easy. A lot of things came out about the disasters they had lived through; their appalling journeys. There didn't seem to be a specific event, though, that I could pinpoint that might affect a future pregnancy. But there was something else. Something I wasn't expecting...' She pauses.

'Go on.'

'It was one of my patient's fathers who let it slip. He said something to my patient about a test his wife – her mother – took part in, soon after they arrived in the UK. Before my patient was born.'

'A "test"?'

'Yes.'

'What for?'

'Some kind of drug; he didn't say what. So my patient queried it with her mother. And this is the interesting bit.'

I glance at the door.

'Her mum flat out denied it at first. Said her dad was talking nonsense. To the point where even the dad began to backtrack. But when my patient pressed them both on it, her mother got quite agitated, and said she'd been made to sign a form saying she'd never talk about it. And if my patient carried on asking questions they might all end up back in the camp.'

I grip the screen a little tighter. 'How long ago was this test?'

'Forty years.'

'What drug was it? Do you know?'

'My patient couldn't get any more details out of them. All her mum would say is that it wasn't relevant and she should forget all about it. I checked her mother's records: she has no history of fertility issues. And there's nothing in there about any trial. Which is totally against the regulations.'

I feel a tingle at the back of my neck. I stare at the stained glass. The spirals come together in the shape of a face.

'Do you think this could be related to those referrals?'

'Well, it's only one person, and we still don't know the facts. Maybe you can find out more.' She pauses. 'But something about this definitely doesn't smell right.'

CHAPTER 38

We're meeting at the clinic in Earl's Court. I messaged Senka last night. My final appointment of the day happened to be in Battersea: a missed termination. I'm finding my duties increasingly difficult. As my mouth recites the offence and the perpetrators' legal obligations, I'm painfully aware of my own illegal status, convinced it must be obvious to all. I've tried the distancing techniques; not one is working. As I listen to these women, pleading for their babies' lives, thoughts of my own mother steal in, pleading for mine.

I arrive early, but Senka is already waiting, with Talli and another nervous-looking woman.

'Talli, you know,' says Senka. 'This is her friend, who we'll call Parul. For her own protection.'

I smile. 'Pleased to meet you.'

Parul nods but does not smile. She tries to be subtle, but she keeps staring at my eyes.

The doctor marches out of her room, followed by a skinny girl in a ripped pink corset and scuffed thigh-high boots. The layers of make-up can't disguise her age: she's barely a teenager. She walks straight past us. Parul visibly wilts.

'Good evening,' says the doctor.

'Parul, this is the doctor I told you about,' says Senka. 'Doc, this is Talli's friend.'

The doctor nods at her. 'Shall we?'

She takes us into a different room, one with pale-blue walls. There are fresh flowers in a vase. A mountain of books and files obscures a wooden dining table; two plates perch perilously on top.

'Please, take a seat.'

The doctor scoops up a faux-fur blanket flung over the sofa.

I wonder if she actually sleeps here. Or just grabs fleeting naps.

Talli and Parul choose the sofa; Senka and I take the chairs.

'Thank you for coming,' says Senka to them. 'I want to reassure you that whatever you say here will be treated in total confidence. Your families will not be compromised. I know this is a concern, and I don't want you to worry.'

Parul's lips tighten.

'I asked the doc to be here, because I think it's important we have a medical opinion. Also, to alert her to other potential cases.'

The doctor nods.

'Shall we start with Talli?' Senka continues. 'She's asked me to speak for her, to help with the language. Please correct me, Talli, if you think I'm getting anything wrong.'

Talli nods.

'So ... Talli asked her cousins to talk to their parents about the areas we discussed. Including whether they'd ever been asked to take part in any "tests".' She pauses. 'Her cousins were understandably anxious. They've grown up in this country – they know how lucky their parents were to be resettled here. They didn't want to stir up trouble.'

Talli's eyes flick to Parul's. She squeezes her hand.

'According to Talli's older cousin, there were no tests, or anything else, for that matter, that might account for her difficulties conceiving. Talli believes she was telling her the truth. Her other cousin said the same thing. But when Talli saw that cousin again later, on her own, she said her mother had mentioned something, but forbade her from speaking about it.'

Senka swallows. 'Her mother made her swear; she was very frightened. She told her that if she broke her word, they'd be in serious trouble.'

The doctor's jaw hardens. I think of the skinny girl we saw earlier. She must see and hear unimaginable things every day.

'Talli contacted two other women who live in the same community, who she'd been told were also struggling with fertility issues. One refused to have the conversation. The other was Parul.' Senka smiles at her. 'And we're very grateful that she's here.'

Senka turns to Talli. 'Are you happy with what I've said, Talli? Is that a good reflection of what you told me?'

Talli nods.

'OK. In which case, Parul: it's over to you. In your own time.'

Parul takes a breath.

'Before I begin, I need to explain something, so you understand how ... difficult things were for my parents. They didn't want to leave their country. But the storms grew angrier, every year. And when that last monsoon came, the tides swallowed their land. They had no option left but to go.' She sighs. 'So they got on a boat. Like millions before them. They spent everything they had, and it took them many months to reach this country. My mother said she was convinced they would die. So when they finally made it, they didn't care what was asked of them. They would have done anything. Anything at all, just to earn the right to stay.'

'We understand,' says Senka. 'And I'm sorry. No one should be forced out of their home.'

I glance at her. My chest tightens.

'You know, my mum, she ... she didn't want to talk about this. Not at first. But her heart is breaking for me...' Parul looks down. 'She had so much joy being a mother, she wants me to become one, too. So when I told her why I was asking these questions ... Well. She agreed.'

Talli whispers something to her, and Parul nods.

'When my parents arrived they were separated, and taken for an interview. My mother's English wasn't as good back then, so the border officials fetched an interpreter. They asked her lots of questions: where she had come from, why she had left, who she was travelling with ... Then they took a sample of her blood and asked about her medical history: vaccinations, any illnesses she'd had, that kind of thing. Whether she had children. When she said no, they asked her if she wanted them.' Parul swallows. 'My parents knew about the one-child policy from other migrants. They were happy to agree if it meant they could stay. She told the officials this. And then one of the immigration officers mentioned the resettlement programme.'

I glance at Senka.

'He told my mother that a few people – only a few, very lucky people – were sponsored by the Party each year. They were given a job and a home and, as long as they complied with certain conditions, after a few years, they could apply for resettlement status. And that was when he brought up the test.'

Talli is hanging off Parul's words. I wonder how much of this she knows.

'Well, my parents had expected to be stuck in the camp ... This was beyond their wildest dreams. He told her they'd developed a contraceptive implant that never needed topping up. That they'd already completed the initial safety tests, but they wanted to see how comfortable it was over longer periods of time—'

'How "comfortable"?' the doctor interrupts. 'That's what he said?'

'Yes.' Parul pauses. 'My mother had heard about implants. She knew some women that used them, although they only lasted for a few years. She thought this would be a good thing, because it would mean she could do her job without worrying about getting pregnant. So when he asked if she was interested in taking part in the trial, she jumped at it. He told her she'd need to have some screening tests, to check she was suitable, and then they brought her lots of forms to sign.'

'Were those forms translated for her?' asks the doctor. 'Did she know what she was signing? Was she informed about any risks?'

'I...' Parul falters. 'I'm not sure...'

The doctor's face darkens. 'What happened next?'

'She was taken away for the tests. And then, they put the implant in.'

'What...? Straight away?'

'I believe so, yes.'

Senka mutters something.

'They told her she'd need to attend some medical appointments. Keep a diary about women's things, you know...'

'Did the implant have a name?' I ask.

'She didn't say, but we assume it was Destine.'

'Did your mother mention if she experienced any side effects during the trial?' asks the doctor.

'No. Although I didn't ask.' Parul's face pales. 'Do you think it could have affected her, somehow?'

'We can't say anything yet for sure, Parul. Did she have any difficulties herself conceiving, do you know?'

She shakes her head. 'Quite the opposite. It used to be their joke. She said that as soon as they made up their minds to start trying, she deactivated the implant and fell pregnant with me straight away.' A cloud passes over her face. 'They don't laugh about that anymore...'

Senka leans forward. 'You said your mother was reluctant to discuss this at first. Why was that?'

'The officials said there was only a limited number of these implants, and that people were being specially selected. That it had to be kept confidential at all costs, and that if she broke the agreement, there would be consequences.'

'What kind of consequences?'

'They didn't specify, but...' She swallows. 'My mum was clear what they meant.'

'Parul,' I say, 'how long ago did your parents arrive in this country?'

'Forty-five years ago.'

Doc's eyes widen. And I know why.

The implant was inserted into Parul's mother twenty years before Destine was legally approved.

CHAPTER 39

After a quick debrief with the doctor, Senka and I head to the café. We take a table at the back and sit, staring at our drinks.

'Experimenting on migrants with untested drugs. Well, this is a new low. Even for ONE,' Senka spits. 'God knows, hadn't those women suffered enough?'

I clutch the mug, squeezing my fingers until they burn. This is the organisation I have dedicated myself to. The government I serve.

'They think they can get away with treating them like lab rats. Because they're powerless. Hasn't this always been the way, exploiting the vulnerable? The mentally ill, or people whose skin is a different colour? Women too poor to say no?' Her words punch out, angry and sharp. 'I told you, didn't I, that it wouldn't just stop at the illegals? Well, here's the proof. These families are resettled. They can't be ignored, they live in this country, they have rights.'

My brain throbs. I'm no longer a bystander. I am complicit in this discovery. I have acted against the state. When the Ministry finds out – and it is a question of when – there will be no mercy.

Senka clatters her spoon onto the table. 'Why aren't you saying anything? Aren't you appalled?'

'Of course I am! I'm just trying to think...' My leg jiggles. 'We don't know what impact those tests had on these women. It's the daughters who are having problems, not their mothers...'

'That's why you have to find out more. It's obvious there's a connection. This might be the catalyst we need.'

I have to find out more...?

My foot jiggles faster. I should never have let myself get dragged into this.

The moment that second restriction on Senka's profile comes off, my parents face imminent arrest and I'm probably up for enforced sterilisation, and yet here I am, running around town with an insurgent, helping her dig up dirt on the Party.

'Can you get hold of anyone connected with those trials?' continues Senka. 'A researcher, or someone from the firm that makes Dest—'

My knee knocks the table, spilling coffee everywhere. I grab a napkin.

'Look, Senka, I gave you the information you asked for,' I say, furiously mopping my lap. 'It's not my job to investigate.'

'What are you saying?' Her face contorts. 'This is about what's right and what's wrong, Kai. About helping these women and holding those responsible to account.'

I exhale. 'I know, but—'

She throws up her hands. 'Who knows how many women have been affected. There could be hundreds ... thousands. This isn't going to end unless we do something. I'm not asking you to wade in there, all guns blazing. We need people like you inside the system. People who can find things out.'

'I'm sorry, Senka, I already told you, I'm not brave, like you. I'm totally out of my depth, here. I can't even do my job properly anymore. I need to focus on figuring out some resolution for my parents...'

'Your parents will be fine—'

'You keep saying that, but you can't restrict your profile indefinitely. It's going to have to be released at some point. But I get it, right? Why should you care...?'

Senka sits back. 'So that's what's really bothering you. You think I'm punishing them.' She glares at me. 'You think what they did was OK?'

'No, of course not. But I reckon it would help, if...' I sigh. 'You told me I needed to open my eyes. And I did. But you won't even let me try to explain ... She was ill, very ill—'

'Don't.' It's like the crack of a gun. 'It's not the same, and you know it. I'm not interested in bullshit excuses.'

Maybe I should stop there. Our relationship, if I can call it that, is fragile enough.

But then I think of Dad. How devastated he was. Mum's face...

'How come you're so ready to take their side? They've lied to you your entire life. They only told you the truth because I forced them to.'

'Look, if I could change things, I would. But ... After you were born, Mum suffered with postnatal depression; it went on for months. She thought she was a failure as a mother.'

Senka snorts. 'Clearly she was.'

'Come on, that's ... Will you just hear me out? They had no idea about the centres, I promise you. They were told you'd go to a good family, that you'd be loved. Dad was heartbrok—'

Senka holds up her hand. 'I don't want to hear it. Nothing changes the fact they chose you over me, and from that moment on, each day has been a fight to exist. That's the only truth that counts.'

She scrapes back her chair.

'This conversation is over. Don't ever bring it up again.'

I reach out my hand. 'Senka, please...'

'I'll see what I can dig up on those trials myself. While you figure out if you've got any moral courage.'

As I watch her march to the door, I recall something my grandmother once said. I never really grasped what it meant, until now.

She said that sisters are the worst enemies.

Because they know where best to strike.

CHAPTER 40

My afternoon appointment is at a family-planning clinic five miles south of Oxford. On impulse, I decide to call in to Mum and Dad's before heading back to London. Attempt to restore some equilibrium while I lick my wounds.

The tram whines past the rain-soaked turrets of Magdalen College, more grey than golden. These landmarks used to be greetings, ushering me closer to home. But my memories are now tainted; the filters that my parents so carefully constructed ripped off. My argument with Senka has only rattled me more.

I keep turning over all these allegations about the Party. I have no idea how to get involved without making things worse. If I'm arrested, there's no hope for my parents. Senka promised she wouldn't make me do anything I didn't want to. So why was she so furious when I refused? It's always there, hanging over me: her birth record.

The unspoken threat.

I step off the tram and make my way past the produce stalls and e-scooter stands. The rain has abated to a constant drizzle that seeps into my clothes. Wafts of incense emanate from a shop doorway. The same golden Buddha gazes out that enticed me as a girl, although its face is now chipped: I glimpse grey welts beneath the gold.

I turn into our road; the familiar window boxes trail yellow, pink and scarlet heads, flattened by the rain. Suddenly, an animal creeps out from behind a garbage bin. A thick white ruff offsets its copper body; black whiskers twitch on a pointed nose. It stops in the road and stares at me with dark amber eyes.

Something about it reminds me of Senka. Stalking in the shadows, smart and adaptable. With a talent to survive.

The fox slips under a garden fence and disappears.

As I approach the corner, I hear voices. One higher-pitched, increasing in urgency, the other an intransigent drone. I round the bend and my stomach drops.

A van is parked outside our house, back doors open.

A black Ministry van.

I dive through a gate and crouch behind a low brick wall. I tear the chip out of my screen and crush it under my heel.

I crawl over to a buddleia bush and press myself between its branches, spearing my thigh. Through the leaves I make out two ASRs – autonomous security robots – marching down our path. My father is between them, arms stretched out in front of him. Black cuffs around his wrists.

My eyes dart to the house. My mother is braced against our front door.

The Ministry official resumes their monotonous drone. The timbre tells me it's a woman's; I strain my neck to see, but the hedge blocks my view.

Disparate words break through:

'Infringement ... Section twenty-five ... Constitution ... quota...'

I know them off by heart, these offences against the state, the laws they have broken. The threats to comply, the permission to use force.

Mum suddenly drops to her knees and lifts her cuffed hands, as if in prayer. An image flashes into my head of that mural in St Margaret's Church: mother and child.

The ASR hauls her up by her wrists and drags her towards the van. The cuffs must be cutting into her, but she bucks and thrusts. Over the booming threats of the security robot, I hear her howls of rage, her pointless protests.

My father shouts something to her from the van doors. I imagine him pleading with her to see reason, not to make things worse.

One of the machines shoves him forward. Dad turns to her one last time and climbs into the back as my mother starts to scream.

I cram my fist into my mouth. The buddleia leaves tremble.

The robot forces her into a restraint harness, oblivious to her kicks. It picks Mum up as if she were a loaf of bread and throws her into the van.

I stay there long after the doors have closed and the van has driven off. Tears scorching my eyes.

I think of that fox strutting across the road.

And curse myself for being so stupid.

CHAPTER 41

I zigzag up side streets, away from the city, my feet carrying me to a destination as yet unknown. I keep my head down, hood up, trying to avoid the cameras. Where can I go? I have no home anymore: they will be waiting. I think of Niko, alone in his charge-basket. All I possess is my work bag and one set of clothes.

I soon find myself on the outskirts of town. It takes me a moment to recognise where I am. I spot a sign for Donnington Bridge: not far to the e-bus terminal. Any transport's a risk, but they'll know I came by train. I hurry over the bridge and on, up the Abingdon Road, until eventually I reach the terminal. I scour the bays and buildings for any signs of security, but as far as I can tell, it looks clear. I creep up to the destination board, panic pricking my skull. What options do I have beyond ONE's far-reaching eyes? Even if I manage to dodge the cameras, their scouts will be everywhere.

And then an idea hits. I just pray that untracked payment device Spice gave me still works.

I loiter behind one of the charging bays and wait for my bus to arrive, checking every person that comes in. Despite the rain, I dig out my sunglasses and cover my face with my mask.

When the bus finally pulls in, I take a seat at the back and curl myself into the window. I try counting, but I'm ambushed by images of Mum on her knees, or being forced into the restraint harness; Dad being shoved into the back of the van.

The motorway spools on, past crop fields and reservoirs, woodlands and solar farms. Every few miles, Party hoardings shout slogans:

Crops are precious: reduce waste!
Conserve water, conserve lives.
Plant a tree. The future is in your hands.

Each time the bus slows, I'm convinced it's a security block, and I scan the road for ASRs or black vans. At one point, a man gets on, staggers down the aisle and slumps next to me. I think he's been drinking. I tighten my mask and retreat further into my coat. He attempts to strike up conversation; I ignore him, pretend I'm asleep. My fidgeting gives me away. After hurling abuse at me, he lurches to a different seat.

I get off at the penultimate stop and switch to the overland. It's rush hour and the carriages are rammed. The train races across the city, exhausted commuters bustling on and off. My eyes sidle over their faces as sweat prickles under my shirt. Security scouts don't announce themselves; they could be anyone. I try some subtle breathing exercises, but it's only when the train empties that my heart finally slows.

I peer out at the dilapidated buildings, the derelict parks. I'm struggling to remember the exact stop. Just as I'm certain I must have missed it, I recognise the slaughterhouse with its graffitied, barbed-wire walls. I punch the red button. The train brakes.

I creep along the platform, bracing myself for the flurry of guards, the slam to the ground. But the station appears to be empty. I find the gap in the railings; as I squeeze through, a brown shape scuttles into a bed of weeds and I let out a squeal. I hurry towards the terraced houses, neck swivelling. The sockets of empty windows stare back at me, as plastic sheets rise up in doorways like ghosts.

About halfway down I spot a possible contender: the door has boards, not sheeting; a few tiles are missing, but the roof is reasonably intact. I wrap my jacket around my arm and knock out the remaining fragments of a downstairs window, cringing as the glass smashes to the ground.

I check the street again.

No movement. Only the groans of houses.

I suck in a breath and hoist myself up on the ledge, arms quaking.

And slide in.

My feet land on rotten boards and the curled remains of a curtain, like a long-dead bird in its nest. A pungent smell emanates from what's left of a sofa. I keep perfectly still as my eyes adjust to the gloom, my ears straining. The skeleton of a staircase leads up to the next floor, fractured steps powdered with plaster. A dank draught coils round my neck.

I heave a surprisingly solid bookcase over to the window and wedge it against the frame. I pick my way towards the kitchen, careful to spread my weight. Most of the fittings have been ripped out; a plastic table and a stained brown sink are the sole survivors. A utility room leads to the back door. I return to the kitchen and squat down on my haunches, clutching my bag, trying not to touch the wall.

The light outside diminishes, clouds morphing quietly into dusk. Bats flit past the small box window on their silent hunt. The only sounds are the occasional hoot of an owl, the buzz of blood in my ears. I try to imagine Niko here with me, snuggled into my lap. Curling my fingers through his fur.

Minutes thud slowly past. My thighs ache so I allow my bottom to slide to the floor. My stomach growls, and it occurs to me that I haven't eaten since this morning. I cuddle my knees to my chest, resting my bag on top like a table. I try to resist, but my head sinks lower until eventually my eyelids close.

◆ ◆ ◆

My parents are in the back of the van. Dad's head is cowed, a gag stuffed in his mouth. My mother holds out her arms, beseeching me with cuffed hands. As she begins to speak, the doors slam shut. The doors keep slamming, like gunshots, ricocheting off the houses.

My eyes snap open. Nothing. Just inky black.

Another slam.

I bolt to my feet.

They're at the door.

CHAPTER 42

I fumble for my screen, wave its light across the kitchen and rush to the back door. There's a screech of metal and then a snap. Adrenaline surges. That's the boards being prised off.

I wrench the door handle; it shrieks in protest but doesn't budge. I yank it again, slam my boot into the doorjamb; chips of wood and paint flake off to the floor. I keep kicking, until it eventually gives way, and I lurch into the yard.

The light cannot penetrate beyond a metre. It's a riot of bushes and weeds.

'Kai?'

My heart stills. Senka.

I tear through the undergrowth, arms flailing, my legs snagging on branches and thorns. I make out an old shed that has fallen in on itself; a tangle of creepers coils up a brick wall behind.

'Don't be stupid, Kai.' Closer now. 'We can help you...'

I pocket my screen and throw myself at the vines. Tendrils snap as I claw at them, my feet scrabbling for purchase in the cracks. I manage to fling my arms over the wall, but no matter how furiously I pedal my legs, I can't heave the rest of my body up.

A light sweeps round behind me, illuminating the bricks. I manage to hoist up a leg. My lungs are screaming and my elbows are scraped raw.

All of a sudden, someone seizes my foot.

'Give it up!'

I use all my remaining strength to kick her off, but her grip tightens, and she hauls me down.

I land with a thud on my side. 'What the fuck?'

'Being a fugitive really isn't your forte.' She thrusts out a hand. 'Come on, get up.'

My shoulder is on fire. 'Screw you.'

'I had nothing to do with their arrest.'

'Yeah, sure...' I try to catch my breath.

She stands over me. 'You're not thinking straight. Why would I do that? You're no good to me in a cell.'

'Maybe thought didn't come into it,' I pant. 'Maybe hate overruled judgement. You've wielded that profile over me like a weapon for weeks. And now you've got what you wanted. Your birth parents will be sentenced for their crime.'

'Don't be ridiculous. I could have given them up months ago. Why risk myself, or the others?'

I roll onto my front and push myself up, wincing as pain sears down my arm.

'You knew I was pulling away. Now you've got me where you want me. I'm an outcast, like you.'

'Exactly.' Her eyes flash. 'And that makes you useless to me.'

I stagger past her, towards the house.

'How did you even find me? You're as bad as them. You must be tracking me.'

'For your own protection, yes. Did you tell your parents anything that might betray us? Locations, names...?'

'Of course not.' I veer round. 'I kept my word, like a fool.'

She follows me into the kitchen. 'You won't last five minutes out here. You've only made it this long because of me.'

I grab my bag. 'I don't care. I don't want your help. Let them come.'

I stumble over the boards into the front room. Spice is perched on the rotting sofa.

'Nice place you have here.' He smiles. 'Although, you've let it go a little...'

I ignore him. Waves of giddiness wash over me.

He catches my arm. 'You look like you could use a meal.' He extracts a twig from my hair. 'Possibly a wash.'

Patterns swirl behind my eyes.

'Kai, are you OK?'

Red and orange squares. Green and blue circles. The throbbing in my head gets louder. A voice echoes.

Someone's tugging at me.

But I am cast loose, nothing to hold on to.

Spinning out to space.

◆ ◆ ◆

The smell comes first. Actually, a stench.

Something digging into my back.

A twilight room with a broken ceiling and grubby walls.

And it hits me where I am.

'Steady...' says Spice as I scrabble to sit up. 'We don't want you going down again.'

He slides his arm underneath my back and gently lifts me up. I feel myself blushing, like an idiot. A sharp pain in my shoulder makes me flinch, and I remember Senka dragging me off the wall.

Spice smells a lot better than the sofa.

'Drink this.' He hands me a water bottle.

I hesitate.

'Don't worry, you won't catch anything.' He eyes the sofa. 'At least, not from me.'

I drain it. I didn't realise how thirsty I was.

Senka is watching me, arms crossed, by the kitchen door.

'We should get moving,' says Spice. 'That site in Bermondsey's the closest. It's pretty basic, but at least she can rest up, grab some food.'

'I'm not going anywhere,' I say. 'Not with her.'

Spice glances at Senka, then at me.

'Look, there's an easy way to settle this,' he says. 'Someone in your office must have got to the profile before we did. Have you noticed anything? A colleague trying to get close to you? Anyone who might have clocked something was wrong?'

I stare at him. He doesn't look as if he's lying. Maybe he doesn't know what Senka's done.

I humour him. 'There's a woman I sit next to ... Aisha Osundo, but I—'

'Well it isn't her, that much we do know—'

'Spice!' Senka glares at him.

Spice eyeballs her back. 'Don't you think we're past that? It's time she knew.' He turns to me. 'Aisha put the second restriction on when yours came off.'

My head pounds. Aisha is one of *them*?

'OK,' he says, 'we all need to calm down. Figure out who we can trust.'

'Well that's easy,' I say. 'Because I don't trust anyone.' I point at Senka. 'Especially you.'

She sighs. 'Look, I don't hate you. Maybe I did, when I first saw that birth record. And all the fantasies I'd nurtured as a kid about what happened to me came crashing down. But one thing I've learned from your Party is that hate doesn't solve anything. It just eats you up.'

I look into her face. I want to believe her, but it's too much of a coincidence. She could easily have told Aisha to release the profile.

'There has to be a way out of this,' says Spice. 'Remember: the Ministry has no idea you're illegal.'

I give a bitter laugh. 'Really? How long do you think it'll take the security squad to get that out of my parents? In any case, staff who cheat the system don't come back.'

'Then you give them something,' says Senka. 'Something they want.'

'What, exactly?'

'You know that better than anyone.' Her eyes meet mine. 'You just have to decide.'

CHAPTER 43

The overland heads back into the populated zones. My gaze darts to every passenger who gets on.

A suited man in his forties.

A mother and her baby.

A nurse in a crisp blue uniform.

My heart is thudding so hard I'm worried it's going to trigger a medi-alert before I get near Westminster. I picture the nurse rolling me onto the floor and pumping my chest, pinching my nose as she gives me the breath of life. Strapping me to a stretcher and carting me off to the nearest wellness centre as my eyes roll back in my head.

Given what I'm about to do, it's quite appealing.

The train drops down towards the river and I see the blue-and-white drapes of Tower Bridge. I've rehearsed what I'm going to say, over and over. It doesn't stop the fear bleeding through my veins. I think of my colleagues' reactions, their superior, salacious stares.

I always knew there was something wrong with her.

What a nerve!

You could tell she was a traitor by her eyes...

We race along the embankment, each bridge we pass curtailing what little time remains. Whenever I feel myself wavering, I think of Mum and Dad, languishing in some squalid prison cell.

I have to do this. No matter the cost.

Before I know it we're at Blackfriars, and all too soon I glimpse the stark white clockface on Elizabeth Tower. My belly responds with a loop.

I heave my bag over my arm and step out onto Victoria Embankment. At least the throbbing in my shoulder seems to be easing off. Five security patrols huddle outside the Houses of Parliament Museum. I keep my head down and force my feet to move, counting each step as security cameras swivel. Alerts must have already been sent.

As I approach the ONE Party complex, a manic fancy takes flight that all will be well. They will respect my track record and know I am loyal. A discreet tap on the shoulder, a polite summons to a conference room. My case will be heard.

There's a sudden whooshing noise.

My legs buckle as I'm slammed from behind.

I drop face down on the pavement; blood trickles from my nose.

'DO NOT RESIST.'

My shoulder screams as my arms are yanked behind my back and the cuffs snap on.

'I am not resisting!'

I thought I'd shouted it, but maybe it's like nightmares where nothing comes out.

A foot thuds into my back as robot hands search me.

'Kai Houghton, you are being arrested on suspicion of treason, an offence under the Crime and Disorder Act.'

I crane my neck round; it's a security official I don't recognise. 'I'm reporting to the Party of my own free will. I claim the right to speak with a minister.'

There's a sigh. It might be a laugh.

'You are in breach of your Ministry duties and have therefore forfeited the right to petition.'

An ASR yanks me up. I remember to breathe.

'This isn't a petition. I have urgent news to report on a case. Security level A: severe threat.'

My accuser whispers into his device.

I summon some residue of courage. 'You don't have the clearance to refuse me.'

The official's eyes swerve to mine. His lip curls. 'Is that so?'

He jerks his head.

The machine hurls me into the cage of a waiting van.

CHAPTER 44

We drive a short distance and the van brakes, hard. I lurch against the bars, my cuffed hands powerless to help. It's dark in the cage; the windows are tinted so I can't see out. It must be sound-proofed too, because all I can hear is my own panting as numbers spin uselessly round my head. It's all deliberate, of course, to disorient you. Make you distrust your own senses. I knew fear had a smell, but not a taste.

Sharp, like lemon. But more bitter.

The vehicle jerks forward, slamming my head against the front of the cage, and veers left, round a bend. We must be going down. There are no hills in Westminster. But there are basements.

The van keeps turning as we descend. How many levels are there? I think of Mum and Dad disappearing down our street in a van like this one. I wonder if they were as terrified as me.

Finally, we come to a stop. The doors fly open, and I am hauled out. Other vans are lined up between concrete pillars: dozens of them. I am marched through at least three security gates, down a poorly lit corridor, green doors on both sides. Apart from our steps, it is completely silent. An ASR unlocks one of the cells and shoves me in. There's a bed with a wafer-thin mattress, a toilet and a sink. A camera on the ceiling.

The door clangs shut.

◆ ◆ ◆

I am thirsty. Very thirsty.

I've asked for water at least ten times, but I have no idea if anyone or anything is listening. Nothing comes. I eye the tap and decide against it. My wrists are burning and my arms won't stop trembling. I tap my toes in rhythms of five and try to decipher the scratched symbols and words on the wall. Numerous curses about the Party. Several encircled Vs.

I count the seconds, quietly whispering the numbers: tens, then hundreds, then a thousand. I'm nearly at three thousand when I hear the clatter of footsteps ringing louder until they stop outside my cell.

A machine unlocks the door.

I am led through a maze of corridors until we reach one where the cells are spaced out at greater distances, and the gangway is better lit.

The ASR pushes me through a door and instructs me to sit on a chair facing a small table. Two empty chairs wait opposite. A camera winks at me from the wall.

A different security official strides in. Silver hair, olive skin, narrow mouth. Judging by her insignia, she's high ranking. Two guards follow.

'Name?' she barks.

'Kai Houghton.'

'Kai Houghton, did you work as a representative for the Ministry of Population and Family Planning?'

Did.

I suck in a breath. 'Yes.'

'You took an oath to investigate and bring to justice any transgressions of the Population Planning Act. To monitor families and ensure they remain within their allocated child quota. To bring down the force of the law on those who do not.'

'Yes, but I—'

'Silence!' She slams the table. 'And yet you not only failed to take the appropriate action against two adults who committed a birth crime and concealed it through subterfuge for more than two decades, you also chose to aid and abet these criminals by withholding evidence. Neither the transgressors nor their excess child have been apprehended.'

So they don't know that excess child is me. Yet.

'You have reneged on your duties and deceived the Ministry.' She leans closer. 'What is your defence?'

'During my investigation, I discovered—'

'What investigation? Where is your report? Why did you make no arrest?'

'Because I discovered an even greater security threat, which I decided to—'

'What "threat"?'

'Intelligence on a lead operative within the terrorist network that calls itself FREE.'

A smirk flickers across her face.

'First, you take advantage of your position and abuse the privileges granted to you. And now you claim to have intelligence on our enemies.'

She presses both palms on the desk and hunches forward.

'This is nothing but a desperate ruse, a pitiful attempt at a bargain plea. You are a disgrace to the Party. You have betrayed your country and will face the consequences. Just as your parents are facing the long-overdue consequences of their crime.'

She grates back her chair.

'The operative's code name is Shadow.' I gabble out the words.

She stiffens. 'Who gave you that name?'

'She did.' I swallow. 'Shadow is my sister.'

CHAPTER 45

I don't know how long I've been in this cell: it could be midday or midnight. There is no natural light to gauge, only an oblong yellow glimmer round the edges of the door.

I think of Mum and Dad, in a cell like this one.

Of Senka, scheming away with Spice.

Her name certainly generated a reaction. I was instantly escorted back to my cell. At least they brought me water. And something resembling food: lukewarm and mushy. I tried to sleep, but it's pointless; I'm just going to have to tough it out. I sniff under my arms and grimace. I definitely smell.

My ears prick up: footsteps.

A thud and a click.

It's the silver-haired official. She doesn't look happy.

'Get up. It's time to move.'

◆ ◆ ◆

I'm back in an interrogation room. This one's bigger, with a false window. The chairs facing me have padded seats.

When the door eventually opens, I nearly choke.

A woman in a bottle-green trouser suit strides in, her trademark bob capped at her jaw. The gold ONE emblem nestles at her throat.

On instinct, I try to get up.

'Stay where you are.'

The minister doesn't bark or shout. She has no need to.

'You can go,' she says to the security official.

The official opens her mouth to protest, but shuts it again and leaves.

Minister Gauteng inspects both chairs before lowering herself down with a sigh.

I see her constantly on my screen, but I've only ever seen her in person a handful of times.

And never alone.

Her mahogany eyes skirt the walls, pause on the camera and settle on me.

'I knew something was off with you, Houghton, right from your induction. I could smell it: the fetor of desperation...' Her nose wrinkles. 'Always trying too hard. Regurgitating our protocols, like some ... bot.'

Damson nails prick the table.

'You claim that Shadow is your illegal sibling. And you have information on her.'

I nod.

'And that this is all a result of your own, private "investigation".'

I nod again and fix my gaze between the table and her throat.

'Shadow has evaded all of our missions: no one has ever seen them. And yet, a junior birth counter with no intelligence experience whatsoever claims to have succeeded where eminently more qualified colleagues failed.'

I slow my breathing. 'Well, to be honest, I didn't exactly find her. She was the one who found me.'

Gauteng's eyebrow arches. 'Please enlighten me.'

'I first saw her profile just over three weeks ago. It was a shock. To discover that my parents could have committed such a crime. They were always so ... loyal.'

A welcome pulse of expensive perfume permeates the cell.

'Of course, I realised there was a conflict ... And I did consider handing the case over... But I felt that I should be the one to investigate.' I make myself look up. 'Because, as their daughter, I was more likely to elicit the truth.'

Gauteng's eyes burn into me.

'And they did confess. Straight away. Which was ... difficult.' I swallow. 'So I followed up the leads I had. The wellness centre, where the profile was first traced. My mother's clinic. Both drew blanks. It was my sister that brought us together. She engineered the whole thing.'

'Why would she do that? She knows how hard the Party has worked to find her, what a prize she would be.'

'I don't know, I ... I think she believes she can turn me. Make me her "asset"...' I shake my head. 'Two sisters, fighting for the same cause.'

Gauteng frowns. 'This woman is a highly dangerous subversive. You should have brought this to our attention straight away.'

'I wasn't sure at first who she actually was. She only revealed that later. Had I known, I would most certainly have reported it.'

'So how was she hidden? After the birth?'

I hold my voice steady. 'She was reallocated.'

The minister's eyes narrow. She fiddles with her sleeve. 'Reallocations were forbidden for second births.'

I glimpse a flash of silver on her wrist.

'That's what I'd understood, too. But, it appears there was an ... unofficial policy. For certain reasons – medical or psychological – some births were allowed to go to term.'

'Well that's the first I've heard of it.'

'My mother said she handed her baby over to the authorities, assuming she'd be reallocated to a family. But what Shadow claims is that there was such a surfeit of excess children, they couldn't find homes for them. So they were sent to secret institutions around the country. Called reallocation centres. And that's where she grew up.'

'"Reallocation centres"?' She barks a laugh. 'These conspiracies of theirs grow ever more fanciful.'

'She says they have sources. People who worked at the centres. They were ordered to destroy all records. But even so, FREE have a list.'

'What list?'

'Of profiles and birth records that were deleted. They somehow recovered them. She showed it to me. It runs into thousands.'

Minister Gauteng flicks her wrist. 'Fakes.'

She gets up and strolls to the false window.

'These allegations are almost certainly without foundation. However, given their inflammatory nature, I will pursue them with the appropriate agencies. I take it you haven't discussed this with any of your colleagues?'

I hesitate. 'There is one other staff member involved, but she doesn't know any details. She restricted the profile on my behalf.'

'Yes: most irregular. Ministry Representative Osundo took it on, I believe?'

'I explained to her that the case had reached an extremely sensitive stage, and I needed to keep the information classified for a few more days.'

Gauteng's mouth pinches. 'You put your colleague in a difficult position. Ministry Representative Osundo is well respected, but she is resettled, and could easily be compromised. She took an unwise risk on your behalf. Why did you not come to your superior at this point?'

'In my head, I knew that was the protocol, but...' I glance at my hands. 'Given who my sister is ... and who I am ... I was worried I wouldn't be believed.'

She returns to her seat and meets my gaze. 'So, when exactly did you and Shadow first meet?'

'Just before the two-week expiry lifted.' I frown. 'I still find it hard to believe ... Who she is, what she stands for. How someone my complete opposite could have been born from the same womb.'

'But she was. What's to stop me thinking you're colluding with her? Perhaps you're already in her sway.'

I shake my head. 'I have dedicated my life to upholding the Ministry's values. My loyalty has never been in doubt, until now. Shadow has no concept of the perils of the old ways, the cost of her so-called "freedom". We may be genetically related, but she is no sister of mine.'

Minister Gauteng studies me, flexing her fingers one by one, like claws.

'If I'm allowed to continue meeting with her, I could bring you information, Minister. On the campaigns they're planning. Maybe I could even deliver her to you...'

My cheeks burn under Gauteng's glare. It feels as if I'm in one of the doc's machines, being scanned on the inside.

'I can't decide if you're stupid or hopelessly naïve. She won't hesitate to kill you if she doubts your intentions ... Why put yourself in danger? Loyalty? Or guilt?'

'I know my parents committed a crime, and they must pay for it. But I nurture a hope the Ministry may look more favourably on their sentence if I can bring the product of that crime to you.'

A smile glimmers. She strokes her Party emblem.

'You will report directly to me. I'll brief your superiors. Given the appalling optics, we've already contained the details of your parents' arrest. You will return to the office, but speak to no one about this, do you understand? Your reprieve depends on it.'

'Yes.' I summon the words. 'And my parents?'

'Will continue to be held in custody. There may be options, pending the outcome of your investigation. Obviously, I can make no guarantees. Apart from one.'

Minister Gauteng leans over the table.

'If you are lying to me, the consequences will be dire. Make no mistake about that.'

CHAPTER 46

I walk into the office, hands tingling with adrenaline. Rain smashes against the windows, adding to a percussion of fingers clicking keys. I drag my feet under the newly restored metal hands towards my desk.

I cannot believe I am here, that I survived my interrogation. That Gauteng is giving me this chance.

Maybe I am brave, after all.

I ready myself for the stares. Even though Gauteng said she'd contained it, I know how furiously the Ministry jungle drums beat, what a delectable nugget this must be. A birth crime concealed by one of their own; the adult sibling, still at large.

But they are silent. Heads down, tapping away in their cubicles, industrious Ministry bees. Aisha is conspicuously absent. Only one person looks up: Hellie. Her gaze snaps back to her screen. A slow flush rises in her pallid cheeks, as if she's standing too close to a fire.

And I hear it again: that monotonous drone on my parents' doorstep, reciting their crime.

Was it her...?

I drop into my seat as heat surges through me. I try to focus on the numbers and words, but instead I see my mother in that harness, being thrown into the van. It's all I can do not to storm over and grab Hellie by her skinny throat, squeeze out her confession. But that won't help anyone, least of all my parents.

My business with Hellie must wait.

The hours trudge past, minute grinding after minute, but I immerse myself in my list of tasks until at last, I'm able to leave.

I walk out to the Embankment, the rain slanting into my eyes and watch the waves thrash against the banks. A state information board flashes: the Thames Barrier has been shut for high tide; rainwater is being channelled from drainage ponds into reservoirs. The flood risk is amber, expected to change to green.

Gulls scream overhead as they wheel across the river. I inhale the salty breeze, relishing the slap of moisture on my face.

I am outside. I am free.

I head back towards Parliament Square. Raindrops bullet the pavement and slosh into the gutters; a phalanx of umbrellas pushes past. The stone path leading up to St Margaret's is saturated with puddles, and water squelches into my shoes.

I press myself through the heavy wooden doors and throw back my hood.

An elderly lady is sitting near the altar, a serene smile on her lips. Two vergers are embroiled in hushed discussions in the nave.

I hurry down the aisle towards the organ pipes, light a candle on the rack and walk back five rows. I shuffle along the pew to the middle and sit down. I pull out the embroidered prayer cushion stored under my seat and slide onto my knees.

I kneel in silence, cradling my head in my hands, listening to the vergers' whispers and the sputter of wicks. Wait for the tangles of fear and regret to exhaust themselves and subside.

I recite words I have not spoken since I was at school. They are engrained, like all childhood rituals, despite the years. They bring comfort. Not because I believe God may hear me. But because they make me feel closer to Mum.

One hand lowers. Slowly. Reaches underneath the pew in front.

My fingers stretch left then right, and touch a small box, secured under the seat.

I place my bag onto the floor and make a show of extracting some tissues. I dab my eyes, slip the box and the tissues back in, and resume my prayer.

◆ ◆ ◆

I walk to my stop on the Parks line. Water gurgles down the kerb as commuters scurry by. The overland pulls in, and I secure a seat by the window. We speed past a rainy blur of familiar monuments and trees; I greet each one as if it were an old friend.

Like Niko, I genuinely thought I may not see them again.

I arrive at my block and call the lift, but instead of going up, I head down to the basement. I squeeze between two recycling bins and take the box out of my bag.

It's exactly as Spice promised: a new UPD and my pager.

Congratulations! You made it. Welcome home. We have your back. Hellie Manson is your snitch. Be careful.

I was right: Aisha must have found out.

Underneath is an address, and the name of a consultant.

It's a reproductive-health centre. Which just happens to be on my patch.

CHAPTER 47

The health centre is a small building tucked behind a park filled with outdoor gym equipment and robotic trees. Stone steps lead up to wide glass doors; walls inlaid with shells and stones soften the clinical white. I navigate a clutch of green and purple chairs and head to the reception.

'Ms Houghton?'

A woman in a pale-yellow shirt looks up and smiles. A silver dandelion clock clings to the wall behind her.

'Dr Whitton will be with you shortly.'

I have registered with Dr Whitton for a consultation about freezing my eggs. Something Gauteng, if she checks, will swallow, given the looming threat of my incarceration. I managed to contrive a meeting at a family-planning clinic half a mile away, ostensibly to congratulate the staff on their performance. Motivational visits are encouraged when our schedules allow. As I heaped praise on them for their Destine adoption rates, I kept thinking of Talli and Parul.

I take a seat next to headshots of smiling staff and printed paragraphs with pink-and-blue swirly edges. No headshots in the clinics I visit: it's best to be anonymous. On closer inspection, I realise the swirly cuttings are patient testimonies, all effusive. You don't see many of those at family planning clinics, either.

But the objective here is to encourage life, not terminate it.

I count eight couples and two single women in the waiting area. The reluctance to make eye contact is at least familiar. A doctor with wavy silver hair strolls into reception, accompanied by a woman, presumably his patient. His moustache and beard are carefully groomed; the tortoiseshell glasses look expensive. The woman listens to him, all nods and smiles. After a brief word with the receptionist, he heads my way.

'Ms Houghton.' He thrusts out a hand. 'Delighted to meet you.'

Not often I receive such a warm welcome. A striped bow tie peeks out from behind his white coat.

'Thanks for squeezing me in, Doctor.'

'My pleasure.'

I follow him into a large, brightly lit consulting room where another dandelion blossoms, this time a print: seeds parachute out in white tufts, the green receptacles burgeoning with fruit. Underneath, in gold lettering:

One child, many options.
We can make your dream come true...

He clasps his hands. 'So, Ms Houghton, I have some rather boring forms I need to go through, I'm afraid, just to get a feel for what you're—'

'I better stop you there, Doctor. I came here under slightly false pretences. I'm investigating a matter, on behalf of the Ministry.'

His smile withers.

'I apologise for the somewhat unorthodox approach, but it is a little ... sensitive.'

'Oh. I see...'

'Please, don't be alarmed. It's only an information request. I need to ask you about the increase in referrals, for your resettled patients.'

'Ah ... Now I understand.' Relief rushes into his face. 'I'd begun to wonder if my messages had gone astray. I've been flagging my concerns for some time.'

I keep my voice level. 'I didn't realise you'd already brought this to the Party's attention. Which department was it?'

'The Health and Care Excellence team.'

'Well, that explains it. I'm afraid that team aren't celebrated for their prompt communication.' I attempt a conspiratorial smile. 'However, I can assure you that I'm very keen to hear what you have to say.'

He sits back and takes a breath, as if he's about to deliver a tutorial.

'Well, this level of referrals – it's not typical, in my experience. And I've been practising here for thirty years. As you're probably aware, we have a large resettled population here. I noticed that referrals in this community had risen quite substantially over the past few years.'

He pauses.

'It isn't always possible to diagnose a specific cause, that's one of the frustrations in this job. We'd attempted IVF, without much success; most had suffered recurrent implantation failure or pregnancy loss. I wondered if there was a common link that could explain it. So I went back over the patients' records.'

He pushes his glasses up his nose.

'Initial blood results hadn't raised many flags. Hormone levels were in the normal range. Ovulation levels were good. The ultrasounds, however, had picked up a range of issues. And that's when I noticed the pattern. I'd conducted endometrial biopsies on quite a few of these women. And all of them were indicating problems with the lining of the uterus.'

'How does that affect fertility?'

'A healthy lining is vital to a successful pregnancy. In these women, the lining did not appear to have formed properly.

Which means that the embryo cannot implant, so the lining breaks down and sheds. And pregnancy fails.'

'Do you know what might have caused it?'

'Nothing I could pinpoint straight away. Sometimes we don't ever know what causes malformations in the reproductive tract. But, when I took into consideration their family history, it gave me an idea.'

I feel a pulse of excitement.

'When talking through the patient's history, we discuss a range of factors that may impact fertility, before deciding on the best treatment. Lifestyle and diet, sexually transmitted infections. Environmental exposures. If any risk areas come up, we carry out further tests so we can deal with them before progressing to the next phase.

'We also ask them about their parents' medical histories, in case there are heritable conditions we aren't already aware of. Given most of these patients' families had migrated to the UK under extremely challenging conditions, we could not rule out exposure to chemical contaminants, either during their parents' journeys or in the countries they had left – most of which have been devastated by severe weather events or flooding.'

I remember Dr Trowsky mentioning this before. 'Like dangerous toxins, you mean?'

'Yes. Certain environmental exposures can be very harmful to a foetus. I was particularly interested in determining the presence of any EDCs: endocrine-disrupting chemicals. They can persist in soil or water for years, and, if ingested, they have the potential to accumulate in the body. Some can cross the placenta from the mother to the developing foetus, with serious consequences. The foetus is particularly vulnerable because the immune system hasn't fully developed and organs are just being formed.'

I try to marry his words with what I already know.

'So you're saying that even if they weren't pregnant at the time, these chemicals could have affected their babies later on, in the womb?'

'Exactly. The mother might not even know she'd been exposed, because she may not have noticed any symptoms herself. Which is why we run the tests.'

Maybe we've got ahead of ourselves. Maybe this has nothing to do with the implant.

'The patients' blood results came back negative for the toxins we usually test for. However, not all EDCs remain in the body. And the patients may have been exposed to a toxin that we don't currently test for. That's why I contacted the Health and Care Excellence team. To see if they had received any reports of a similar nature from other consultants working with these communities.'

'So you still don't know what's causing it.'

He shakes his head. 'No.'

I bite my lip. 'Can they be treated, these women?'

He sighs. 'As it stands, sadly, there's little we can do. We've tried IVF and IUI, but ... Well, with implantation problems, the odds are very much stacked against them. Their only guarantee of success is to use a surrogate.'

I think of Parul. Of Talli's cousins. All those other daughters who may be suffering in silence.

I have to risk it.

'Tell me, is there any chance, that...? Could a contraceptive device cause similar types of issues? If there was some reaction in the mother to the drugs?'

His forehead creases. 'I've never heard of any cases. I mean, the synthetic hormones used in the implant are technically

EDCs. They mimic the body's natural hormones to prevent pregnancy – that's their role. But they don't hang around in the body, and these women would have deactivated the implant in order to conceive, so the drug wouldn't have been in circulation.'

I try to smother my urgency. 'Do you know if your patients used the Destine implant before trying for a family?'

'I'd need to check. But, given its ubiquity, almost certainly.'

'And what about their mothers?'

He frowns. 'Unlikely. Given their age.'

'You would hope so...'

He tips his head. 'I'm sorry...?'

I take a deep breath.

'Doctor Whitton, I'm about to share something with you. Something confidential. And I need you to swear you won't speak to anyone about it without my prior authorisation.'

His eyes widen behind his glasses. 'I took an oath. If a patient of mine is at risk, and I don't inform them or do anything about it, I am violating that oath.'

'Oh, I hope you will do something about it, believe me ... But, given the sensitivities, it has to be managed in the right way.' I grasp the arms of the chair. 'I have interrogated the data. Fertility issues in resettled communities are being replicated in centres across the country – they just either haven't noticed yet, or the information is being sat on, like yours.'

I pause.

'I have reason to believe that a large number of migrant women were coerced into taking part in the clinical trials for Destine, in return for resettlement. And that whatever happened to them during those trials has somehow led to these fertility issues in their daughters.'

Dr Whitton's eyes flit to the door, as if he's half expecting a security squad to come barging in.

'This is a serious accusation. Very serious indeed.'

'I don't make it lightly.'

'Aside from the fact that there are *very* strict rules about how participants are recruited for clinical trials, there have been no reports of any safety issues with Destine over the past three decades. What's your evidence?'

'So far I've only heard reports from a handful of women whose mothers took part. People are understandably frightened; we suspect they were forced to sign NDAs. Threats were made about reprisals if they broke them.'

'How many women?'

I hesitate. 'Two.'

Air expels through his nose. 'I'm sorry, but that's hardly—'

'You said earlier, that hormones could affect the foetus...'

'Yes, but these women couldn't have become pregnant if those hormones were circulating. Not unless the quantities were very small.' His bow tie quivers. 'And hormone levels were tested. The deactivation function was proved to be robust.'

'Well, maybe it wasn't so robust during the trials, but that never came out. Do you know anyone who was involved?'

He barks a laugh. 'Goodness, I mean we're talking, what, thirty, forty years ago...?'

'I appreciate that. But your networks reach far into this industry, Doctor Whitton. You're very well connected, you know people – people who might be able to provide further insights.'

He sits back and rests his elbows on the armrests, making an arch with his fingers.

'It seems to me that you came here with an agenda, Ms Houghton.'

'I did, Doctor. An agenda that I believe is the same as yours. To help these patients by getting to the root cause.'

He smiles, but he's not happy.

'My question is, on whose authority are you acting? Obviously not the Health and Care Excellence team's.'

'I'm leading my own investigation. It's not clear yet who's implicated, which is why this has to remain confidential for now. But I need help.'

He blinks at me behind his glasses, and I prepare myself for his excuses.

'I hope you don't mind me asking, but ... Your heterochromia – was it congenital or acquired? It's so rare these days to see it, particularly the whole iris.'

'Congenital.' A slow flush heats my cheeks.

'I apologise. My intention was not to embarrass you. My interest was purely professional.'

'No offence taken.'

He clears his throat. 'Egg cryopreservation is relatively straightforward, but you will need several more visits before the egg-retrieval procedure itself. Blood tests, ultrasounds ... Medication for ovarian stimulation. I will be in touch about those. Should you wish to contact me, you can make further appointments via my secretary.'

'Thank you, Doctor Whitton. I really appreciate this.'

'I make no promises. But let's see what my network throws up.'

CHAPTER 48

It's all I can do not to hug Aisha when she arrives. I cling to my seat and make do with a smile.

'Ministry Representative Houghton, how nice to see you.' She flashes me a grin.

'You too, Ministry Representative Osundo.' I cup my hands. 'I hear you've been busy.'

'A little hectic – but all under control. How about you?'

'Oh, you know...' My eyes flick over to Hellie's desk. 'Somewhat stressful. But nothing I can't handle.'

My screen lights up with an incoming call. 'Excuse me a moment.'

The number isn't familiar.

The title is, though.

I summon some saliva. 'Ministry Representative Houghton, how can I help you?'

'The minister would like to see you.' It's Gauteng's private secretary.

'Of course, when would best suit?'

'Now.'

❖ ❖ ❖

I raise my finger to the keypad and enter the code I was just given for the executive floor. A hundred thoughts flare in my head. I fumble the digits and have to enter it again.

Just string her along with the areas we discussed...

What else did Senka say?

Only you can bring her this information. Remember, you're the one in control...

My guts are screaming that they're nowhere near any measure of control.

The lift shoots up, sucking air from my ears as my heel drums the floor. I've spent my entire working life on the first floor of this building. This past week has brought me to an underground level I never knew existed, and now to the top.

I step out onto a plush natural weave, which carpets the executive holding pen, with doors leading off on four sides. I take refuge on a sofa partly concealed by bamboo palms and try to distract myself with the living art. Yellow-rimmed snake plants dart out of frames, fighting with white-veined philodendrons. Peace lilies coil around a portrait of the Mother; their sickly blooms remind me of a coffin spray.

There's a click, and a door opens. A stick-thin Ministry official appears dressed in black. He looks like a crow, staring down his beak at me, pausing fractionally on my eyes. 'Follow me.'

He leads me down a corridor lined with ONE Party luminaries. I avoid their contemptuous stares. He presses his palm to a scanner, and we pass through another door, into an open-plan area that's surprisingly spartan, just the occasional plant on a desk. There must be about twenty people, all glued to their screens. As I pass, not one of them looks up.

The secretary jabs his hand at a wall of glass.

'The minister is waiting for you on the roof terrace.'

I slide back the door and stop. For a second, the view eclipses my fear.

Domed gardens and majestic waterfalls stretch along the riverbank. Green terraces nestle into tower blocks that are linked by skywalks shimmering above the colossal branches of robot trees.

'Impressive, isn't it?'

I spin round. Minister Gauteng is bent over one of her planters, scrutinising the neat rows of spinach and lettuce. She prides herself on having one of the highest office yields. I've heard she takes more care of those vegetables than she does her own son.

'This city used to be a concrete sprawl, mired in fumes. Stinking of the shit they dumped in that poor river.' Her nostrils flare. 'It's a wonder anything survived.'

'Indeed. And we have the Party to thank for that.'

I nod at an army of asparagus spears, resisting the urge to count them. 'They really thrive up here, don't they?'

'Most do.' She plucks out a weed and tosses it over the railing. I watch it spiral down. 'There are always one or two that don't make the grade.'

She leads me behind a vertical wall of planters, beyond the reach of office eyes.

'So: a week already.' She dusts the soil off her fingers. 'What do you have for me?'

I've been briefed on a range of distractions.

'Shadow is busy with a new campaign. It's the resettlement centres.'

'More attacks?' Her tone sharpens.

'Yes.'

'Where?'

'I don't know precise locations yet, but I'll find out. In her last message she wrote about needing to help free those who couldn't help themselves.'

'Anything else? What about these alleged records of excess children? Have you managed to get access to those?'

'No, but she knows I want to see them again. It's just that communication this week has been a bit intermittent.'

Gauteng's lips part, revealing the tips of her teeth. 'You're really not doing her any favours...'

She extracts a small screen from her pocket, taps some keys and shoves it under my nose.

It's as if I've gripped an unearthed wire with wet hands. The picture has been taken from above, dimmed by the paltry square of light.

My mother is sitting on a bed in a cell. A green jumpsuit sags from her body like shed skin. Her hair is tied back, accentuating the bones in her thin face. She stares at the wall, clutching the mattress as if she is steadying herself on waves I cannot see.

'Sentences for a crime like hers can be indefinite.' Gauteng snatches the screen away. 'And I can put you back in a cell, anytime I choose.'

'I'm su—' My voice fails. I try again. 'I'm sure I'll see Shadow again, soon.'

Gauteng braces an arm against the railing. I glimpse the same flash of silver under her sleeve, only this time I notice black studs.

'Remember what I said, Houghton. Unlike you, I'm true to my word. Initiate contact and bring those records to me.'

CHAPTER 49

I arrive early for my eleven o'clock meeting at the reserve. It must be well over thirty degrees already, which is hot, even by May's standards. They say another heatwave is coming, and temperatures in London will top forty degrees. I just hope Dr Whitton's contact shows. The doctor came good. I knew he would. He put me in touch with an old university friend called Marik, who just happens to work for Eridian, the manufacturers of Destine. Marik's understandably twitchy, and at one point, I thought he might bail. But Dr Whitton assures me Marik will come.

The sun shimmers off the water, and I spot two avocets foraging, sweeping their upturned bills through the water like scythes. A couple of bird-watchers nod at me, telescopes hoisted over their shoulders as they march past. The Wetlands Reserve was my idea: a weekend choice in keeping with my interests. Our rendezvous is at the reed hut, a bird hide about a mile down one of the more remote trails. Too far for most amateurs, and it's late and hot enough for the assiduous birders to be on their way.

I walk down the trail, Dad's old binoculars bumping against my chest. My insides roil. Every time I think about my parents, Mum's picture derails me. They won't make it; I know they won't. Not unless I persuade Gauteng to intervene. So I paged Senka last night. Told her she had to give me something concrete to keep Gauteng at bay. She promised me she would.

I turn onto the boardwalk, trying to soften the clump of my boots. The door to the hide squeaks open; it's empty. I lower myself onto a bench and lift the binoculars to my eyes.

Only a short stretch of path is visible through the slit, curving round beyond the water. I watch three oystercatchers stabbing the silt for worms as a cluster of cobalt damselflies flits past. An olive chiffchaff alights on a bulrush and warbles an insistent refrain. The minutes tick past in a chorus of buzzing and chirps.

Just as I'm thinking Marik might have pulled out after all, I hear steps coming down the boards, light and quick. My fingers tighten around the binoculars. The door opens and shuts. I count two steps, the rustle of a coat. A welcome waft of air on my cheek. It's getting hotter in here; the sweat's already trickling down my back.

'Nice morning.' The voice is male. 'Seen much?'

I keep the binocs clamped to my face. 'A pair of avocets. Oystercatchers.'

The bench creaks. 'Any chicks?'

That's the code.

'No. Not that I've seen.'

I lower my binoculars. A wiry man with a sharp nose and dark eyes gazes back at me. He looks a little like a water bird. A very tired water bird.

'Marik?' I whisper.

His head jerks. 'No names. This is extremely dangerous for me.'

The tightness in his voice betrays his fear. It's catching.

'I know. And I'm extremely grateful you came.'

He wipes the sweat off his forehead and takes off his rucksack, his eyes darting round the hide. He crouches forward and peers through the slats, as if he's worried a Party birder might be lurking on the shore.

'I'm only here on the strict understanding that you keep my

name out of it. I can't risk my family. I won't testify. I'll deny everything.'

I've already agreed to this. 'I understand the risks. You have my word.'

He hugs the rucksack on his lap, not entirely convinced.

'Dr Whitton vouched for me. You know what's happening. That's why we're here.'

Marik turns to me. He takes a long slow breath and nods.

'So, first you need to understand exactly how the implant works. The contraceptive chemical that Destine releases is called DST. It's a combination of two synthetic hormones: progesterone and oestrogen. Synthetic hormones like DST have been used for decades in pills and implants to block ovulation, but what makes Destine different is the mechanism it uses.'

'The chip.'

'Yes. The microchip was designed to work for decades, not years, with a remote switch so the wearer can turn it on or off.' He looks at me. 'The chip itself is made of silicon and contains a series of drug reservoirs. Membrane seals on these reservoirs melt to release tiny doses of the hormones.'

He checks to see if I'm following.

'Both the drug and the mechanism were evaluated in those original clinical trials. To establish their safety and efficacy. And both passed with flying colours. The implant was highly effective in suppressing ovulation, with no safety concerns.'

'What about side effects?'

'Nothing unusual, the same as many other contraceptive devices: occasional spotting, some nausea. Mood swings and headaches. A slightly increased risk of blood clotting.'

'And the deactivation – were any issues reported with that?'

'Not in the trials, no, the return to fertility was also good, after the implant was deactivated. Pregnancies proceeded normally, or at least in line with the control group. Which is why the regulators gave it the green light.'

'So, tell me: why were migrants coerced to take part in those trials?'

Sweat beads his face. 'Look, I knew nothing about that; it all happened decades ago. I was just a lowly student back then, trying to get my PhD. The only thing I remember being unusual was how fast it all happened. There was a lot of pressure coming down from the executive to get Destine into phase-three trials. But it wasn't an easy brief. They needed to recruit over a thousand women of reproductive age who they could study over a fifteen-year period. I didn't know until afterwards, that...' He swallows. 'That they were part of the resettlement programme.'

'How long afterwards?'

'Not until they were well into the trial. It was the diaries. Electronic diaries were used to keep track of things like whether the participants had had any bleeding or spotting, that kind of thing. Part of my job was to collate the results. Many of the questionnaires had been auto-translated, which led to some interesting phrases. I commented on them one day to my supervisor, you know, as kind of a joke...' His jaw tightens. 'That's when I learned that almost all the participants were resettled. When I asked why, I was told it was so we could test responses in women from different ethnic backgrounds across a range of ages. And most weren't using other implants or IUDs, which meant they could be recruited more quickly. He was quite matter-of-fact about it.'

'Didn't you think it was odd – to focus on that community?'

'The trials had been approved by the regulator, and I was a newbie at the bottom of the pile.' He sighs. 'I took it for granted that the required consents had been obtained and trial protocols had been followed.'

A whooper swan glides past the hide, its elegant, snow-white wings skimming the water.

'So when did you realise something was wrong?'

He glances at the rucksack, still clutched in his lap.

'The start of this year. We launched a follow-up clinical study using a smaller sample of the original participants. To check the implant's efficacy up to the onset of menopause. We used data from medi-patches, as well as patient e-diaries and questionnaires. Obviously, one of the areas we asked about was side effects.' He gazes through the narrow wooden slit. 'I remember reading that first report. I just assumed it was a random one-off response. About two hours later, I read the same question, phrased differently. And then it came up a third time. And I knew.'

I look at him. 'What was the question?'

'Whether the implant could have somehow affected their daughter. Reduced their chances of having a baby of their own.'

Despite the heat, the hairs on my arms stand up.

'So I accessed other participants' families' medical records. It didn't take long to discover this was happening to a lot more than three families.'

A gaggle of greylag geese planes onto the water, splashing and honking, their orange beaks outstretched.

'I went straight to my boss. I proposed we start a case-control study immediately: send out new questionnaires to the trial mothers and their daughters. So we could investigate a causal association between the use of the implant in mothers and fertility issues in their daughters.'

He shakes his head. 'Well, that's when the shutters came down. A week later, I was told in no uncertain terms that no further questionnaires would be sent and no data could leave the building. And neither I nor my team should converse about this with anyone. Then they slammed us all with a fresh batch of NDAs.'

'Really?'

'Oh, yes. It was made abundantly clear that if any of us put a step wrong they'd send in the legal heavies.'

'So, what happened? They just ignored it?'

'Not exactly. I was asked to carry out a retrospective study internally using what data we had, cross-referencing with medical records, so the information would be contained.'

A little grebe upturns with a splash, making us both jump. It surfaces a few metres away.

'Well, that confirmed it. Records showed that the daughters of the original Destine trial participants were experiencing significantly more adverse fertility outcomes than the control group. A substantial number had been diagnosed with abnormalities in the uterus, leading to infertility, spontaneous abortion and implantation failure during IVF.'

I grip the bench. Exactly the same issues that Dr Whitton mentioned.

'By this stage, everyone was really jumpy. I had to triple secure every report, every email. I had senior people, I mean *very* senior, breathing down my neck, challenging me on everything. You could hear a pin drop in that lab; we hardly dared talk to each other. Because we all knew: these adverse effects must have been caused by the implant, in the womb. And remained hidden until decades later, when those daughters had grown up and wanted to start a family. Our reproductiv—'

I silence him with my hand. Someone's strolling down the path by the hide.

We wait for footsteps on the boardwalk, the squeak of the door.

No one comes.

Marik's eyes dart to mine and back to the water. 'I think I should go.'

He unzips his rucksack and extracts a thick brown envelope.

'I managed to make hard copies, which is just as well.' He swallows. 'Everything on the system has either been locked down or disappeared.'

'What's in there?'

'Participant questionnaires. Study outcomes.' He pauses. 'A report on the animal trials.'

I frown. 'What animal trials?'

He shakes his head and stands up. 'I'm sorry, I really need to g—'

I grab his arm. 'Please, Marik. It's important I understand. Don't worry, that was just some twitcher going home.'

He hesitates and sits back down.

'After those study results, we ran some research trials with mice, to explore the effects of different doses of DST during pregnancy. Their gestation period is only twenty days. You see, the development of our reproductive systems is governed by a series of genes that are active at specific time points in foetal development. Anything that disrupts these genes can have significant and permanent adverse effects.' He pauses. 'The evidence from those trials was conclusive: DST exposure in the pregnant mothers led to increased abnormalities in the uterus of their female embryos. It effectively reprogrammed the development of their reproductive organs. Which in turn led to infertility problems in the offspring.'

I feel a prickle on my neck. I think of my own chip quietly secreting hormones into my veins.

He turns. 'When I went back and looked at the uterine

biopsy reports for daughters of the original Destine trial participants, the same structural anomalies had been observed.'

'But how did they get pregnant if the hormones were circulating? Anyway, I thought the implant was supposed to be deactivated?'

'It was...' He visibly deflates. 'We now know it only takes a very small amount of DST to damage a foetus and cause severe alterations. Small enough not to prevent a pregnancy. The deactivation function must have failed; we don't know why. They're testing that now. One possibility is that the seals malfunctioned, and there was some leakage from the cartridges.'

'But why wasn't this picked up in the trials? I thought you'd said they'd tested it?'

'They did, but no DST was detected. Whether it was masked by something else in the blood samples, or there was a problem with the hormone assay tests, we just don't know.' He sighs. 'As for the daughters – only children up to three were tested, and no problems were identified. They never set out to look for impacts beyond that age.'

I stare at the envelope as my mind skids from one bombshell to another.

And a terrible thought stalks in.

'These effects ... The implant ... This only happened during the trials, right?'

Marik doesn't answer. His eyes are fixed on a tufted duck floating towards us.

'No changes were made to the implant mechanism because the trials were judged to be a success. Therefore the same problem could still, in theory, be happening...'

Trills and honks amplify to a dissonant screech.

'But ... but the implant has a ninety-percent adoption rate. We're talking—'

'Twelve million women, of reproductive age in the UK. Wearing it right now.'

I stare at him, trying to grasp the number; the digits flap through my head, like a bird struggling to take off.

'We don't know exactly how many babies have been affected since the implant was introduced. But, worst case, tracking female births over the past twenty-five years...'

He hands me the envelope. He's gripping it so hard his knuckles have bled out.

'It could be as many as seven million.'

Seven million...

I remember what Dr Whitton told me. If he's correct, and this damage is irreversible...

Practically an entire generation of women in this country will never be able to give birth.

CHAPTER 50

The Smart Mart is rammed with people topping up with produce on their daily shop. I wander down the aisles, picking items off shelves, robotically checking quota ratings. Ministry slogans shout at me everywhere I turn:

Less haste, less waste!

Conserving is serving.

A healthy quota makes a healthy family.

Not if there's no family to feed, it doesn't.

I fill my basket and move to the back of the shop. My stomach thuds as I catch sight of Spice. He's examining a packet of insect burgers. He does not look at me, we do not speak. His eyes flick to a *staff only* sign posted on a door. He waits for a couple of shoppers to go by and swipes a card over the keypad. The lock clicks back.

I step into a narrow passageway piled with containers of flour, pulses and other dried goods. I abandon my basket on a tub of pasta.

'Well, look at you,' says Spice, his teal eyes glinting. 'Congratulations. I knew you'd make it.'

A small part of me leaps.

'Better get going.' He nods at the stairs. 'She's pretty excited.'

I paged Senka the headlines after I got home from the reserve. Her reply came immediately:

Will fix up a meet.

Spice mounts the wooden staircase in long, easy strides. I follow him across the landing, through a white, stained door.

Senka is standing with her back to me, near the blinds. She

marches over, grasps my shoulders and pulls me into a hug. I stiffen. It's entirely unexpected.

She steps back and smiles. 'How are you feeling?'

'Absolutely petrified.'

'Don't worry, you'll get used to that.'

Spice grins. 'I think surviving two interrogations with Minister Gauteng does warrant a few nerves…'

'What did I tell you? It's in her genes.' Senka turns to me. 'Thank you. For all of it. I know how stressed you've been. First your parents, and then your arrest … I just wanted to say, that…' She swallows. 'Well, it took some guts, going back to the Ministry. But you did it. Not only did you nail the interrogation, you brought us the evidence we need.' She pauses. 'It may not count for shit, but … I'm proud of you.'

Heat pricks behind my eyes. I blink and look away.

She digs into her pocket and pulls out a USB.

'Profiles and birth records. Just a sample: obviously not including mine. You think that will satisfy her?'

'I'm not sure Minister Gauteng is ever satisfied.' I close my fingers around the stick. 'At least this will give her something to chew on. Until we figure out the plan for Destine.'

'She'd have been fresh in, wouldn't she, when the reallocation centres were operating? Clawing her way up the food chain. Perhaps she's implicated.'

'Possibly. Either that or she's using it as leverage.'

I shrug off my coat and reach into my bag for the nail scissors. I carefully unpick the coat's seam until the slit is wide enough. Spice moves over to the window and peeks through the blinds. He looks primed. Charged.

I slide the envelope out and hand it to Senka, relieved to be rid of it at last.

She pulls out the documents and pores over each page. I watch her eyes zigzagging across words, taking them all in.

'Jesus. Jeee ... zuss!' She looks up. '*Seven million?*'

'And more every day...'

Senka thrusts the papers at Spice. 'Even for the ONE Party, this is just ... It's fucking genocide is what it is.'

Spice's face hardens as he reads. 'It's definitely not treatable?'

I shake my head. 'Not according to Dr Whitton.'

Senka tugs her hands through her hair. 'Even seven million doesn't cover it. What about the daughters of all those mothers they've snuck those things into? The migrants in the camps, or the ones who've been deported? Excess children, like me? I'll bet they're not counting their babies.'

'And twelve million women we know of are wearing that implant as we speak. How many of those are trying for a baby? Or are already pregnant?'

Senka stares at me. 'Just think. If Destine had been launched a few months earlier, you could have been one of those daughters. So could I.'

We lapse into silence while Spice finishes reading.

'Well, this is it,' he growls. 'The Party's nemesis ... The population will nosedive, even if we act now. Do you think it was deliberate?'

Senka exhales. 'That would be madness, even for them: sabotaging your own population. It's demographic suicide. If you've no one to rule over, you don't have power.'

'Maybe they didn't intend it to work quite this well. There was a hard-line lunatic fringe back then, remember? What was their slogan? "Stop Battery Hen Britain", that was it. They claimed we were heading the same way as the Easter Islanders.'

He turns to me. 'What's your opinion? What did this Marik think?'

'That it's a cataclysmic fuck-up. They still don't understand why the leakage wasn't picked up or how to stop it. But Marik wasn't involved in the original design, he was just a student. From what I can gather, Eridian's instructions came from the very top.'

'We need to get those implants banned,' says Senka. 'Every day, more women are having them inserted, and more of their daughters will be affected. It's an outrage. The Party have been sitting on this for months.'

'Marik says they're stalling while Eridian runs more tests. They don't want to report anything until they've figured out how to fix the implant.'

'One thing's for sure,' says Spice. 'They'll never come clean about what's happened. It's too major a risk; they know how dangerous this scandal could be.'

Senka looks at him. 'So they'll find a scapegoat.'

'It'll have to be a bloody big scapegoat.'

'Exactly.'

He meets her gaze. 'Ah ... don't tell me ... "FREE Exposes Pregnant Mothers to Hazardous Toxins"; "Terrorists Concoct Devilish Plague To Sterilise Children"...'

I gawp at him. 'They couldn't pull something that big off...'

'Just you watch. There's no limit to their stories, and the public just swallows them.'

'Well, this is it, our moment,' says Senka. 'We need to make a move before they do. Let's see what Nieran can access, using these documents as a start. But it can't be us that breaks it, they'll just shut us down. We need someone senior, on the inside. Someone official who's prepared to call it out, who'll be believed.'

Spice raises his eyebrows. 'And who exactly do you have in mind to blow that rather large whistle?'

'Not Marik,' I say. 'He's made that clear, and we have to respect it. He's already taken a massive risk.'

'There must be people who are worried. You know how it works – if ONE can't pin it on us, they'll look for a sacrificial lamb, someone high enough up the ranks to satisfy the baying hounds.' Senka glances at me. 'We just have to locate them.'

'Don't look at me, I don't have any clout with the upper echelons. Particularly now Gauteng has her eye on me...'

'Actually, having a direct line to her might help.' Spice nods. 'That gives you power. It may not feel that way, but it'll make others nervous. More keen to press their case, in readiness for the purge.'

I rack my brains. My network doesn't extend to the real power holders. And I certainly wouldn't trust my boss. But something's nagging at me. Something someone said...

'In the meantime, we need whatever evidence we can lay our hands on. Spice, you follow up with Nieran. I've already put the word out about testimonies from resettled families. Kai: it would be good if you could tap up your doctor friends, too.'

The memory unlocks. That's it: Dr Trowsky's contact, Yasmine.

I helped someone who knew how to pull strings...

I still have friends at the Ministry, powerful friends...

Senka's still talking: '...get together a report for the news networks: ask them to verify it before hitting up the UN.'

'OK,' I say, 'it's a long shot, but I might have a lead – from someone who worked with the Ministry. As it happens, a settler. It could be nothing, it was only a passing comment.'

'Great,' says Senka. 'Where are we going?'

'"We"? Are you crazy? Security squads will be everywhere.'

'I'm called Shadow for a reason. They'll never know.'

CHAPTER 51

I remember Yasmine is an early riser, even on Sundays, so I arrive in Mortlake just before seven. I'm pretty sure I haven't been followed. Yasmine's road is a short walk from the station, next to a park. It's a little cooler today, thank goodness; if the heat wave came early I was worried she may not go for her run. Almost every house on this street is an eco-module: living walls with built-in water collection, passive cooling and plant-purified air. The buildings' sloped exteriors look like ships' hulls, giving the impression of a fleet grounded in harbour.

I stop three houses up from hers and loiter out of view of the camera positioned on an adjacent wall. I have donned my exercise gear and do some flexes as if I'm limbering up for a run. Planters jut out from Yasmine's house, brimming with leafy heads. Someone passes a downstairs window. I only catch a glimpse, but I'm sure it's her.

Ten minutes later, the door opens. Yasmine's copper hair is tied back and she's wearing running shorts and trainers. She braces one hand against the wall and pulls her leg up in a stretch.

I drop to a crouch as she jogs onto the pavement and fiddle with my laces. She sprints past with a cursory glance.

I catch her up. 'Mind if I join you?'

She turns. Her surprise darkens as she remembers. 'What on earth...?'

I hold up my hands. 'I just want to talk, I'm not carrying anything. You can check.'

Yasmine scowls. 'I told you to leave me alone.' She breaks into a run.

I jog a short distance behind her. Yasmine's steps are light, her breathing steady. Unlike mine. She turns left onto Sheen Lane, just as I thought. Heading for Richmond Park.

She slows to cross the road.

'When we last met, you mentioned someone got you transferred out of reallocations.'

She glares at me. 'This is harassment. I should call the police. I'm sure your Ministry colleagues would love to know about your illegal search.'

'Someone you'd helped.'

Yasmine's eyes stay fixed on the road. She doesn't respond.

'I'm guessing they were Ministry.'

She steps off the kerb. 'I don't know what you're talking about.'

She weaves across the tramlines, dodging the cyclists and scooters, pumping her arms.

I up my speed to a sprint. It takes me a while to catch up with her.

'Let's not waste time,' I pant. 'You regret what happened at those centres, I know you do. There must have been things you witnessed ... terrible things. Decisions you were forced to make. This is your chance to put them right.'

'Leave me alone.'

A stitch needles my insides as we pass another runner. My lungs are burning, but I keep going; we're nearly at the park.

Sweat gleams on Yasmine's forehead as we approach the black metal gates. Even she is breathing hard. I spot a herd of deer to the right of the path, ambling out of the trees. The stag at the front stops and tosses its antlers. A man in a green shirt sprints past the Mother's Pond towards Sheen Cross Wood.

I fall back, checking to see which way Yasmine goes. She

glances round to see if I'm still following. I bend over and rest my palms against my thighs, catching my breath. As Yasmine approaches the gate to the wood, I resume my jog. I wait until she's well into the trees, then accelerate to a sprint.

I reach the gate, and the man I saw earlier steps out from behind a clump of ferns.

'Guess I got the running genes, then.'

The camouflage is so good, I barely recognise her. Senka has swept back her hair, and whether it's stealth wear or cosmetics, her face looks entirely different: bulked and blotchy. She winks at me and speeds off.

I lumber up the track behind. Senka has already caught up with Yasmine. As we flank her, Yasmine slows. Her head swivels to Senka and back to me.

'We only need a few minutes, Yasmine. My friend here had intimate experience of a reallocation centre.' I gulp a breath. 'You had no choice what you did back then. But now you do.'

Yasmine's face drops.

'That log looks pretty comfortable.' Senka links her arm through Yasmine's. Yasmine tries to pull away, but Senka's grip tightens.

'Stop! I'm not ... You can't do this.'

'Please, don't make things difficult.'

Yasmine tries to wrestle free. 'I told you, I'm not getting into this.'

They thud onto the log, side by side.

'Some memories never leave you, do they?' says Senka. 'Especially the tough ones. They cling to you. Like a bad smell.'

Yasmine eyes the fence. She's thinking about making a dash for it.

'Christmas was always bad. I don't know how old I was: seven, maybe eight. The nice carers usually went back to their families on Christmas Day, if they could. So we were left with the not-so-nice ones who didn't want to be there.'

I feel myself tensing. I haven't heard this before.

'It must have been later on, because it was dark outside. And there was that stale stench of leftover food. Both carers were asleep in their chairs. One was snoring like a bear. I think they'd been putting away the wine...'

Yasmine stares at Senka as if she's some kind of ghost. Senka lets go of her arm.

'The lounge was crammed full of kids, fidgeting and bickering. They'd put on the same film they always did – about the nativity – and it was turned up really loud. So me and my friend decided to go to the room where they put the babies. We often went there, just to get some privacy. Sometimes we'd play with them, or pick them up if they were crying.'

Yasmine is hanging on every word.

'As I opened the door, this icy wind cut into my face. We both gasped, it was *freezing* in there. There were ten cots in that nursery, and no noise was coming from any of them. All they had over them were sheets. And I realised: the windows had been left open.' Senka swallows. 'I went over to a cot. This tiny baby was lying there, eyes squeezed shut. Its skin was grey. I reached my hand to its cheek ... It was so cold. I could see the frozen trails of snot and tears. I lifted it out and cuddled it close; it was lighter than a bird. But it didn't matter how long I hugged that baby, it didn't stir...'

Yasmine brings her hand to her mouth.

'Five of them died, in that room. On Christmas Day.'

'Who are you?' Yasmine's voice is a rasp.

'I'm one of them. All of them. Does it matter?'

'I'm sorry ... Those things should never have happened. I

tried telling them. I tried to show them what was going on, but no one wanted to know. I swear to you, I tried...'

Senka is completely calm. 'How many others do you think died? Or were sold into slavery, for slower deaths?'

'Please. I did my best for those children. I did what I could. I just want to live out my days, whatever's left of them, with my family.'

Senka turns. 'That's all we wanted, too. But we never got the chance.'

I stare at Senka, in her strange disguise, and something inside gives way. Something that's built up over all these years, layer by layer, like a shell.

I thought it was there to protect me.

'We can't make this right,' says Senka. 'But we can at least stop pretending it didn't happen. Seek justice for the abandoned. And hold those responsible to account.'

'It's not that simple.' Yasmine sniffs. 'The mothers of those children never knew about the centres. And if you haul this out into the open, the Ministry are bound to retaliate. Those mothers have their families to consider; they don't want the Ministry knocking at their door.'

'That won't happen, if we do things right.' Senka leans closer. 'And you know someone who can help us.'

'The person you mentioned, Yasmine, they had an excess child, didn't they? And you found a home for them. Made their crime go away.'

She shakes her head.

'Who was it, Yasmine?'

'I can't, I'm sorry—'

'Just give us a name. It's important. More important than you know.'

'It was a long time ago. Please, I beg you, don't drag me into this—'

'Your niece, Farah. She longed for a baby, didn't she?'

Yasmine freezes. I glance at Senka.

'But it wasn't straightforward.'

'What do you—?'

'She had an implant put in without her knowledge. At the camp. Which is why she couldn't get pregnant.'

Yasmine's face pales. 'How do you know this?'

'Because I was the one who arranged to get it removed.'

Yasmine's neck slumps, as if her head's suddenly become too heavy. She looks out across the park. Some of the deer have lain down in the grass, just the other side of the fence. The stag, though, is watching us, his broad chest rising and falling.

'She asked me to take her baby and find it a home. Not breathe a word to anyone. She said she would help me. I was thinking of my family. So I said yes.' She twists a thick silver band around her finger. 'But no one wanted the babies anymore. It was twenty years ago, the rules had changed.' She sighs. 'So I took her daughter to a centre. I never told her. And she never asked.'

'Which centre?' asks Senka.

'Dartmoor.'

Senka stiffens. 'Whose child was it, Yasmine?'

She licks a line of sweat above her lips. 'They're powerful now. They'll come after me and my family.'

'We won't give up your name.'

'It'll be obvious; I'm the only one that knew.'

'We'll do everything we can to protect you.'

'You can't, not from her. Believe me.'

Senka clenches the log and exhales. Her patience is thinning.

'This isn't just about what happened, back then,' I say. 'It's about what's still happening, Yasmine. To women and girls all over this country, and beyond. Girls like Farah. And it's not only enforced implants.'

She holds my gaze for a moment. And sighs: 'Gauteng.'

My mouth dries.

'*Minister* Gauteng?'

She nods.

The Ministry's figurehead. The symbol of restraint and sacrifice.

The woman that judged me from the moment I stepped through the Ministry's doors.

CHAPTER 52

I stalk through the wood, twigs snapping under my feet. It feels as if a tram is racing through my head. All those terrifying sermons about duty. The endless criticism, nothing ever good enough. That interrogation ... Gauteng made me feel like some traitorous miscreant, a stain on the Ministry's name. When she'd committed exactly the same crime as Mum. And hidden hers, too.

'Hey, wait up!' Senka jogs up behind. 'Jeez, you walk faster than you run.'

I turn round. 'I'm so sorry, Senka.'

She frowns. 'What do you have to be sorry for?'

'What you've been through. Everything you've had to endure...' I blink furiously. 'And now, Gauteng. The hypocrisy of it all...' My fingers curl into a fist. 'I am so angry.'

She takes a step closer and gently mops a tear from my cheek. 'Good.'

A squirrel twitches its tail and scoots along the branch above us as cumulus clouds scud across the sky.

'You should have heard her. The threats she made about my parents...'

Sentences for a crime like hers can be indefinite...

'No wonder Gauteng was so keen to get her hands on those records.' Senka eyes me. 'She must be worried. Well, we've got her now. I've already paged Nieran. Your next meeting should be pretty interesting.'

'I can't believe how brazen she was.'

'Others in the Party must know about the list. For a start,

your interrogation would have been recorded. We can play on that, ramp up our demands.'

I think of the camera in that cell. And I remember something...

'You know what, she has this weird bracelet – with black studs. She doesn't wear it to be seen, like normal jewellery. It's tucked under her sleeve.'

'Does she?' Senka smiles. 'That'll be a jammer. Those black studs are ultrasonic transducers, emitting white noise. They block surveillance. We use them all the time.'

'She wore it in the interrogation. And the last time we met.'

'Now you know why...'

Heat flames through me. I picture shoving Gauteng over the rails of the roof terrace. Hurling her precious planters down after her.

'I'd better split.' Senka hangs back; we've almost reached the boundary of the wood. 'Keep an eye on your pager. We've got the perfect leverage now for Destine. With Gauteng forced over to our side, things will be a lot harder for the Party to shake off. This could be the scandal that finally sticks.'

Just the thought of confronting Gauteng sends a frisson through me.

I look at Senka and hesitate. 'That centre, on Dartmoor. Was that where you...?'

She nods. '"Home sweet home".'

'I suppose it's all been demolished.'

'That's what I'd assumed, but someone told me they'd seen a derelict Ministry building on the moor, all fenced off, just a few years back. The offliners have a camp near there. Apparently, it's just been left to rot.'

There's a beep. Senka grabs her pager. She lets out a whoop.

'Nieran's got it!'

'The birth record? You're kidding me. Already?'

'I don't suppose there were many Gautengs. Here.' She hands me the pager. 'This was your result. You read it.'

My eyes swerve to the box saying *Mother.* Gauteng's name is on there for all to see. The father has been left blank.

I check the other details and look up.

'Her daughter's only a few months younger than you.'

'What's her name?'

Mpho

'Not sure how to pronounce it. Looks like Umfoe...'

'Give it here.' Senka scans the record. 'It's African. It's pronounced...' She takes a sharp breath.

'What is it?'

She grips the screen and swallows. 'You pronounce it: "mm Poe".'

Poe. The friend she talked about. The one who was sent overseas.

Her eyes mist over.

'You really think it's her?'

She swipes a hand through her hair. 'The date, the name. It all fits.' Her gaze drops to her wrist. 'And there's one way to find out...'

CHAPTER 53

Dr Trowsky's face falls as soon as she sees me. She hurries across the tiles, pulling me away from the reception.

'You need to leave, right away. We agreed you wouldn't come again. You only bring trouble.' She tries to shepherd me to the exit.

'Has something happened?'

She eyes the other patients in the waiting area. 'Don't make me call security.'

'Please. It's important.'

'It always is.' She mutters something under her breath. 'Two minutes.'

As soon as her door is shut she wheels round. 'Every time you waltz in here, you want something. And when I give it to you, it's me that has to bear the consequences. You know I was visited by some Ministry heavy?'

Shit...

'They grilled me – about your mother. I was half expecting to be chucked in the back of a van.'

I feel a stab of guilt. I should have warned her.

'I never gave up your name, I promise...'

Her brow creases. 'What kind of daughter are you?'

'I've been trying to protect my mother, you know that.'

'Then how come you're here? Not holed up in some cell?'

I exhale. 'It's complicated...'

I stare at the contraception poster, with the cartoons. They now seem even more obscene.

She holds up her palm. 'Look, I don't know what your game

is, or who you represent, but I'm just trying to do my job the best way I know how, and I'm treading a fine enough line as it is. I can't afford to be caught in your crossfire.'

I grate a tooth across my lip. She's right: I'm putting her in danger.

But these are her patients; she needs to know.

'The thing is, what we discussed last time ... It's worse than we'd feared. Much worse.'

She blinks at me.

'The trial your patient mentioned was for the Destine implant. The synthetic hormones are what's causing the fertility problems. Which means the daughter of any mother who wears it during her pregnancy could suffer the same fate. Not just those who took part in the trial.'

'What?' She frowns. 'How?'

'The hormones are leaking, even when it's deactivated. Not enough to prevent a pregnancy, but enough to damage a developing foetus ... and make a female infertile.'

I hand her a copy of Nieran's charts, which have built on Marik's estimates.

'With every day that passes, another eight hundred Destine daughters are born. That's what we're calling them. The resettled communities were just the first to be affected.'

'Good God...'

The projected population crash is shocking to see. In a matter of years, the country's fertility rate drops off a cliff.

Dr Trowsky lays the papers carefully down. 'You're *sure* it's the implant?'

I nod. 'But the Party aren't saying anything. Until they find a solution.'

She grinds her nails into her forehead. 'I've inserted that

device into literally thousands of women. Because I thought it would protect them. Save them the agony of an enforced termination. Isn't there enough blood on these hands…?'

'It's not your fault. You're a good doctor, who cares for her patients.'

Dr Trowsky stares at the wall. 'All these years, I've tried to do my best, I've worked so hard…' Her voice falters. 'I came into this profession to nurture life, not to end it. Countless times I've wanted to throw it all in. But you know the thing that always stopped me?'

I shake my head.

'My patients. If a new doctor came in, who'd been indoctrinated by their training, who never knew what it was like before … Some ardent Party recruit might judge these women, when they were being forced to make the worst decision of their lives. At least I understood. I could talk to them and put my arm around them. Show some compassion. Sometimes even cry with them…'

I think of my own role in her patients' lives. Rapping on doors, preaching the rules at them, deaf to their pleas.

I thought I was doing the right thing, for the greater good.

That the ends justified the means.

'I sent those women to clinics like yours. You acted in their best interests within the confines of the law and you helped them, including my mother. If anyone is at fault, it is me.'

There is a curious release in saying it.

I've heard so many accusations about ONE over these past weeks. It has been building, this dawning realisation. Now, there can be no more denying it.

The Party I have dedicated myself to is corrupt. Built on layers of lies.

'I need your help, Doctor, to expose this. And doctors like you, who can work with us to compile the evidence, vouch that this is real. When members of the medical establishment speak up, people will listen.'

Dr Trowsky takes a breath. 'We have to get this device out of pregnant women's arms. And anyone else who may be trying for a child. I swore an oath. We cannot be silent, if there is to be any credibility left in our profession.'

I hold out my hand. She looks at it for a moment and grasps it.

'Be careful, Doctor. Only talk to those you trust. We need you.' I push back my chair and stand up.

'Wait a moment ... Do you want a child one day?'

I glance at my belly. 'I used to think so...'

'In which case, you're not going anywhere.'

She walks up to me and prods my left arm, just below the shoulder.

'If you have a girl, you don't want to risk her being made infertile. So let's get this thing out.'

CHAPTER 54

My stomach lurches as the lift ascends, bile souring my throat. I've spent the last few minutes at my desk swallowing waves of it, my fingers scurrying aimlessly across keys. I'd taken great pleasure rehearsing this meeting: imagining the different ways I could drop the bomb and then picturing Gauteng's response. Her brazen denials and fervid counterattacks giving way to fury. Culminating in delicious, smouldering compliance. But now this meeting is upon me, my bravado has absconded. Gauteng is not one to cower in the face of opposition.

Gauteng's secretary doesn't bother with words, just waves me listlessly through the doors, doubly affronted by the impertinence of my 'last-minute' request and then being obliged to fulfil it. It's either that or the heat. Although, unlike in our cubicles, the executive floor's hi-tech cooling system doesn't appear to be struggling. A red extreme heat warning has been issued; it may only be nine-thirty, but the temperature's already climbed to thirty-four degrees. People have been told to stay inside; the public cooling centres are operating night and day, and the fire brigades are on high alert. Two wildfires have already been reported in woodlands south-east of the city.

I step onto the balcony: it's like walking into a furnace, and I'm momentarily blinded by the glare. Bright yellow shapes swirl behind my eyes and I count them in a frenzy of threes. There's a slow hiss of water that must be coming from the irrigation tubes. As my eyes clear, I see her, inspecting her produce; a leafy mist clouds her head.

'This better be good. I'm supposed to be in the PM's briefing.'

Even knowing what I do, my reaction to this woman is visceral. Every nerve and cell wired for flight, not fight.

She straightens. Beads of sweat glisten on her forehead. 'He won't be happy.'

I take a breath and remind myself I'm the one in control.

'I apologise for the short notice. But what I'm about to tell you couldn't wait.'

I glance at the railing and imagine her plummeting over, her trouser suit billowing out around her legs like sails.

She leads me away from the doors, under the shade of the vertical planter.

'Shadow made contact. They're planning something huge. It's the Destine implant: she claims there's a problem. And they're going to expose it.'

I study her face for a reaction.

She frowns. 'What problem?'

'The hormones are leaking when it's deactivated in pregnant mothers. Damaging the babies in the womb.'

Gauteng's lids hood her eyes. 'The stories they come up with. Honestly, it defies belief.'

'Their sources claim the damage makes it virtually impossible for those daughters to conceive.'

She snorts. 'What "sources"?'

'Research reports from scientists, patient testimonies ... Shadow said they've spoken to doctors and consultants, too.'

Gauteng shakes her head. 'Utter nonsense...'

It still amazes me how convincingly she can lie. But this time, I won't be taken in.

'I checked some stats myself, before I brought this to you.' I pause. 'It does appear that fertility referrals in certain communities are rising.'

Gauteng's gaze slides over me. 'Oh, dear. She's really got to you, hasn't she?' Her gaze lingers on my eyes. 'I suppose I shouldn't be surprised.'

She delves into her pocket and pulls out her screen.

Here comes the counterattack. It's not Mum, though. Or Dad.

It's Marik and I, in the hide.

'Do you *honestly* imagine we don't know what's going on, Houghton? This supposed "scientist" you met is an agent of FREE. Those reports were cooked up, for your benefit. You're being groomed, by your sister. And you're fool enough to fall for it.'

I stare at her. 'No ... That's not true ... A research team verified it, they conducted experiments with mice—'

'These are the weapons they use: disinformation, distortion of the facts...'

'I saw the referrals myself—'

'Hasn't your training taught you anything?' Her eyes flash. 'They take one bit of data and twist it. We know referrals are rising. Our medical advisors have diagnosed the cause and it's nothing to do with the implant. This is the briefing I'm missing right now. The Ministry of Health Security gave the executive team the heads-up weeks ago.'

Is this another punt by Gauteng to derail me? Or is it possible what she's saying is true?

'Your sister's playing you, Houghton. When you're the one supposed to be playing her...'

My brain starts frantically shuffling events.

Talli, Parul. Dr Whitton. It was him that initiated contact with Marik, not Senka. Those conversations were real. Weren't they?

Dr Whitton was Senka's lead...

Sweat pricks my collar.

I won't ever lie to you...

I think of that hug, after my arrest.

Our first meeting.

It's hard for you to recognise deceit, because it's all you've ever known...

'Your usefulness has expired, Houghton. Shadow is running rings round you. You've brought me nothing. It's time to terminate this arrangement and send you back to your cell.'

'*No.*' I grab her wrist. The bracelet digs into my fingers: a sharp reminder. 'There's more...'

She shakes me off.

'I have my own image to show you.'

Her cheeks flush red.

When was the last time someone other than the prime minister gave her an order?

I clench my hands to stop them trembling. 'I should advise you that what I'm about to share is in the hands of people who, if I fail to return, or am harmed in any way, will load it onto the MPFP system and then send it to every state news network and social-media site in the country.'

She squints at me, as if I'm one of those weeds trespassing in her planter.

I brandish my screen.

I watch her eyes widen, her mouth sag a fraction. Exactly as mine must have done when I first saw Senka's profile.

Her tongue probes the recesses of her mouth. 'I see your sister's creatives have been hard at work.'

Another doubt flickers. But this, at least, I know is real.

'You must have dreaded this moment, your entire career. I'm sure the PM would love to see this flash up on his dashboard.'

'Any fool can forge a birth record. You think I haven't seen fakes like this before?'

My chest constricts. This is it, the clinch.

'It's a lovely name, you chose. I believe it means "gift".'

She seizes me by the throat. The movement is so quick I don't even have time to register it.

'Don't you dare...'

'You had Mpho reallocated...' I gasp. 'She was sent to a centre ... They were both there...'

She jerks my neck loose. 'What are you talking about?'

'Shadow – she grew up with your daughter. At the centre in Dartmoor. They were friends.'

Gauteng's face hardens. I can see her calculating. Deciding.

'These are wild accusations. You cannot prove a thing.'

'That's where you're wrong.'

I reach into my pocket and hand her a small, sealed bag.

'The Victorians called it mourning jewellery: a personal memento of the person they had lost. But in this case, she was still alive.' I force myself to meet Gauteng's gaze. 'Your daughter made a friendship bracelet for Shadow. Braided it, using her own hair.'

Gauteng gawps at the bag. She slips her finger inside and touches the hair.

A tern soars past, riding the thermals, the black tip of its wing almost brushes the railing.

I rummage in my pocket for the stick. 'This USB contains a sample of the profiles and birth records in FREE's possession. Including your daughter's.' I give it to her. 'They're genuine. You can check.'

She closes her fist round the stick and clears her throat. 'Well, I must say, I'm not often wrong about people. It seems you've finally discovered your backbone … What are your demands?'

'My parents cleared of all charges. My sister's profile deleted from the system.' I swallow. 'And the truth. About Destine.'

She leers at me. 'I can give you the truth. But it's nothing to do with that implant.'

Even now, Gauteng cannot acquiesce.

'If I were you, Houghton, I'd have another chat with your—'

'Minister, I'm sorry to disturb you.'

We both wheel round. It's her secretary, the black crow.

She exhales. 'Didn't I make myself clear?'

'I apologise, but the prime minister is asking for you. He's quite insistent. The briefing's about to start.'

The gold fingers of Gauteng's Party emblem sparkle in the sun.

She glances at me. 'We'll resume this discussion later. In the meantime, why don't you join us? You might learn something.'

CHAPTER 55

We leave Gauteng's office, her secretary scuttling ahead through a never-ending maze of security doors that branch off to each ministry's HQ. I replay Gauteng's words in my head, analysing, questioning, trying to make sense of what I heard. I cannot believe Dr Whitton would lie to me. Or that Marik is an agent. But Gauteng did not falter. What is this alternative explanation she claims their medical advisors have found?

Eventually the secretary stops and presses his ear to a panelled door, as if he's checking for a heartbeat. He palms it open and ushers us into the ministerial briefing room.

It's packed. The cooling system may be going at full throttle, but the temperature is noticeably warmer. All eyes are on the podium.

The prime minister is flanked by Union Jacks, the Party logo gleams behind him on a wall of green. An uneasy silence is punctuated by the squeaks of chairs and an occasional cough. I recognise a few faces from the reels: ministers, directors, state press.

Gauteng signals for me to sit. She strides down the middle and takes her place on the front row. The prime minister inclines his head to acknowledge her, or perhaps her lack of punctuality.

He takes a breath. 'Good morning. Thank you all for joining me; I know schedules are busy. I need to update you on an important advisory I received from the UK Ministry of Health Security. This was the subject of an executive meeting at the end of last week.'

He pauses. His forehead gleams under the lights.

'A new variant of the human herpesvirus family has reached our shores. It is called HHV-6C.' He emphasises each letter. 'Early studies suggest that this virus may negatively impact the fertility of some women.'

My heart stills. A hushed murmur breaks out. The state news reporters furiously type away.

'Now, without wishing to get too technical, the way this virus works is by infecting the lining of the uterus, which can make things much more difficult for a pregnancy to progress. Given the seriousness of these symptoms, combined with the potential rate of transmission, the Ministry of Health Security has designated this human herpesvirus a variant of concern.'

I search for Gauteng. The back of her head is silhouetted by the lights.

'We don't yet know precisely how transmissible this new variant is. However, studies show that it is passed on in saliva or mucous droplets through coughs, sneezes and touch, so we urge everyone to wear masks and to wash their hands thoroughly...'

There's an immediate rustling as people in the audience ferret in their bags and snap on masks.

'Specialised testing systems will be set up under the guidance of the Ministry of Health Security. I want to reassure you that trials are already in progress to establish if current antiviral medications are effective and, should it be required, investment has been allocated to support the clinical trial of new medicines.'

People aren't looking that reassured. It's hardly surprising, given the headline tracking along the wall screen:

New Variant of Human Herpesvirus May Cause 'Serious' Fertility Issues in Women.

'I want to take this opportunity to thank all of our scientists, medical practitioners and health agencies across the country for their unflagging diligence and hard work in bringing this new variant to our attention. I am positive that we will beat this virus' – he thumps the podium – 'as we have beaten others before it. And we will beat it together, as ONE.' He gives the podium a final thump.

My ears are ringing. I cannot believe it.

'Thank you, I think we'll move to questions.'

Hands shoot up at the front. The PM points at someone; I think it's a state news reporter.

'Where did this variant come from?'

'A very important question, thank you.' He shuffles his papers. 'As far as we understand, the virus was not brought to the UK by a single "patient zero". The evidence suggests it arrived on multiple occasions from illegal migrants and spread onward each time. We fear the virus may have been circulating in some resettlement centres, undetected, for years.'

What? My hand flies to my mouth.

'Infections have been traced to three centres in the south-east, with a further ten cases identified in one community neighbouring a centre. We believe the virus may have been transmitted after migrants were "broken out" by the terrorist group FREE...'

Voices erupt as more hands shoot up.

'...assure you that multiple surveillance systems are in operation and security will be tightened around all resettlement centres and illegal migrant landing sites.'

Gauteng swivels round in her chair to face me.

I'm suddenly desperate for air.

I push my way through the throng and out into the corridor.

I don't know what to believe anymore. What is or isn't real.

I hurry to the nearest lift, which mercifully descends without a code, and collect my bag from my desk. The cubicles are empty: everyone must be in the auditorium watching the briefing. As I'm on my way out, my screen buzzes.

It's Dr Whitton.

'Ms Houghton, I hope I'm not disturbing you.'

'Not at all.' My pulse is throbbing. 'Actually, I was hoping to speak with you.'

'I wonder if you could pop by this morning, to go through the results of your blood screening? Nothing for you to worry about; we just need to discuss a couple of things. A slot has become available at eleven-thirty, if that's any good to you?' He pauses. 'Our air-cooling system is very efficient, but if you'd rather not travel in the heat, I totally understand.'

'No, no, that'll be fine.' I swallow. 'I'll see you shortly.'

I knead my fingers, trying to quell the ceaseless swells of panic, and focus on the colourful testimonies on the wall:

I can't thank Dr Whitton and his staff enough. They supported us through a long journey...

Baby Marie is the light of our lives...

I glance at the other two women waiting. Why are they here?

Because of a virus, as the prime minister claims? Or because their mother wore an implant before they were born?

One of the women glances at me and adjusts her mask as she solemnly scrolls down her screen. Maybe the news is already out.

This was supposed to be the day we set our plan in motion; the day I took Gauteng down. I didn't secure a thing.

The only arrow that hit its mark was Mpho.

On the way here, I penned numerous drafts to Senka, my questions carefully phrased so they wouldn't betray my doubts. I deleted them.

In the end, I sent just three lines:

G still denying everything.

Gave her the evidence.

Suppose you've heard the news...

Dr Whitton marches around the corner, with a middle-aged man in tow. The doctor mutters something to the receptionist and nods. The poor man looks as if he's itching to get out of here.

The doctor beckons me with a perfunctory smile. When we reach his office, he doesn't even wait for me to sit down.

'We have a problem,' he says. 'A big problem.'

'I know...'

He frowns. 'Did Marik contact you, too?' He mouths the name, as if he's frightened of saying it.

'No, I thought you meant the virus. I attended a briefing this morn—'

'We'll get on to that. Marik called me. He sounded genuinely scared. He thinks he's being followed. They've frozen him out at work, his research study's been canned ... They told him, and I quote: it was "no longer relevant".'

A million thoughts explode in my head. How could I let that snake-tongue make me doubt?

'Even his closest colleagues seem afraid to go near him. His boss threatened him again with lawsuits if he speaks to anyone. He thinks they already know. He's worried about his family. His wife said she'd seen a man loitering outside their house.' He tugs at his beard. 'Frankly, I'm worried too.'

Fear curls in my belly. That photo Gauteng showed me ... This is my fault.

Dr Whitton sighs. 'Marik wanted me to ask you ... no, to *beg* you not to circulate those papers. For the sake of his family.'

'It's too late for that. I'm sorry. I haven't released his name to anyone beyond our immediate circle; everything is anonymised, the same goes for you...'

Dr Whitton's head sags. 'I see.'

'But I do know someone who can protect him, and his family. Get them offline until things calm down. Tell him not to worry. We'll sort it.'

'Really?'

I nod. 'So, what about this virus, then? Does it actually exist?'

He slides a paper across his desk. 'I received this earlier. It's been circulated to every centre in the country. I've been getting calls from colleagues all day.'

From: UK Ministry of Health Security
UKMHS Designates New Human Herpesvirus Variant
of Concern
Dr Hannah Shaw, UKMHS Director of Clinical and
Emerging Infection

I skim the first part, which covers what I've already heard. Dr Whitton has highlighted two paragraphs lower down, presumably for my benefit:

HHV-6C infects the lining of the uterus, activating natural killer cells leading to production of chemicals called cytokines which make implantation of a fertilised egg much more difficult.

I look up. 'I don't understand ... What is this?'

'The perfect cover story. If I hadn't spoken with you or Marik, I'd be none the wiser. Viral infections of the reproductive tract are well documented. New strains are a frequent occurrence: it's plausible.' He nods at the paper. 'Keep reading.'

Diagnosis of this infection can only be made by specialist uterine biopsy as the virus evades detection in blood or saliva tests.

Any suspected cases of HHV-6C must be referred to the UKMHS immediately, which will oversee the processing of all biopsies and the dissemination of results.

Details of this new variant remain classified until current studies are concluded.

'They're locking it down. I'm not even allowed to conduct my own biopsies.'

I slap the paper down. 'But we *know* it's a lie. Marik said—'

'It doesn't matter what he said. The Ministry of Health Security has sanctioned it. Why do you think Marik's being shut out? They're trying to discredit him.'

So this is it: the Party spinning their new truth, exactly as Spice and Senka predicted. Making their enemies the scapegoat. The next set of blinkers for a public all too willing to believe.

The doctor's eyes lift to mine. 'They'll never disclose the real problem. And anyone who tries to will disappear.'

I drum the chair. 'You'd better tell me how I can get hold of Marik. We need to make arrangements, right away.'

CHAPTER 57

As soon as I get on the train, I notice it. Almost every person is wearing a mask, despite the heat. The hum of the ventilation system is accompanied by the occasional muffled mutter. Passengers eye each other, keeping their distance.

I listen in to a conversation: '...Geoff told me it must be that centre near Dover. The one that was in the news. He reckons they're probably in London by now. Who knows how many more are running loose, coughing out their germs...'

The woman next to her shakes her head. 'It's criminal, that's what it is. Imagine, your Denise not being able to have a child.' She adjusts her headscarf. 'You know how fast these things spread. If they don't get a grip of it soon, it'll be everywhere.'

My mind reels. The scale and speed of this is breathtaking. I think of all the 'facts' I've been fed over the years, the conspiracies denied, the counter-accusations about FREE.

How many of FREE's reports were actually true?

The train slows to a stop. The doors open and a wall of heat slams in. A teenage girl gets on; sweat pimples her forehead. She makes for an empty seat, next to the passenger with the headscarf. The woman rushes her bag onto the seat.

The girl blinks at her. 'Can I sit here?'

The woman keeps her eyes at waist height. 'It's taken.'

'Excuse me?'

'She said, it's taken.' Her friend fixes the girl with a stare. 'Unless you have a mask.'

The girl frowns in confusion. Maybe she hasn't seen the news.

I stand up. 'You can have my seat.' I smile at her behind my mask.

'Oh ... Thank you.'

The mouthy woman lifts her gaze, lingering for a second on my eyes. 'The prime minister told us to wear masks.'

'I know, don't trouble yourselves,' I say. 'I'm getting off.'

As I head across Parliament Square, I notice a crowd has gathered by the statue of the Mother. A man draped in a Union Jack is standing on a box, punching the air. Sweat drips down his face. His head is already crimson from the sun.

'...because *our* country belongs to *our* people. And we don't need illegals coming over here, infecting British mothers, do we?'

'No!' comes the reply.

The people in front of him wave their placards:

Take your virus home!

No room for vectors!

One sign has a grotesque drawing of migrants in a boat with a red cross scrawled over it:

Stop the spread!

Children race around the square, the painted Union Jacks on their faces melting into smudges of red, white and blue.

How did this happen so fast? It's only just been announced.

Headlines scroll across a hoarding:

Infertility Virus Spread by Illegal Migrants.

ONE Party Cracks Down on Rebel People Traffickers.

And it dawns on me: of course, it's all been prearranged. The Party are using this to lock down the centres, turn away more boats, accelerate deportations. Any residual public sympathy for the plight of climate migrants will evaporate.

I hurry along the pavement, keeping my eyes on my feet. By

the time I reach the gates of St Margaret's my shirt is drenched.

It's a relief to be inside, away from the sweltering clamour; the cool air welcomes me like a kiss. The sun lights up figures in the windows: Jesus on the cross, soldiers and disciples, kings, queens and saints. A stained-glass history of persecution and power. I stumble past the cloaked stone effigy of a noblewoman and slump into a pew.

'No candle today?'

My head swerves round as Spice slides onto the bench beside me.

'What do you think of your government's latest show? They really pulled out all the stops, didn't they? At least they're predictable.'

I clench my knees, as tears threaten. 'Today has been a complete disaster.'

He nudges me. 'Come on, it can't have been that bad.'

'Gauteng denied it all, didn't seem the least bit worried ... The only part that got to her was Mpho. She was so convincing, about Destine. She made me question myself again, despite everything. The conversations I'd had, the reports I'd seen. Whether any of this...' I flap my hand '...is real.'

'Of course she did. That's standard operating procedure. Did you give her the USB and the bag?'

'Yes, but we got interrupted. She didn't agree to anything.'

'That doesn't matter. Things are in motion. I'll bet she's checking it all out as we speak.'

I exhale. 'Why do I let her get to me? It's like she holds this power over me, even when my brain is telling me it's all lies.'

Spice scans the aisles and edges a little closer.

'Don't be so hard on yourself, Kai. She's a bully. And you can't underestimate what they've put you through.' He rests his hand on my arm. 'From the moment you could read, ONE's been wiring your brain a certain way. Everything you've been taught, everyone you've met ... The posters, the reels, wherever you go ... It's relentless. Your whole life you've been told how to think: what's real, what's fake, who's good, who's bad. Conditioned not to challenge, or think for yourself. And to accept it as normal, when the reality is, you're living in a toxic echo chamber.' He shakes his head. 'I used to work for them, you know, in robotics. Coming out was tough. You need a decade of deprogramming just to escape them. The Party's like some kind of narcotic. Once you're out, your brain has to learn how to rewire itself. It's a full-scale withdrawal. And right now, you're doing cold turkey.'

His words soothe me.

'It was different for Senka. She was outside the system from the off, she had no choice in the matter; she saw the world as it was. Plus she had Mila and the other carers from the camps before she went offline. It took me a long time to adjust. I still struggle with it sometimes...'

'You don't look as if you're struggling.'

He smiles. 'Well, as we both know, appearances can be deceptive.'

He stretches his arms behind his head. His T-shirt rides up and I glimpse a tattoo on his bicep just under his sleeve. It's the symbol I've seen before: a bird hovering over an eye.

'What is that? Some FREE insignia?'

'This?' He glances at the tattoo. 'Offliner. The dove, for peace and freedom. Defying the ever-watchful eye...'

'Ah ... a dove.'

'The clue's in the name: Spice, as in spice imperial, technically a pigeon, but hey, same family. And then there's Grey and Barb ... As in Barbary? The names are mostly used by offliners who have regular contact with the online world. I pity the poor sod that gets Wompoo Fruit.'

A laugh erupts, despite everything. I'm about to ask him what his real name is, but I stop myself. Spice is who he is to me.

'Listen, we need to help Marik. Get him and his family somewhere safe. He thinks the Party knows he was the one who leaked the story. They're following him, they even went to his house.'

'I'll make arrangements.'

'Thanks.'

My phone buzzes. I'm tempted to ignore it, but it might be Gauteng.

'Let me guess: is it her? Your duplicitous boss?'

'Her secretary.' I frown. 'Apparently, Minister Gauteng's taking me to dinner.'

CHAPTER 58

I can see why Gauteng likes this place. It's like eating in a greenhouse. Vines trail down polished wood panelling; ferns spill over pots suspended from the ceiling. A planter of vegetables and herbs sits in the middle. I grasp my thighs to stop them jiggling and stare at the menu board, trying to drum up an appetite. It feels like some kind of test: the choices are exhausting.

'I'm kicking off with a margarita, which I highly recommend,' says Gauteng. She's wearing a ruby trouser suit, with lipstick to match. 'They grow or forage all their own ingredients. Unusual combinations, but they hit the spot.'

She's acting as if we're out to seal some casual business transaction. Maybe for her this is. The way the waiters fawn over her, she's clearly a regular. Human waiters, too. This is not going to be cheap.

I try to remember the last time I went out for dinner. It must have been Mum's sixtieth. She smashed a glass after too much sparkling wine; Dad and I had a hell of a job getting her on the tram.

It rushes up inside and consumes me: a yearning for my tipsy, giggling Mum. Not the prison version that haunts me.

It gives me the courage I need.

'That's working, I assume.' I nod at Gauteng's jammer bracelet. 'Did you check out the USB?'

Gauteng peers at me over a moth orchid, clinging to its stick. 'Naturally.' The dark-pink petals gape like jaws.

A waiter appears with two margaritas. I wasn't aware I'd ordered one.

She takes a sip. 'Mmm. Chilli and grapefruit. Quite a kick.'

She puts the glass down. 'I'm curious: do you think you make your parents proud?'

'I'm sorry?'

'Your parents. Are they proud of you? Truth be told, my son is a bit of a disappointment. There's nothing exceptional about him at all. I used to wonder whether Mpho would have been stronger. Perhaps that's the punishment for having two. You get stuck with the first one that comes along, even if they're average.'

I take a gulp of my cocktail. No doubt she intended an insult. If only she knew...

'I presume you had the hair tested, too.'

She twirls the stem of her glass slowly round. 'Where is she now? Mpho?'

My gaze retreats to the young couple on the table behind. The girl keeps fidgeting with her mask. 'We don't know.'

'I want to see this centre you mentioned. In person. With Shadow.'

'That was never part of the deal.'

'I can make her profile disappear. Have your parents released, without charge. I just have to say the word.'

'What about Destine?'

She smiles, a ruby rip across her face. 'You know, it's funny – I could have sworn you and I were in the same briefing...'

I delve into my bag and hand her the folder.

'More gifts? What is it this time, a finger?'

I nod at her margarita, my heart pounding. 'You might want another sip before you look inside.'

She frowns. 'You expect me to review this *now*?'

I nod. She heaves out a sigh and opens the folder, making a show of how pointless she thinks this is.

I watch her skim the first document: the anonymised medical reports. She peers at the biopsy results, barely acknowledging them. But when she gets to Marik's study, she slows. The questionnaires and mouse trials have Eridian's name stamped all over them. Her finger moves down the report and stops at one particular paragraph. Her eyes dart to mine, and return to the page.

The waiter arrives to take our order. Gauteng doesn't look up. I shake my head at him with an apologetic smile. I begin to wonder if she's actually bothered to review any of this material before; she must have been sent it. My hand keeps wandering to my cocktail, but I resist and drink water instead.

She flicks to the fertility rates and population projections, which culminate in Nieran's killer graph: Destine's demographic nosedive.

She stares at the graph for a long time and puts the documents down.

She inhales through her nose. 'I'm going to ask you a question. And everything depends on your answer.'

Gone is the dismissive tone. The sarcasm. Perhaps the Ministry of Health Security watered their projections down.

'Are these fakes?'

'You know they're not.'

Her eyes don't waver. 'Do I?'

Electric impulses catapult round my brain. And I recall what Marik said, about instructions coming from the very top. I thought he meant Gauteng.

'I'll ask you again. And if you lie to me, it won't matter how loud you shout about Mpho, I will take you, and your parents, and your terrorist sister, down with me, into the abyss. Are. These. Fakes?'

I slowly shake my head. 'The prime minister is lying. The Ministry of Health Security is lying. There is no infertility virus. Why do you think they're controlling all the biopsies for HHV-6C?'

Her body sinks into the chair.

'You didn't know?'

Could the Party really have lied to their own ministers?

Her eyes return to the plummeting curve. 'No.'

I swallow. 'Every Destine daughter will suffer the same fate. A generation of mothers is already lost. The problem is, it's hidden. The damage skips a generation, from mother to daughter, which is why they've only discovered this now. The migrants who were forced into taking part in those trials are just the start. We have to act now. Otherwise, the population in this country will go the same way as the bison did, and the bears.'

'Extirpated,' she spits. 'By our own hand...'

The waiter creeps back to our table and gives her a questioning glance; she swats him away.

'Wasn't Destine the prime minister's project?' I ask.

'He owes his position to it. Which is why he's going nuclear; he can't afford for this scandal to get out. The migrant protests are a powder keg waiting to explode. It's all part of his plan. Zero tolerance on immigration. He won't hesitate to remove any threats. Permanently.'

She throws up a hand. 'God, it's so obvious ... And yet I was the fool who was duped, not you.' She sighs. 'OK, let's think. We need to be smart. The whistle blower at Eridian – where is he?'

'Somewhere safe.'

'He'd better be ... How many doctors do you have who'll testify?'

'Enough to be credible. More will speak out if they know there's official backing. We've located some of the original trial participants, but they're running scared. We need people to come forward from Eridian. We can't rely on the whistle blower alone.'

'We'll need a hell of a lot more than that ... Who else have you shown this to?'

'At the Ministry, you mean? No one.'

'Good. Keep it that way.'

She gathers up the documents and slides them back in the folder. 'I have work to do. A lot of work. But what I said before stands.'

She taps the folder with a scarlet nail. 'Before I act on this, I need to see the reallocation centre. And I want Shadow to show it to me.'

CHAPTER 59

Flames consume the perimeter, dark tunnels of smoke billow into the sky. The camera angle widens: beyond the barbed-wire coils and metal fencing, several accommodation blocks are on fire. People are running everywhere: migrants clutching possessions, military personnel, uniformed guards. Through the smoke, I glimpse ASRs jetting water into the blaze.

I turn up the volume and cuddle Niko closer.

'Bomb-disposal teams are already on site at this resettlement centre near Dover, working with security forces to extinguish the fires. It is believed several improvised incendiary devices were transported across the perimeter by drones, which ignited on impact. The incident follows the prime minister's briefing on Monday that revealed the "infertility virus" as it has been dubbed, originated in a resettlement centre...'

The newsreel switches to crowds of masked campaigners marching down Whitehall towards Parliament Square. I've been trying to block out their shouts all day.

'Meanwhile, in central London, hundreds of demonstrators marched on the city to voice their anger...'

The camera zooms in on their placards:

Britain is full: stay away!

We don't want your virus!

'The prime minister has appealed for calm, reassuring the public that the Party is doing everything within its powers to prevent the spread of the virus...'

I've never seen this scale of protests before, certainly not broadcasted on state media. The moment any demonstration gathers pace, it is quashed.

Gauteng warned me about this. The PM is actively fuelling the discontent, covertly supporting radicals, to accelerate his agenda and drown out any rumours about Destine. Buying time for whatever 'solution' he's planning.

The prime minister wants to pull up the drawbridge, once and for all.

My screen buzzes. It's Dr Trowsky. I mute the reel.

'Have you seen what's happening? Unbelievable. Same old polemics: us against them.'

She sounds quite breathless. I hope she's being careful about this call.

'Where are you?' I ask.

'In the middle of a wood. Don't worry, I'm using one of my husband's old devices. I was visited again. A different one this time. Asking whether I'd contributed to certain "reports". It was made very clear that if I'd shared any data with "unauthorised sources", I could have my licence revoked. And worse...'

I think of Dr Whitton, and the others. Have they been visited too?

'I'm sorry. We knew this might happen. Things should ease shortly. I can't say any more, but I promise you, there is a plan.'

Senka agreed to Gauteng's proposal. Spice tried to dissuade her. The truth is, Senka wants to go. To show Gauteng the prison where her daughter was sent. Force her to finally acknowledge what the Party did.

'Well, I hope to God you're right,' says Trowsky. 'I had another stream of calls from patients today, asking how they could get checked for the virus. I had to send them off to the state testing facility, even though I know it's pointless.'

'And that's all you can do, for now.' I hear the shrill notes of a woodpecker in the background. 'At least it won't do them any harm.'

'No, but inserting more implants will. I've changed to a different brand for first-time contraception users. We often suggest temporary options anyway, so they can see how they get on.'

I'm distracted for a second by the newsreel: the prime minister is live. I watch his lips move, his hands sweep in emphasis, his ruddy face crease with concern. How many interviews have I listened to without questioning them? How many speeches have I applauded? It's easier to recognise his deceit, just watching, without his artful volleys of words.

'The real challenge has been pregnant mums,' continues the doctor, 'or patients of mine who've started trying. Almost all are on Destine. I can't just sit back and do nothing while those hormones leak into their wombs. The line I'm taking is: I've heard an update is coming. And those without an implant will be prioritised.' She sighs. 'I just hope I get them out in time.'

'Careful, you can't be too obvious. The Party clearly suspects.'

'I have a duty of care, remember? As you once pointed out.'

I finish the call with a familiar churn in my belly. Doctors like Trowsky and Whitton are putting themselves and their families at risk. Does Gauteng really have the intention, or the clout, to take on the PM?

I still don't trust her. Not one of us does.

Two more days, and we'll be in Dartmoor.

CHAPTER 60

Pink and purple heathland stretches to the horizon, flecked with gorse; the sky is a cerulean blue wisped by clouds. If I've got this right, the reallocation centre should be less than a mile away, on a decommissioned military firing range. I check the map reference again, as we stumble past honeyed clumps of heather, hoping my navigational skills hold up. No one uses maps anymore, apart from offliners, and the peatland bogs on Dartmoor are notorious. Huge expanses have been rewetted and restored, which is great for carbon sequestration, but I don't fancy sinking to my armpits in one.

'Please God, tell me we're nearly there.'

Steener has been whinging for most of the past hour, huffing along behind me. The sweat is dripping off him; dark patches flood his shirt. Just as well the temperature has dropped, otherwise I honestly don't think he'd have made it.

'Not far now.'

'That's what you said half an hour ago.'

If he doesn't shut up he might end up being the next 'bog body' to suffer an untimely death. After spending most of the night awake fretting, I'm already on edge. At least he's here, although he took some persuading. I had to be sparse with the details, luring him with the promise of a potential scoop. When Senka asked me if there was anyone in the forces that we could trust, there was only one choice. Thankfully, the prospect of meeting Gauteng seemed to excite him. I can't deny it: I'm relieved he came.

We wade through the bracken; new green fronds climb

through last year's copper ferns, some of their tips still coiled like chameleon tails. As we approach a scattering of moorland ponies, one lifts her velvet head, her mane ruffling in the wind. Her nostrils flare and she gives a low whinny. A white foal trots over, spindly legs splotched with brown, and nudges its mother with its nose.

As we move past the ponies, I see it: a bare brick hulk rearing up from the moor like an insult, tiers of windows gawping. I think of Senka and shudder.

'Is that it?' Steener wheezes.

'It has to be.'

I pick up the pace. Most of the windows are broken, the bricks stained with dirt and moss. A barbed-wire fence surrounds the perimeter, red-and-white signs posted every few metres:

Ministry of Defence Property: Keep Out.

Stone steps lead up to a wood-panelled door. One of the panels near the bottom is missing; a splurge of graffiti covers the rest. I picture Yasmine, walking up those steps with Senka in her arms.

It could have been me.

'Now what?' says Steener.

'We wait for the others.' I nod at his pack. 'Rest up, have a drink.'

He grunts. 'This better be worth it.'

I turn my back on the centre and inhale a lungful of fresh moorland air.

A brimstone settles on a lilac spike of flowers; an orange-tip flutters to another. I close my eyes and count my heartbeats in fours. Prepare myself for what's to come.

After a few minutes, the birdsong is eclipsed by a high-pitched whirr.

Steener cocks his head. 'You're kidding me. They get bikes?'

The noise grows louder, more of a clattering now, tyres bumping across earth. The moorland ponies we saw earlier whinny and take off.

Three e-quads appear in the distance. As they get closer, I make out Spice in front, his braids flying out from beneath his helmet.

'Jesus,' says Steener. 'Is that her? In the middle?'

I squint at the bike. 'I think so.'

'Who's that on the left?'

'Her bodyguard.'

The quadbikes brake in a skid of dust. Gauteng's bodyguard leaps off and immediately starts scouting the area. I catch Spice's eye. He gives me the faintest of smiles and mutters into some ancient radio device. There's a crackled reply.

The minister pulls off her helmet and stares at the building.

'It really *does* exist.' She mops her forehead with her sleeve.

Steener leans closer and whispers in my ear: 'I've heard she's quite a terror.'

Gauteng's gaze flicks to Steener and back to me. 'Who's he?'

Steener clears his throat and steps forward. 'Detective Inspector Steener, Foeticide Division. At your service.'

Gauteng frowns. 'What's he doing here?'

'He's just an observer,' I say. 'In case we need evidence.'

Steener's smile widens to a grin. 'Discretion is my speciality.'

Gauteng scowls and reaches into her pack. She pulls out a device.

My hand flies up: 'Hang on—'

'A simple camera: no functionality. Your friend here's already checked: he's very thorough.' Gauteng turns to Spice. 'When will she arrive?'

Spice takes a swig from his water bottle and wipes his mouth. 'She's already inside.'

He shoulders his pack and walks over to a gorse bush in front of the fence. He glances back over his shoulder.

'One at a time.'

The fence has been cut behind the gorse, the hole just big enough for a person. Spice pins back the branches and nods at me. 'After you.'

I crouch down shielding my face with my arm and prise myself through. Gauteng's not the only one desperate to see inside this centre.

When we're all through, Spice turns to us. 'Wait here.'

He heads for a ground-floor window. Gauteng's bodyguard ignores the instruction and ducks down after him. Spice checks the frame for glass, levers himself up and swings his legs in.

Gauteng raises her camera and starts filming. A minute later there's a terrible grating sound. The doorframe rattles. There's another wrench, and the door bursts open.

I trudge up the steps and stop. A dank, musty smell emanates from inside. The hallway is dark and silent. No baby cries. No chatter.

Gauteng pushes past. Plaster has flayed off the walls, exposing rotting board beneath. A door to what must have been an office has been left ajar, as if waiting for the next batch of babies to arrive. I follow Gauteng in. Outdated monitors and screens slump on desks, cables coiled behind; folders lie abandoned on shelves. Gauteng swipes off the dust and inspects one.

She shakes her head. 'I can't believe they didn't clear this place. They must have left in a hurry...'

Her bodyguard is wedged beside her, eyes swivelling from windows to doors.

I flick through a folder: printed lists of food and provisions, verified with dates and signatures. Steener's busy with a camera of his own, snapping pictures of the files.

I peer inside a cupboard, its rusty lock hanging from a hinge. The shelves are strewn with empty medicine packets and bottles. I pick one up: some kind of sedative. Still a couple of pills inside.

Spice leans his head round the door.

Gauteng glances up from her reading. He makes her wait.

'She's ready for you. Leave the cameras here; you can pick them up later. Try anything stupid and you lose them. For good.'

CHAPTER 61

We follow Spice down a filthy tiled corridor, green fire-exit signs hanging at odd angles from the ceiling. He stops outside a battered brown door. Gauteng's lips tighten.

He knocks once and opens it.

A teenage girl is standing beside a row of beds. She has long, dark ringlets, honey skin and piercing blue eyes.

Gauteng stares at her. Her forehead creases.

'Hello.' The girl holds out an arm. 'Welcome to my dorm.'

I'm staring, too. I didn't know Senka's choice of stealth wear would be this...

I drag my gaze away from her. The beds are crammed together, almost touching; the bleached remains of giraffes scamper across their sheets. The walls must once have been white, but have grimed yellow; the border is faded, but I can still make out their shapes, gliding around the room:

I remember running my fingers along their necks, fuzzed with fluff and dirt...

Senka's swans: her first memory.

The boy that never moved.

Senka points at two beds, near the middle. 'Those were ours...'

A tattered comic lies on the floor beneath one, pages open, as if its reader has only just left.

'We started out near the window, but managed to move when they made it all girls. You didn't want to be by the window. Not in winter.' She shakes her head, and her ringlets bounce. 'And *definitely* not by the door.'

Bad things happen when no one's watching...

Gauteng can't take her eyes off Senka. I wonder if she's guessed her disguise.

'We used to sit on our beds at night, and Poe would patiently plait my hair while we told each other stories ... Dreams of what we'd do when we got out. I desperately wanted my hair to be like hers.' She touches her curls. 'No matter how tight she did the braids, it never was. One of the many things I loved about her...' She looks straight at Gauteng. 'Poe never realised how beautiful she was.'

Senka walks round behind us. 'Our bathroom was this way.' She waves us on, like a tour leader. 'Each dorm had their own; it was meant to slow the spread of infections. As we were all shunted in together for meals and "play time", that never really worked.'

We move to a room across the corridor. The basins are encrusted with dirt and the taps are missing; a weathered blind has severed itself from the rail. The toilet bowls are stained black, the seats either broken or sliding off.

I glance at Gauteng. Her face is rigid, like a bot's.

'You've come as her, haven't you?' she says to Senka. 'Mpho?'

Senka's cheek twitches. 'I'll show you the nursery, next.'

Senka takes us to another dorm, with cots instead of beds. A blue potty lurks in the corner.

'We used to come here and play with the babies. We'd change their nappies, too. Sometimes they were left on their own for hours.'

My eyes drift to the windows and it wells up inside.

I lifted the baby out and cuddled it close ... But it didn't matter how long I hugged, it didn't move...

I want to hug Senka in my arms. Drag her away from this place.

'What happened to Mpho?' Gauteng's voice is a rasp.

'You're asking *me*?' Senka's eyes flare. 'They were your policies, weren't they? Or are you going to claim you didn't know?'

'I was in Resources ... It was only later, when I transferred over, that I heard rumours about these centres. I never knew they sent Mpho here. They told me never to ask.'

'Your daughter was incarcerated for thirteen years because you couldn't ask a question? What kind of mother are you?'

Senka veers round to Spice. 'I need some air.'

Steener raises his eyebrows at me. I don't think he can believe what he's witnessing.

'Actually, why don't you all come?' She gives Gauteng an acid smile. 'Then I can show you the gardens.'

She leads us through the kitchens and out the back. A mossed stone path snakes between garden plots. Some hardier produce still persists amongst the weeds: bloody stalks of rhubarb, spring cabbages. Gauteng doesn't give them a second glance. A toy car has been almost entirely consumed by ivy. We march past the beds, past the creeper-ridden greenhouses, down towards some sheds.

'Where are we going?' asks Gauteng's bodyguard.

'You'll see.'

Eventually, Senka stops outside a brick building with a cracked oak door. A padlock lies on the ground in front. Senka stares at the door but doesn't move.

Spice touches her arm and whispers something. She clenches her hands and nods.

The latch has rusted: Spice has to force it. A waft escapes: damp earth, vegetation.

Inside, it is completely dark.

Senka flicks on a torch; the light bounces off the walls, casting strange shadows. Spice passes me another torch. Three haybale covers have collapsed by the door; the stains suggest the hay was never used. Two grain troughs are mounted on a platform, connected by a chute, a stepladder leading up each one.

Senka beckons Gauteng to the nearest ladder.

'Wait...' The bodyguard steps in front of her.

Gauteng hisses something at him and pushes past.

Steener nods at me. 'Shall I take a look at the other one?'

I swallow. 'It's OK, I'll do it.'

I take hold of the ladder and mount the first rung. A cobweb trembles by my hand, and a spider scuttles out. I bolt up the rungs, stifling a scream, pacing myself with Senka. As I lift my foot for the ninth rung, the ladder shudders.

'Jesus...' I cling on, gripping the sides.

It's Steener, clambering up behind.

Senka squints at me through the gloom. 'You OK?'

I hug my body into the steps. 'I'm fine.'

Steener heaves himself up beside me. 'Can you budge over a bit?'

The stepladder is only just wide enough for two.

'OK, but no sudden moves.'

I unpeel one arm from the ladder, shuffle along and angle my torch over the rim.

A square black void swallows the feeble light.

As my eyes adjust, I see the grain has rotted to earth and mulch. The trough must be about half full.

A groan escapes Gauteng on the other ladder. 'God, no!'

I swerve round: she's gaping at the trough.

I strain my torch further in.

Buried in the soil, are specks of white.

Steener inhales.
Bones.
Tiny human bones.

CHAPTER 62

The unseen. The unheard. The abandoned.

I skate down the ladder, my knees smashing into the steps.

I need to get out; I need to breathe.

Gauteng and Senka are shouting at each other; her bodyguard is halfway up their ladder, yelling at her to get down.

I stagger outside and start to count.

But the fours don't work.

Gauteng lurches through the door and casts around, her eyes wild: 'I didn't know, I swear it ... I didn't know!' Her hair is taped to her face with sweat.

I rush up to Senka and throw my arms around her.

'I'm so sorry. It should have been me.'

Her back heaves against my fingers. 'The fault was theirs. Not yours.'

Spice emerges and lifts his hand to Senka's cheek. She clasps it for a second and steps away.

'They covered the bodies with woodchips and straw. Then let the microbes do their work. It almost broke Mila when she found out...' Senka stares at the garden. '"Human fertiliser".' Her mouth trembles. 'They used it on the plots.'

Gauteng crushes her fingers to her lips and whispers something. Maybe a prayer.

'No ceremony. No graves to mark their passing.' Senka's voice is monotone. 'No record they ever lived.'

'What happened here?' Steener's witnessed many horrors in his career, but even he looks sickened.

'Abuse. Neglect. Disease...'

The bodyguard's head suddenly jerks round. Spice looks up, too.

I hear it: a very faint buzzing. Like a mosquito. But even deadlier.

Spice's radio erupts; only garbled words get through:

'...at least ... carrying ... away...'

The bodyguard bellows at Gauteng: 'Get back inside, now!'

She freezes. 'The camera...' She dodges past him and races back up the path. He tears after her as the buzzing gets louder.

'Everyone: take cover! Shut your eyes.' Senka shoves me through the shed door.

Spice is barking at the radio: 'Repeat! Repeat!'

Steener throws himself down next to me. 'What the hell is going on? Are those drones armed?'

The buzzing is directly above us.

Spice drags the door shut. 'Cover your head, keep your mouth—'

An explosion thuds his body into the wall; light bursts through the cracks.

I feel the ground tremble against my chest and hands.

'Spice!' Senka scrabbles over as debris pellets the building.

The trough nearest us groans. Soil and dirt shower our bodies.

'Stay down!' Spice pushes her flat. He swipes the dirt from his eyes and shuffles on all fours to the door. As he inches it open, acrid smoke drifts in.

'Shit...'

I hear cracks and splintering, another boom and then a crash.

Spice hauls himself up and turns to Senka: 'Wait here.'

'Spice, no...'

I scurry to my feet as Senka dashes out after him.

Flames surge through the reallocation centre; at least half of it is on fire. Smoke streams from the first-floor windows, ballooning from the roof in a swirling black vortex. Sparks fly up, searing the clouds; I can feel the heat from here.

I catch up with Senka and see the bodyguard stumbling through the smoke, Gauteng sprawled in his arms. Blood gushes from her forehead. He kicks open one of the sheds and carries her inside.

Spice reaches the shed, just as the guard launches himself out.

'You fuckers!' He smashes his fist into Spice's face then sprints towards us.

'No!' screams Senka. 'You've got this wrong.'

He reaches his hand behind him.

I lunge in front of her, as his arm thrusts forward.

A split-second glint. A mute thump.

His head yanks back. Something red flies out of his hand.

I slump against Senka.

'Jesus, Kai!' She catches me and folds me down onto the grass.

Steener's eyes bulge. He rips off his shirt and balls it against my side. His naked stomach is as pale as a child's.

A man shouts. I hear a dull thud amidst the fire's roar.

Senka tucks her jacket round me and strokes my face.

Her fingers are wet. I blink at her.

'You're going to be OK, I promise.'

She's sad, and it's all my fault.

I try to wipe her tears.

'Don't move...' She clutches my hand. Her face spins.

Or is it me who's spinning?

Someone's lifting my legs.

Sweat leaks out of me, but I'm so cold.

'Kai, stay with me...'

Numbers glitter and dance, melt into beautiful patterns...

The roaring gets louder.

I'm shivering. Can't stop.

'Don't close your eyes, Kai.'

Where is she? So, so cold...

I—

UK Government Accused of Gross Negligence for Failure To Act as Millions of Women Face Prospect of Infertility

By Fadziso Noko

Al Jazeera

Since its release twenty-five years ago, the UK government's Destine contraceptive implant has been hailed by the ONE Party as the 'life-long, hassle-free' answer to birth control, and deemed to be one of the Party's 'crowning successes'.

But research reports secured by Al Jazeera have linked the DST hormones secreted by the implant with adverse effects in the daughters of women who wore the implant during pregnancy. Specifically, the studies show that the hormones caused structural anomalies of the uterus in these babies who are now being dubbed the 'Destine daughters', and that this is leading to much higher rates of infertility and early miscarriage. If these reports are true, the UK could face a demographic catastrophe on a scale never seen before.

'In view of the seriousness of these adverse effects and their risk to future human life, the issuing and use of this implant should have been stopped with immediate effect,' claimed one report, compiled by an association of doctors and consultants. 'This failure to act constitutes gross negligence by the Ministry of Health Security.'

A spokesperson from the UK government commented that there was no evidence to suggest that the implant was defective, and that allegations made by 'a handful' of UK doctors were 'unjustified' and 'a dangerous distraction'. The spokesperson said the UK Ministry of Health Security (UKMHS) would shortly be issuing a specialist technical briefing containing early analysis of HHV-6C, a new variant of the human herpesvirus family, which, they claim, is responsible for causing uterine anomalies in some women.

However, a British fertility specialist, who declined to be named, said he had seen no data to support the UKMHS's claims about HHV-6C and that a medical product alert should have been issued to withdraw the Destine implant straight away.

A WHO (World Health Organisation) spokesperson told a virtual news conference they had requested access to research and patient data on the Destine implant and on HHV-6C, which they stated is in fact not a new variant, but that the UK government has declined their requests.

CHAPTER 63

There's a faint tinkling. Sailboats in harbour.

A waft of air.

Beeps – constant as a heartbeat.

My eyes nudge open.

Blinds flutter at a window. Primrose-yellow walls.

'Well, there you are.' A woman.

I squint at her. I know that face.

She smiles and squeezes my arm. 'Good to see you back, Kai.'

Senka…

My eyes drop to the cannula taped to my hand. A line snakes over the blanket and up behind my head.

'You're in the trauma unit in Exeter.'

A purple bruise flowers out from my veins.

'They're doing a great job.' She nods at me. 'You're going to be just fine. You might feel a bit groggy as the anaesthetic wears off. The pain meds should kick in though. Don't worry if things are a little confused.'

Anaesthetic?

'Do you want some water?'

I suddenly realise how parched I am. 'Yes. Please.'

'OK, let's sit you up a bit.'

She presses a button, and the bed pushes into my back.

She holds the cup to my lips. The water tastes so sweet. I gulp too much and cough. Pain spears my right side.

'Oh, Kai. Is that sore?'

I grimace as my hand slides down my ribs. My torso is swathed in bandages.

'Tell me ... what happened.'

Her eyes search my face. 'What do you remember?'

I curl my fingers into the blanket. 'Flames ... smoke pouring into the sky.'

'That's right, there was a drone attack. A fire. At the centre.'

Centre...

The word unlocks a flood of images: dormitories ... cots ... gardens...

Troughs.

I moisten my lips and swallow. 'Gauteng – she went back, didn't she? For the camera?'

'Yes, she did.'

'She was bleeding.'

'Don't worry about Gauteng; a rafter nearly got the better of her, but she's a tough old bitch. She's giving the poor nurses hell.'

A chuckle escapes and I wince.

'Sorry. God, it's good to see you laugh.' Senka's eyes shine.

'The bodyguard ... hit Spice.'

'Spice is fine. And then, what...?'

'Kind of hazy ... No, wait...'

A snarl. Mad eyes.

'He was going to hurt you.'

She nods slowly. 'And do you remember what you did?'

I comb my memory, but it's like sifting rubble in the dark.

'You dived in front of me,' says Senka. 'That man stabbed you instead of me.'

My eyes widen.

'He must have got the knife from the shed. It lacerated your liver.'

A knife?

My fingers tentatively probe the bandages.

'You lost a lot of blood and went into shock. Steener got you and Gauteng helicoptered out, and they rushed you to theatre. Without him, things could have been a lot worse.' Senka grasps my fingers. 'You risked your life, Kai.'

'I remember him. Barrelling down the path. I didn't even think, I just … did it.' My eyes lift to hers. 'And I'm glad.'

A tear wets the sheet.

I clear my throat. 'You're sure Spice is OK?'

'A bit beaten up, nothing major. He was a little upset about his nose. I told him the swelling would go down eventually.' She smiles. 'As it happens, he asked if he could visit you. Not really advisable, given the security situation. But he was quite insistent.'

I feel my face flush.

'What happened to the bodyguard?'

'He didn't make it.' She takes a breath. 'He thought the drones were ours. He would have killed us … Gauteng didn't have a chance to tell him, but she knew who'd sent them. Which is why you have a guard at your door. Someone close to her must have snitched. Told the PM what she was up to.'

'It was *him*?'

'The perfect opportunity, if you think about it. Take out Gauteng and me in one fell swoop, destroy the reallocation centre and still come out looking the hero … "The vanquisher of FREE"…' She shakes her head. 'There's been nothing in the state press about it. He hasn't dared confront Gauteng publicly. Which means he can't have everything sewn up, or she'd be locked up by now.'

There's a knock, and the door opens. A nurse in a blue-and-white uniform bustles in.

She frowns at Senka. 'Why aren't you wearing your mask?'

'Sorry. I forgot.' Senka yanks one out of her pocket with a barely disguised eyeroll.

'How's our patient?' The nurse glances at the monitor.

'Conscious and coherent,' says Senka.

'Excellent.' The nurse turns to me. 'You need to rest. Don't exhaust yourself. I'll be back in a few minutes to take some bloods. The doctor will pop by later, after we've done your scan, but he was very happy with how the operation went. As long as we keep you free of infection, he's confident the liver will heal nicely.'

'That's great news,' says Senka.

'Thank you so much. For everything.' My words seem rather paltry given the circumstances.

'I should probably take the hint and let you sleep,' says Senka after the door closes.

'Quickly, tell me the plan.'

Senka lowers her voice. 'Gauteng is firming up her support. She claims she has a game changer: someone seriously high up in the Ministry of Health Security. Who'll testify the virus is a fabrication.'

'Do you know who?'

'No. She's playing her cards close to her chest. We sent our report to the international press; a few have covered it. The UN's asking questions.'

'That's encouraging.'

Senka sighs. 'I just hope we can trust Gauteng to do the right thing. I have to say she's played a blinder on Dartmoor, which gives me hope.'

'Really?'

'Not only did Gauteng get the cameras, she went one better, thanks to you.' Senka grins. 'She gave Steener the go-ahead to launch an investigation, after he received an "anonymous tip-off". Forensics are all over it.' She nods at me. 'Finally, we might get justice. The reallocation centre, sheds and gardens have been designated a crime scene.'

CHAPTER 64

I am sitting in Gauteng's luxury eco-apartment on the fortieth floor of the Helix Tower. She sent for me after I was discharged, promising a big announcement. The tower's award-winning design is a silver-and-green living spiral; each floor sports extensive balcony gardens, encircled by silver ribs that harvest water and generate solar power. From what I've gleaned, the inside is pretty impressive, too: top-end eco furnishings and views over London that rival the Party's executive floor's. Gauteng just informed me that the plush sofa on which I'm reclining is made from recycled waste. Then she asked how I take my coffee.

The whole experience is slightly surreal.

A flatscreen on the wall flashes silent news. Sumatra's fires have claimed more lives: toxic smog has been released from peatlands dried out by illegal plantations and drought. The fires have been burning underground for weeks. Poisonous yellow smoke bloats over charred fields as flames devour what's left of the forests.

I think of the centre and look away.

While Gauteng is busy shunting beans into her coffee grinder, I take the opportunity to study her face. Make-up has artfully masked the scrapes and bruising; a flesh-coloured strip on her forehead covers the wound.

She catches me looking. 'My "sporting injury" is healing nicely, don't you think?'

She was lucky her bodyguard got her out. She had two cracked ribs, chest burns and a deep cut on her face. She came to visit me a week ago in the trauma unit, just before she left. She apologised for "the incident" with her bodyguard and told me to rest up as long as I needed. She even brought me chocolate. I think she was trying to be nice.

She eyes my torso. 'How are you getting on?'

'Painkillers are my friend. They signed me off for another two weeks at least. The main thing is keeping it clean; they're still plying me with antibiotics. How about you? Pain still bad?'

'Only when I stretch or twist the wrong way. I try to avoid deep breaths.' She hands me a cup. 'Here you go: Cornwall blend. That'll sharpen things up.'

I inhale the aroma. At least now I can breathe without my entire right side throbbing.

'I have some news for you that should ease things a little.' She smiles at me over her coffee. 'Last night your parents were released. Given everything that's happened, I thought it was prudent.'

I search her face. Is this some cruel tease? 'Are you serious?'

'They're in a safe house. Together. The charges have been dropped.'

Tears rush to my eyes. I hardly dare believe it.

'Can I visit them?'

She shakes her head. 'It's too dangerous. People are watching. Wait till things have quietened down. It shouldn't be too long, hopefully. Not after the little surprise we have planned for today.'

I ache to see them. But at least they're free.

'I'm holding on to Shadow's profile. Just in case. I'll trade your sister's for Mpho's, when all this is done.'

Gauteng's collateral. Protecting her back in case Senka does the dirty on her.

'What news of the Dartmoor investigation?'

'The PM is taking a keen interest, as you can imagine. He's insisted on a press ban. DI Steener confirmed they've found fragments of bone and teeth from over a hundred different children so far...' She lets out a sigh. 'The remains are in the process of being identified.' She pauses. 'I need to prepare myself, if ... if Mpho's are there...'

I clench my palms around my cup. I never thought I would pity this woman.

'Have you asked Shadow about that?'

'I'm not sure she's of a mind to tell me.'

I swallow. 'I believe Mpho may have been sent ... overseas.'

Gauteng's eyes squeeze shut. She knows what that means. But at least Mpho might be alive.

I take a breath. 'What will happen when they identify the remains? Will you tell the families?'

'That depends...'

'On what?'

She arches an eyebrow. 'Who's in power.'

While I've been recuperating, Gauteng has been busy. Not only has she lined up a heavyweight at the Ministry of Health Security, she's managed to get major influencers in the state media on side. She's planned this like a military campaign. Senka and FREE have been part of her special forces, supplying her with intelligence and stirring things up with the international press and the UN. An unlikely coalition.

'You know, I remembered something the other day.' She taps her cup. 'A curious comment you made, after we'd left that horrendous shed.'

'Oh, really?'

'Yes, you were apologising to Shadow. And you said: "It should have been me..."'

The blood rushes to my cheeks. I stare at my coffee. 'To be honest, my memory is a little fuzzy…'

'Yes, I expect it is.' She checks her watch. 'Better get ready for the show.'

'Shouldn't you be there?'

'It's important to maintain distance. Let the PM hang himself with more lies and denials. A few blistering accusations … before swooping in for the kill.'

The protests about the virus have been escalating. The Party has done nothing to suppress them. There've been five more attacks on resettlement centres in the past week.

She nods at the screen. 'There he is – our illustrious leader.'

The prime minister is speaking. She doesn't unmute. Headlines run along the bottom:

Prime Minister Appeals to the Public To Stay Calm…
Security Tightened around Resettlement Centres…
Transmission Rate for HHV-6C Has Increased…

Gauteng shakes her head. 'He's a consummate liar. You're too young to remember that emotional speech he gave about hard choices, when foetal reductions for multiple births were made compulsory. He was practically in tears. I subsequently found out those amendments were included at his insistence, against the advice he'd been given. A former minister even went to his house to petition him on behalf of some women who were pregnant with twins. She brought pictures of them with her, thinking they might stir his pity. So she could cancel their injections.' Her lips purse. 'Apparently, he sifted through them, handed them back and said: "We'd be doing this country a favour if we stuck a needle into them all"…'

I stare at the man on the screen, nodding and wheeling his arms. 'And yet you continued to work for him. Alongside him.'

'Yes, I did.' She juts out her chin. 'We are all products of this regime. Brought up to obey, not to challenge. It took me a while to find my voice. And then learn how to hide it. Until now.'

The image suddenly switches.

Urgent News Broadcast

She jabs her remote and unmutes.

'We're sorry to interrupt our broadcast, but we have news just breaking from the UK Ministry of Health Security...'

The screen switches to a man in his fifties standing at a podium outside the ONE Party complex. He clears his throat and adjusts the microphone.

'My name is David Bashlow and I am the Chief Scientific Officer at the Ministry of Health Security. I have an important announcement to make.'

He grips his papers.

'Three months ago, the executive office of the prime minister instructed the Ministry of Health Security to investigate the potential threat to this country posed by a new variant of the human herpesvirus family: HHV-6C.' He takes a breath. 'HHV-6C is, in fact, not that new. It has been circulating for some time, although it is very rare. Previous tests in a small number of women had shown an association between infection and subsequent difficulties conceiving. However, in all cases, these women had gone on to conceive after receiving fertility treatment. Therefore, the threat had previously been judged to be low.'

He looks up and swallows.

'When we were asked to investigate three months ago, we were given specific details by the executive that "had to be evidenced" in our findings.' He pauses. 'These details had no scientific basis whatsoever. HHV-6C does not cause uterine anomalies. There is no evidence to suggest that the virus was brought here by migrants. And the virus does not cause permanent infertility. These were lies. Intended to mask a different health threat that has not been investigated and should have been: the Destine implant.'

There's a flurry of voices as cameras spark.

He holds up his hand. 'Please, let me finish. The information I presented on behalf of the agency was done so under duress. It was a deliberate act of obfuscation and disinformation by the leadership of our country, and I wholeheartedly apologise. I feel the utmost regret for my actions, and for the disruption, damage and offence they have caused to those women who have been falsely diagnosed, and also to the migrant population who were unjustly blamed and have been targeted with unspeakable acts of violence. Therefore, it is with great sadness that I am tendering my resignation.'

'Ah, Davey…' murmurs Gauteng as cameras explode and journalists scrabble with their mics, barraging him with questions.

I gawp at the screen. I've never seen anything like it. A direct challenge. It's suicide.

'How the hell did you persuade him to do that?'

'I told him I'd look after him. To be honest, he didn't have much choice.'

'Why?'

'David is Mpho's father.'

Destine's Shameful History: Migrants Coerced into Trials That 'Robbed Their Daughters of Motherhood'

By Katarina Spellmann
ONE State News

The government's Destine crisis has taken another shocking turn, with mounting pressure on Prime Minister Karl Andersen to 'tell the truth and resign'. In an interview released today, further allegations have been made that climate refugees were coerced into taking part in clinical trials for the Destine implant over forty years ago, without information being disclosed about its potential risks. A resettled mother, who has asked to remain anonymous, claimed that she was offered resettlement in the UK in exchange for taking part in the trial, and made to sign consent forms she didn't understand. She said that other migrant women like her were also used as 'guinea pigs'.

'My daughter has been told she will never be able to have her own child. Her uterus was damaged by hormones from Destine when she was growing in my womb. I feel so guilty. No one told me this implant could hurt my baby.'

If evidence is found to substantiate this claim, the government could face a fresh set of charges of human rights violations – to add to a very long list.

Thousands take to the streets in Destine protests, demanding PM resigns. Family planning clinics mobbed.

'They knew for months there was a problem' claims Eridian research lead.

Destine implant forced on migrant women in resettlement centres : 'another human rights travesty' says UN spokesperson.

'An appalling abuse of power' says DI after remains of more than four hundred children found at Dartmoor reallocation centre.

'Institutionalised, neglected and abused': one survivor of the 'Dartmoor Deathcamp' tells her story.

CHAPTER 65

It's over.

The prime minister was found dead at his desk yesterday morning.

Unconfirmed reports suggest he had injected himself with a lethal cocktail.

A suicide note was found next to his body, apparently quite extensive, in which he listed his achievements. The concluding sentences were leaked to the press:

> *I have dedicated my life to this country during an unprecedented crisis, and I have made it stronger. Survival requires sacrifice. And we have not only survived: we have flourished.*
>
> *As I resign from office, I resign from life.*
>
> *My work is done.*

An emergency executive meeting was called, and Gauteng was appointed prime minister.

I have been watching this surreal escalation of events from the comfort of my childhood home. Ten days ago, Mum and Dad were finally told they could leave the safe house. I have spent the remaining days of my recuperation with them, witnessing Senka's dream of a ONE Party implosion come true.

Each of us has needed time to heal. To adjust to a world without secrets.

To try to be a family, again.

Gauteng may have only just officially got the job, but big changes are under way.

An official investigation has been launched into the Destine implant.

Family planning clinics are implementing an implant removal programme with immediate effect, including those women in resettlement centres who may not even know they have one.

Counselling and fertility treatment plans are being drawn up for all Destine daughters and their families.

And a taskforce has been assembled to overhaul the Party's immigration policy, including the resettlement centres. I can predict one outcome: women of childbearing age and their families will be prioritised for resettlement.

Gauteng rang me this morning. 'I know you're not back till next week, but I wanted to run a few ideas past you.'

I thought I'd misheard.

'We're getting rid of the Ministry of Population and Family Planning. We need something fresh. I was thinking the "Ministry of Family and Integration" ... What do you think?'

My stomach tightened. 'We need a lot more than rebranding. The Party has always excelled in euphemisms. What will it actually do?'

'Be responsible for the wellbeing and integration of families, no matter where they come from ... Or how large...'

Her words took a moment to sink in. 'You're actually going to do it? Get rid of one-child?'

'Do we have a choice? You've seen that population graph. We're throwing a significant sum into research, but it's unlikely a miracle cure is going to appear any time soon. We'll keep an eye on consumption through the resource quotas. Right now, our biggest challenge is managing the nosedive.'

'Well, I guess I'm out of a job, then ... And I'm delighted.'

'Not so fast. I've earmarked one area specially for you. That's what I wanted to discuss. We're going to publish the excess children's profiles. Make a formal apology. Restore their birth records on the system.'

'That's a big job. Thousands of families could be affected.'

'Exactly. And it's going to require very sensitive handling. As you and I both know ... We have to support the parents and families as well as the excess children. Help them find each other, if they want to. Or help them grieve.'

'That won't be easy. A lot were trafficked. Many abroad.'

'I know...' I heard her intake of breath. 'I gather your inspector friend has connections in this area. Perhaps his team could assist? I hear he's doing rather well. They're making him chief inspector.'

We talked for a long time. About the team I would need, the challenges we would face. The distrust and the lies. Other changes that would have to come. But as I listened to her, something swelled in my chest that I have not felt for a very long time. It fluttered like a newly fledged bird.

Hope.

CHAPTER 66

We amble along the riverbank, checking the ground for rabbit holes. A rowing boat glides past, oars dipping in perfect synchrony, blades catching the sun. Two swans ride its wave and drift towards the bank, their black markings and peach bills offset by flawless white.

Senka glances at me. 'Did you know that swans chase off their cygnets after only five months?'

A light breeze brushes my face. 'Do they?'

'To get ready for the next brood.'

I'm not sure whether she's doing this deliberately. I don't respond.

A rabbit darts across the path in front of us and dives under a tangle of brambles. Some students race by in their swimming costumes, and I think of cool water slipping over my shoulders, the thrill of leaping in. I'd never swum in a river before last weekend. I hovered on the bank, watching Spice frisk through the water like an otter, hair slicked back, droplets sparkling on his skin. He teased me mercilessly until I finally plucked up the courage to jump. The cold surged through my body, stealing my breath away, and erupted in a shout.

I had never felt more vibrant. More alive.

Senka stares across the river, at the meadow. 'I didn't know there were wild ponies here.'

'Oh, yes. They've been around for decades.'

I count seven of them grazing, including a chestnut foal with a white heart on its nose: it can only be a few weeks old.

'We used to watch them from our window, Mpho and I.

Cantering across the moor.' She sighs. 'God, how we envied them.'

I'm beginning to wonder if this is a good idea. Spice did warn me.

Maybe it's too much to expect. Too soon.

We pass a family picnicking on a rug. The dad bounces his daughter on his knee, singing a nursery rhyme that's vaguely familiar; the little girl flaps her arms and squeals with delight.

I see the black metal gate up ahead, and slow.

I nod at Senka. 'That's it. The pub.'

She stares at the gate. Turns back to the horses.

She's about to change her mind.

'OK,' she says. 'I'm ready. Let's go.'

We follow the path under a trellis pergola that is threaded with honeysuckle and jasmine.

'It's stunning at night,' I say, desperate to ease these next moments. 'Fairy lights come on. It's like walking down a magic tunnel.'

Senka keeps moving, eyes fixed straight ahead. I'm not sure she heard.

The garden is busy: nearly all the tables are taken. I spot Mum and Dad at a picnic bench in the corner, next to a weeping willow. Long, shaggy trails of leaves cascade to the grass.

Mum sees us straight away and lifts her hand in a hesitant wave.

Senka's fingers clench and unclench, as if they're limbering up for something. 'Is that them?'

'Yes.'

The look on Dad's face makes me want to cry.

'In my head, I saw them younger...'

What were they like, these parent ghosts of Senka's who gave her up before she could form memories? Who did she wish for, in her dreams?

'I have her nose,' says Senka.

'Yes ... We both do.' I glance at her. 'Do you want to go over? Or get a drink first?'

She exhales. 'No. Let's get it done.'

As we approach, Mum scrabbles awkwardly off the bench.

I clear my throat. 'Mum and Dad: this is Senka.'

They know her name, now it's safe.

Zoe was their cygnet. Senka is the swan.

'Hello, Senka.' Mum swallows. 'Thank you for agreeing to come...'

Senka stiffens.

Their intonation is exactly the same.

A smile skitters across Dad's lips. 'It's ... so good to see you...'

Senka nods but doesn't speak.

We settle ourselves on the bench.

Mum keeps blinking and swallowing. I want to comfort her, squeeze her hand, but I can't.

Dad takes a breath. 'I brought some pictures. Of when you were little. Of course, you don't have to ... It may not be ... What I mean is, only if you'd like—'

'Sure.'

Dad reaches into a bag and pulls out a cream album with gold foil lettering.

Baby's First Year

And I remember: this is it. What I found, all those years ago. It was in a box in their bedroom, buried under clothes. Dad caught me with it. That was why he was so upset.

Senka gazes at the album.

'You don't have to look at them,' adds Mum. 'Unless you want to...'

Senka chews her lip and turns the first page.

The photo must have been taken at the wellness centre, just after she was born. Mum's holding her in her arms. Senka's face is all pink and wrinkly. She's tiny.

Senka stares at it for a long time. Mum and Dad are both watching her intently.

And I wonder: is Senka anything like the grown-up girl they imagined?

Senka flicks to another page. She's lying on her back in a green babygro, tugging at her toes. Her hair is almost white.

She turns another page. And another.

There's a photo of her hanging in a yellow door bouncer, her mouth stretched wide with laughter.

'See how beautiful you were...' says Mum.

Senka doesn't reply.

The last page is the hardest.

Senka is standing on tiptoe, grasping the bars of a cot. Her midnight-blue eyes are fixed on a baby.

A baby that is me.

I grind my nails into my thigh. This is her history, her pain to grieve – not mine.

She gently closes the album and pushes it back. A skein of Canada geese flies past, their bodies aligned in a perfect V.

'I need to say something.' Mum's words rush out. 'I made a terrible decision, a decision that was mine alone, and it will haunt me until I die.' Her breath judders. 'But I *always* loved you, Senka ... I just didn't know how.'

Senka keeps her eyes on the album, her shoulders hunched in.

I wrap my arm around her.

Dad's face collapses. His back heaves. 'I'm so ... so ... sorry...'

Senka slides her hand across the table, and finally looks up. 'It's OK,' she says. 'I know.'

EPILOGUE

'No stone left unturned' Promises Prime Minister Gauteng after Enforced Surrogacy Protests Mount
By Laila Ziani
ONE State News

Prime Minister Maria Gauteng announced today that she would be launching an official enquiry into claims of enforced surrogacy targeting vulnerable women in resettled communities.

Demonstrations organised by human-rights activists FREE have been mounting over the past week. Hundreds of people have taken to the streets to voice their concerns about the exploitation of migrant women in what they claim is an escalating black market in surrogacy.

Campaigners say resettled women are being pressured into acting as surrogate mothers by unscrupulous baby brokers masquerading as legitimate surrogacy agencies. Brokers, they claim, that are profiteering from the misery of Destine daughters unable to conceive.

'The only thing these vile fraudsters care about is money,' said FREE's head of campaigns, Senka Houghton. 'They target Destine daughters, seducing them with the promise of having their own biological child. What these women don't know is that the intended surrogate mother may not have a choice in the matter, has to undergo gruelling hormone treatments and receives only a fraction of their payment. We cannot let this cycle of abuse continue.'

Prime Minister Gauteng acknowledged that the illegal surrogacy trade was 'a significant problem' and promised that her investigation would 'leave no stone unturned'.

THE INSPIRATION BEHIND *ONE*

As with my first two novels, *The Waiting Rooms* and *Off-Target*, it was real-life issues that prompted the premise for *One*. Then came the 'what-if?'

Two ideas came together: What if birth was a crime? How might a one-child policy play out in Britain?

And, with daily reminders of the havoc we are inflicting on our planet, how might the climate crisis affect us, the way we are governed and how we treat other people?

State control of women's bodies is nothing new, it has dogged us throughout history. In multiple countries, people are being dictated to about their reproductive rights. The number may have changed from one to three, but China still has a law stipulating how many children its civilians are allowed to have. During the one-child policy, according to China's health ministry's estimates, over half a billion birth-control procedures were carried out. These included 336 million abortions and 196 million sterilisations. Many of these were forced. Shen Yang's excellent memoir *More Than One Child* was a key inspiration for this book. She writes about the challenges of growing up as an illegal excess child in China, committing a crime just by being born, and how a constant sense of guilt and shame tainted every childhood memory.

Playing God with your citizens has consequences. China's birth rate hit a record low in 2022 and the government is now so concerned that it is actively incentivising families to have more children, to ward off a feared labour shortage and sustain the costs of the country's ageing population. At the other end of the scale is India, which will overtake China in 2023 to become the world's most populous country. Two-child policies currently operate in several Indian states, with penalties including fines, and even jail time, for transgressing fathers, the removal of health benefits for mothers and the denial of state rights for 'excess' children.

It's not just Asia where women's reproductive rights are being challenged. The overturn of the landmark abortion legislation Roe vs Wade last year in the United States caused an uproar. As I write this, according to the Center for Reproductive Rights, no less than sixty-five countries either prohibit abortion completely or only permit it where there is a threat to the mother's life. It seems reproductive rights are still very much under attack.

One also explores another subject close to my heart: climate change. I worked for an environmental organisation on climate change projects for many years.

One depicts a future Britain where climate crises have ushered in a totalitarian regime that enforces strict child and consumption quotas to mitigate further impacts. But, thanks to geography and wealth, even the UK's crises are relatively mild compared to the chaos caused by extreme weather events in other countries. The ONE Party uses this polarisation to justify its laws, emphasising the stark contrast between the stability and security enjoyed by UK citizens and the devastation overseas, ramping up the defence of its borders and incarcerating climate migrants in vast 'resettlement' centres.

Over the past decade, it is estimated that, on average, more than twenty million people have been displaced within their countries each year by disasters including cyclones, hurricanes, floods, wildfires and droughts. Unless we radically accelerate our actions on climate change, soon moving within countries will no longer be possible. People will be forced to migrate across continents as many more areas of land become uninhabitable, causing the largest human migration ever seen. The UN International Organization for Migration projects there could be one billion environmental migrants in the next thirty years. How we manage this globally will reveal much about our humanity.

You can find out more about the issues that inspired *One* and my other books on my website: evesmithauthor.com

I love taking part in book clubs, so do get in touch via the website or social media.

You can also subscribe to a quarterly newsletter that will keep you posted on upcoming events and news. Thank you for reading.

ACKNOWLEDGEMENTS

I owe thanks to many people for their support with this book.

First, my publisher, Karen Sullivan and the incredible team at Orenda Books for their unflagging enthusiasm, support and guidance: West, Cole, Anne, Chloe, Victoria and the design master Mark Swan. I am forever grateful.

My agent, Harry Illingworth at DHH, for continuing to champion me and my writing.

The book bloggers, reviewers and bookshop staff who promote our novels with such zeal even in the most difficult of circumstances, and a particular mention to Patty and Gemma at my local Waterstones, who have been incredible advocates, and to the arch blogger EmmabBooks who is ceaseless in her support.

Thanks to my lovely web designer, Emily Jagger, whose patience runs eternal, and to the authors who provided quotes or encouragement. It means a lot.

And special thanks to the expert scientists who responded to my peculiar brief: to Professor Jo Verran and Professor Sheila Cruickshank for their help and introductions, to Dr Gerry Lee for her imaginative ideas, to Dr Michael Carroll and Dr Viki Male for tolerating all my questions and providing brilliant solutions.

Thanks also to the climate-change experts Ken Wright and Paul Hardisty for checking my assumptions and giving great feedback.

I also want to thank Shen Yang for letting me quote from her memoir, *More Than One Child*. A wonderful thing about writing is that you connect with other authors, and I am so pleased to have connected with Shen Yang.

And now my readers: thanks to Sue Haywood for her ideas, introductions and support.

Bill Hudson, my alpha reader, who has been with me all the way down this long and sometimes rocky road, and is always ready with a keen eye and calm words.

And to all the readers who buy our books: we are nothing without you.

Lastly, huge thanks to my family and friends, for their unwavering reassurance and encouragement. This book tested me, and I probably tested you, but you were still there. Especially my husband and two daughters. Thank you.

3018